little
· IT

Dear Little Black Dress

Thanks for picking up this Little Black Dress book, one of the great new titles from our series of fun, page-turning romance novels. Lucky you — you're about to have a fantastic romantic read that we know you won't be able to put down!

Why don't you make your Little Black Dress experience even better by logging on to

www.littleblackdressbooks.com

where you can:

- ❧ Enter our **monthly competitions** to win **gorgeous** prizes
- ❧ Get **hot-off-the-press** news about our latest titles
- ❧ Read **exclusive** preview chapters both from your **favourite** authors and from brilliant new writing talent
- ❧ Buy **up-and-coming** books online
- ❧ Sign up for an essential slice of romance via our **fortnightly email** newsletter

We love nothing more than to curl up and indulge in an addictive romance, and so we're delighted to welcome you into the Little Black Dress club!

With love from,

The *little black dress* team

Marisa Mackle was born in Armagh, Northern Ireland. She divides her time between Spain and Ireland.

Also by Marisa Mackle

Mr Right for the Night
So Long, Mr Wrong!
Mile High Guy
Manhunt
Confessions of an Air Hostess

Chinese Whispers

Marisa Mackle

little
black
dress

First published in Ireland in 2005
by Dodder Books Ltd.

First published in Great Britain in paperback in 2007
by LITTLE BLACK DRESS
An imprint of HEADLINE PUBLISHING GROUP

A LITTLE BLACK DRESS paperback

1

ISBN 978 0 7553 4372 0

Typeset in Transit511BT by Avon DataSet Ltd,
Bidford-on-Avon, Warwickshire

Printed and bound in Great Britain by Clays Ltd, St Ives plc

Headline's policy is to use papers that are natural, renewable and
recyclable products and made from wood grown in sustainable
forests. The logging and manufacturing processes are expected to
conform to the environmental regulations of the country of origin.

HEADLINE PUBLISHING GROUP
An Hachette Livre UK Company
338 Euston Road
London NW1 3BH

www.littleblackdressbooks.co.uk
www.headline.co.uk

This book is dedicated to Sheila Collins

<u>Wanted: Fabulous Female Flatmate</u>

Should:
1) Be funny (as in amusing, not weird)
2) Lend trendy clothes (but not steal mine)
3) Be young-ish (but definitely not a student)
4) Have a decent day-time job
5) Never forget to buy toilet paper

Should not:
1) Hog the phone
2) Hoover the flat between midnight and 7.00 a.m.
3) Bring strange men home from clubs (or women if that way inclined)
4) Flirt with my boyfriend (if I ever get one)
5) Leave hair in the bath

Oh God, why is this happening to me? I can't stand the thought of sharing my lovely little flat with a complete stranger! Suppose I end up with a raving nympho with a penchant for three-in-a-bed romps or a crazed nut that carefully writes her name on milk cartons? I wish Ellie was still here. Why can't everything be just like before? How did it go so, so wrong? But Ellie is gone now. Gone for good. She moved out this morning. It was for the best, she said. She couldn't continue sharing a place with someone who had slept with her boyfriend. She said she hoped I'd understand and was very civilised about it all. We didn't have a good-bye drink. No. In fact we didn't even say good-bye at all. I just sat in my room staring numbly at the wall as she packed her bags and when I finally heard the front door shut, I looked out the window tearfully as the taxi sped away. Then I collapsed to my knees and howled.

The pain is unbearable. I'm hungover and depressed and feel like I always do when I get dumped, only this is worse. Yes, this is definitely the pits! I've managed to get over my ex-boyfriends by remembering how badly they snored, how they piddled on the bathroom floor and always left the toilet seat up. I'd recall their unbelievable tightness or the way they ogled every passing tart in a low-cut top. But Ellie didn't have any horrible traits, nor did she ever treat me badly. So I couldn't possibly hate her. She had a heart of gold and always tried to set me up with well-meaning men and remembered my birthday and stuff. When I used to work late she'd go into my room to turn on the heating, and when I found out that my ex-boyfriend Greg was two-timing me with his married next-door neighbour, Ellie booked a girlie weekend away to Brighton and wouldn't let me waste one minute more on him. When my budgie, Bertie, died she dug a hole in my parents' garden and we buried him and had a little ceremony. Just the two of us. And then we opened a bottle of wine and reminisced about Bertie's short life before hitting a trendy nightclub because, as Ellie, pointed out, it was exactly what Bertie would have wanted.

Nobody else would have done that for me. I have a big gang of fun but fairly fickle friends who tend to forget about you the minute a man arrives on the scene. Ellie is different though. Some girls ring you just so they'll have someone to go to a club with. But they're much more interested in meeting a potential mate than spending the evening chatting to you and will basically spend the night looking over your shoulder to check out any available talent. But Ellie genuinely cares about other people. She listens. And cares. She cared about me.

So now you know the type of girl Ellie is, you'll probably understand why I can't pin a blown-up photo of her to the door and throw darts at it like I've done with the countless boyfriends who've bit the bullet and fled. This is so, so different. Yes, there'll be other flatmates; yes there'll be other party-loving women who will drift in and out of my life at various stages. But there'll never be another Ellie. I wouldn't mind but I didn't even sleep with her damn boyfriend. I didn't even fancy Connor, although admittedly, when I first met him I thought he was one of the best-looking guys I'd ever seen. So did Ellie. She couldn't wait to introduce us. Her two favourite people in the world. She said she was worried that we wouldn't hit it off. But we did. Oh yes we hit it off all right.

I'd made a big effort for Ellie's twenty-eighth birthday party. She said Connor had lots of hot-looking friends and joked that if I didn't fancy any of them there was no hope for me. She made me get my hair done professionally instead of just doing my usual DIY job and even let me wear her favourite dress so I could make a serious impression. I did it to please her: got my roots done in a top hairdresser and wore a short dress and knee-high boots. When Ellie saw my new look she frowned and said, 'I didn't expect you to make *that* much of an effort'. But then she laughed. She knows better than anybody that I'm an 'all or nothing' kind of girl.

The minute Connor walked through the door I felt like a trussed-up turkey. He was wearing faded blue jeans and a black T-shirt; his light-brown wavy hair had that just-got-out-of-bed look and he was sexy as hell. Desperately intimidated, I immediately rushed back upstairs and changed. When I reappeared, slightly red-faced, I mumbled something about my boots being new and hurting my feet. He nodded sympathetically but he knew. That's just the way Connor is. He knows things about women.

The flat soon filled up with friends of Ellie and Connor's. They all seemed to be media types as

Connor works in TV (although] exactly I have absolutely no ide; a travel writer for a magazine cal Anyway the flat was jammed w people and champagne corks seer every five minutes. At one stage I Connor snogging passionately they disappeared altogether. I was genuinely happy for my flatmate though. After all, she, like the rest of us, has met with a fair amount of slime in her time, so at last things seemed to be looking up.

I mingled with the party set wondering vaguely who they all were, but avoiding anyone who might quiz me about what I did for a living. You see, I never really have a suitable answer to that question. At the moment I'm temping in a really awful stuffy insurance office so I suppose my real title would be 'PA' but I don't feel like a PA. No. I'm not sure what I am but deep down I always had this feeling that I really would get somewhere someday. I just didn't think it would take me this long. Anyway, ever the optimist, I still live in hope that God has something more exciting in mind for me than answering phones, placing files in dusty cabinets, and having to answer to a cantankerous fool and his sorry old sidekick, Cynthia.

So anyway, there I was at the party, terrified of being 'spoken down to', interrogated, and frozen into embarrassment by these ultra-hip creatures with spiky haircuts and funny-coloured shoes. I kept moving around the flat with plates of canapés

pretending
right-no
mea

to be the perfect 'can't-stop-and-talk-[...] hostess. I know it was fairly ridiculous, I [...] I *shouldn't* feel inferior to these people because I know from experience that those in glamorous jobs usually get paid very little but the thing is, these types always seem to know what they're talking about and I don't. Also, I know that people who ask 'what do you do?' aren't actually remotely interested in your job; they're just trying to place you. Trying to figure out if you're worth spending another sixty seconds in their company. I decided not to allow myself be dismissed.

I opted to hang around the fridge (where most people seem more interested in guzzling cold beer than quizzing you about work) when I felt a pair of strong hands grab my waist. I screamed and swung around. Suddenly I found my face buried in a broad black T-shirted chest. 'Mmm, you smell good,' I thought hazily before looking up. My eyes locked with Connor's and drunkenly I tried to focus on them. I remember noticing his eyes were a very dark blue. I've never seen anything like them before: intense, intelligent and utterly mesmerising. But, alas, they belonged to my best friend's new boyfriend. I knew this so I did the right thing, took a step back, offered him a mini quiche and asked breezily whether he was enjoying his evening.

'I am, but I haven't had a chance to talk to you yet, unfortunately. You've been running around all night,' he teased, revealing a set of teeth you could advertise in a dentist's office.

'Well, I can't let Ellie do all the work,' I insisted.

'And besides, you can never totally relax at your own party, can you? I have to make sure people aren't smashing things or having sex in my bed.'

Connor raised an inquisitive eyebrow.

'Anyway,' I hurried along, 'I always find I have a better time at other people's parties. I do like letting my hair down.'

'I can see that,' Connor grinned and looked down at my long blonde hair. The ends of my tresses were floating inside my wine glass. Jesus, how embarrassing! Why hadn't anybody told me I was this drunk? I fished my dripping wet hair out of my glass with a flirtatious smile. Connor looked like he didn't know whether to laugh or not. Suddenly the awkwardness between us dissolved as Killian, a friend of Connor's (almost as good-looking, but not quite) made a surprise appearance and introduced himself.

'You're taken, so get lost,' he gave Connor the elbow. 'Wanna dance, Gorgeous?' He grabbed my hand. I put down my glass and let him lead the way into the living room where a couple of people were stamping on balloons and generally lowering the tone of the party. I spotted Ellie out of the corner of my eye. I smiled and she winked back. This was exactly what she'd been hoping for. She'd been convinced that Killian and I, and Connor and herself would make a great foursome. As in going out and drinking and stuff.

Then something really awful happened. Something really, really terrible. One minute I was snogging somebody (I think it was Killian but due to vast alcohol consumption I simply can't be sure), and the next minute I was face down on Ellie's beautiful handmade rug, which she imported all the way from India, getting sick. And even though I was absolutely sloshed, I was still aware that this was the most embarrassing thing that has ever happened to me. For as long as I live I'll never recover from the humiliation of it all. Yes, just imagine your worst nightmare and multiply it by a thousand. I could tell there was a crowd gathering around me and I heard someone urgently shouting 'Can someone call an ambulance?' Jesus, that was enough to sober me up immediately. I lifted my head and yelled 'No! No ambulance, I'll be fine.' Then Ellie was beside me holding back my hair and she whispered, 'Are you okay?'

'No . . . no, I'm not,' I whimpered. 'Tell all these people to go away and leave me alone.'

Thankfully she did just that, ushered all the excitable party people into the next room and then came back with some old dishcloths and helped me clean myself up. I sat up unsteadily and told her I'd ruined her night.

'Don't be silly,' she laughed good-naturedly. 'It wouldn't be a real party unless at least one person got sick.'

'But your rug . . .' I pointed out helplessly. 'I'll pay for a new one, I promise. I'll write to the people in India, I'll . . .'

'Now listen, don't be daft,' she said calmly. 'The rug will go off to the dry cleaners and come back like new. It's only material.'

'I think I'll go to bed now for a little snooze,' I mumbled weakly and apparently I passed out just after that. I remember half waking up in the bathroom with Ellie holding my head under the freezing cold tap. Then I felt myself being carried to my bedroom by a big pair of strong arms. When I came around completely, Connor was in the room. He was pointing a black object in my face. Something shaped like a gun. 'Jesus, what the f . . .?'

'Hey, I was just going to help you dry your hair,' he said softly. 'If you fall asleep like that you'll wake up with pneumonia. I've also got you a pint of water and I'm going to make you drink it whether you like it or not.'

'Thanks,' I muttered. Even though I felt completely lousy I must admit it was nice to have somebody being so attentive. Even if that somebody didn't belong to me. I sipped the water slowly while Connor plugged the hairdryer into the socket. He started drying the top of my head and the warm blast of air made me drowsy again. I leaned my head against his chest and I'm not totally sure if this happened or not, but when Connor finally switched off the dryer I think that he might have kissed my ear.

'You'll have to take off that dress,' he said. 'You'll ruin it by sleeping in it.'

'S'okay,' I muttered. 'Don't have the energy anyway.'

'Well I'm taking off my T-shirt,' Connor insisted. 'It got soaked earlier.' He stood up and although the room was quite dark when he peeled off his T-shirt, I can assure you he'd give David Beckham a real run for his money.

'I don't suppose you've a big enough top you could lend me?'

I stared at his picture-perfect-tanned physique, opened my mouth to answer, but no words came out. I can't even begin to describe how sexy he looked. I began thinking how lucky Ellie was to have Connor and then it hit me that . . .

'Hey, where's Ellie?' I asked suddenly.

'She's gone to the hospital.'

'Wha . . . at?' I sat bolt upright right in the bed.

'Yeah, one of her crazy journalist friends passed out and hit her head against the glass coffee table in the sitting room. The table's okay but they reckon she'll probably need stitches.'

'Oh my God, the poor girl!'

'Yeah it's pretty bad, isn't it? Ellie drove her to the hospital. She rang my mobile there a few minutes ago and says her friend's going to be okay but they might be stuck in the hospital overnight.'

'Poor Ellie. I feel so guilty. Tonight should have been a really fun night for her. She was really looking forward to it, eh . . .' I paused. 'She couldn't wait for us all to meet you.'

Connor looked away looking slightly uncomfortable.

'Did I just say something I shouldn't?' I asked.

'Of course you didn't,' he said quickly. 'Yeah, there were a few casualties here tonight. The punch was pretty strong; I reckon someone poured in an extra bottle of vodka. Ellie didn't touch any of it so that's how she was sober enough to drive to the hospital.'

'God, I'm a disgrace,' I muttered. 'It was Ellie's birthday. *I* was the one who should have stayed sober and let her enjoy herself. By the way, did you not offer to go to the hospital too?'

'Yeah, 'course I did,' Connor said looking completely offended. Then he sat down on the bed beside me. 'But Ellie thought I should stay with you to make sure you were okay. She was worried about you.'

'That's just typical of Ellie. She puts everybody else first. The girl is a goddamn saint. I feel even guiltier now. I'm a dreadful person for drinking so much.'

'Don't worry, it happens to us all. Don't beat yourself up about it, do you hear?'

'I hear you. Anyway I feel much better now. Thanks for looking after me,' I managed a weak smile. 'Will you be okay now? Where are you going to sleep?'

'Um . . . I'll see if someone can lend me a sweater or something, and then hopefully I'll grab a couple of hours' kip on the sofa,' Connor yawned. 'But first of all I'm going to insist you take off that dress. Go on, I won't look, I promise.'

He turned his back and after much fumbling and grumbling, I finally yanked Ellie's dress over my head. 'You'd better not look,' I warned him. 'I'm not wearing a bra or anything so you are absolutely dead if you move.'

'I'm tempted but I won't,' he laughed.

'Good.'

But nothing is ever simple and somehow the damn clasp of the dress suddenly got stuck in my hair. For the life of me I couldn't untangle it. And asking Connor for help wasn't an option as I was now half naked, as was he.

There was a light knock on the door. Oh fuck, it was probably one of Ellie's annoying friends. Or maybe a couple trying to come in and 'do the business'.

'Don't you dare come in,' I yelled.

Another knock.

'Hey, would you ever piss off please?' Connor ordered and we both started giggling. But the door opened anyway and as someone turned on the light, I let out an indignant scream.

Ellie just stood there in the doorway, saying nothing.

One week later . . .

I was invited to a party last night. By a fat man in a chipper at around 4.00 a.m. Incensed by his cheek, I made a big show of checking my watch and asked who else was going.

'Well, you for a start . . .' he gave a lecherous grin, squirted a big dollop of curried ketchup into his fries and licked his thick rubbery lips, '. . . and me.' Then he paused, took a deep breath and proceeded to release the loudest belch I've ever heard in my life, forcing me to recoil in horror. 'Sorry about that, haha,' he guffawed. 'Anyway, how about it?'

Needless to say I didn't take him up on his miserable offer but as I walked home in the freezing rain I wondered whether my life was always going to be this crap. I mean, God help me, but surely all my Friday nights from now on aren't going to end in some greasy chipper or in an endless queue at a taxi rank? Alone.

I wonder how much longer I'll be single anyway. Just out of interest really. I mean honestly, I'm not one of those desperate women going on lots of dates in the hope I might strike lucky. And my life certainly isn't all about trying to snare some random man so that I can quickly settle into dull suburbia and be the same as everybody else. I couldn't actually think of anything worse. I'm okay with being single. In fact I'm almost content. And for the past few months I've been wearing a DO NOT DISTURB sign over my heart. And I firmly believe you can be happy (if not happier) alone than with a man. Surely there must be nothing lonelier in this world than being paired off with the wrong person? However, I went to a fortune-teller last week and she said something which got me thinking. Initially I wanted to know if Ellie and I would ever be friends again, but the conversation drifted onto love and I was told I would find romance when I least expected it.

The one in the headscarf also said I should go somewhere where I normally wouldn't go. She probably had a point. After all the crowd never seems to change in my local pub and the chance of a handsome stranger walking in and whisking me off my weary feet gets slimmer as the years progress. That's probably why I ended up in a dodgy club last night with Dervala where the wine was so bad I started feeling hungover as soon as I began to drink. Dervala is a complete party animal whom I actively avoided in school but recently started hanging out with again, because everyone else is busy falling in love, or at least pretending to fall in love and giving the impression of being really, really happy. Anyway, when you're single the last thing you want to do is hang out with couples.

Dervala only just used me to have someone to go in the door with of course, although I didn't quite realise I sported the word 'sucker' streaked across my forehead. After our first drink she disappeared off with a Peter Andre look-alike except that he had blond hair. His friend looked like Peter Andre's younger brother, but with dark hair and asked if I'd like to go to his place or mine. 'Both,' I said. 'You go to yours and I'll stay in mine.' He opened his mouth stupidly and closed it again. Your place or mine? Please! Where have I heard that before? Is there nobody in this town with any imagination? Dublin is too small. That's what I think. I really need to find a new place to look for a suitable mate.

Speaking of places though, I urgently need to do something about getting a flatmate. It's not something I'm looking forward to. In fact, I'm dreading interviewing all these people. I mean, you meet someone for like, five minutes and you have to decide there and then whether you can sleep under the same roof as them for a year. And trust them with all your personal stuff! God, even the thought of it is terrifying. I wish I was rich enough to live by myself, I really do. But how am I ever going to become wealthy? Hell I can't even afford to play the Lotto!

But back to the love thing. Of course, I know why I'm single. Because you have to actually physically leave the flat to meet a man, don't you? You've got to put yourself out there, on the market, so to speak. Oh yes. But I have been sitting in my flat instead watching telly for the last few months. I'm even getting the hang of *Emmerdale*, and admiring Patsy Kensit's hair on a regular basis, which is a bit depressing really. So I haven't exactly been sitting in the window display of love, flogging my wares. Why? Well, it's quite simple really. My last few romantic endeavours turned out to be a lot less than successful so I just decided to give myself a break and get to know myself a bit. Mind you, sitting for hours in front of the TV certainly hasn't brought me any closer to finding the real me and it hasn't done my figure any favours either. Every time I see an ad for a chocolate bar I rush into the kitchen to see what else I can stuff my gob with. Why do Cadbury's always seem to advertise during the soaps?

The only way to lose weight is to stay out of the house all day long. Even I know that. Shopping is fantastic exercise and the new shopping centre in Dundrum will be an absolute haven for a shopaholic like me. Also trying on Miss Sixty jeans in communal city centre changing rooms along with stick insect teenagers is a great incentive to drop a few pounds. But unfortunately I've been hanging around the flat wearing baggy jumpers and tracksuit bottoms for far too long, and have therefore put on at least a stone in the last six months. That has to go. The sooner the better. At least when I was a student I could pretend I needed the food to give me energy for my exams. Now I've no excuse.

Anyway, about a year ago I seriously started to look around for a potential mate. Before that I was happy enough having the odd fling and basically enjoying myself. But then everybody started settling down and discussing property prices and crèches at dinner parties so I thought about joining them. That's when I met Mr Maybe. In one of those trendy new cocktail bars. You know the ones with the big windows and long queues outside with everybody breaking their neck to get in. This guy started chatting me up and he was tall, fairly handsome and determined to impress. He insisted on taking my number and to his credit he rang the very next day. Now, I have met many many men who've claimed their undying love in the small hours of the morning, only to disappear without trace once the bar has closed, so I was flattered by this guy's extraordinary eagerness. I agreed to accompany him to a fancy restaurant the following evening. He picked me up in a shiny black Mercedes. Yes, I *know*. I had to pull Ellie away from the window to stop her gawking. It was a great start but sadly not such a great finish.

As soon as I had strapped myself into the passenger seat Mr Maybe started making continuous calls on his mobile phone. He told me he was a band manager. He even told me the name of the band and although I consider myself more of a music buff than the average person, this band didn't ring any bells.

'They're huge in Germany,' he pointed out sulkily and then continued to yap away, choosing to completely ignore my lack of interest. Looking back, I reckon he was possibly on to the talking clock or something. Eventually he stopped but I had received the message loud and clear. Mr Maybe was clearly a VIP. Lucky me. He then parked the car and asked me what I wanted to do. I was a little confused – were we not supposed to be going to a restaurant or something?

I suggested a walk, recommending the South Wall pier in Ringsend because it's quiet and has fabulous views of the sea all the way over to Howth on a sunny day. I thought Mr Maybe would find it all terribly romantic. But no. The walk was nothing short of a disaster. My date kept looking over his shoulder to make sure his lovely car wasn't being vandalised by young thugs, and then to top it all, the heavens opened and it began to pour. Mr Maybe was furious and I began to feel very ill at ease and almost guilty, like the horrible weather was all my fault. We ran back to the car and then he asked if I was hungry. I nodded appreciatively so he started the car. And we drove and drove and drove. Eventually we stopped outside a dodgy-looking take-away with a gaudy neon purple sign hanging outside. At first I thought it was a joke but since nobody was laughing I realised that Mr Maybe was deadly serious. I ordered something vegetarian with fried rice. He ordered chips. Back at his plush Dalkey apartment, with fantastic views of the sea, I tucked into my 'dinner', which had since gone horribly cold. He stuck on a video featuring a lot of Chinese people waving swords about and shouting. Not a word was spoken as we munched in silence. Half way through 'dinner' my date turned towards me and looked meaningfully into my eyes. I returned his smile warmly. Thank God he had relaxed. Maybe the evening wouldn't turn out to be so bad after all. 'Fiona?' he spoke softly. 'Yes?' I answered in what I thought was my most seductive voice. He raised one eyebrow. 'You're not eating all of that fried rice, are you?'

Needless to say we never met up again.

Not one to be deterred by a few mishaps (after all there's nothing for nothing in this life) I met another fella shortly afterwards. He was a man of few words but I didn't mind. He seemed mysterious so I was intrigued. I'd met him in a busy nightclub two nights earlier where the music had been very loud. And let's face it, after a few drinks, men always seem that bit more desirable. However in the harsh daylight of O'Brien's sandwich bar, no sparks were flying. After what seemed like a very, very long silence, he asked 'So, Fiona, do you have any pets?'

'No', I answered truthfully, because I hadn't got my cat Timmy at that stage. 'Do you?'

'No,' he answered back.

And that, believe it or not, more or less wrapped up our brief conversation.

At this stage you're probably thinking that you're lucky compared to me. I must hold the world record for meeting dodgy men. Unfortunately though, I'm only just getting started. Oh yes.

After Mr Maybe and Mr Man-of-Few-Words, I didn't feel like dating for a while. Sitting home alone night after night might have been boring but at least I wasn't getting my heart broken and fretting madly over the fact that 'he' hadn't called. But before long, things started to look up again when I met a vaguely famous actor at the launch of a new shop. He'd been paid by a PR company to come along and say a few words and there'd been a lot of free drink on offer. He was a tad on the short side (aren't all male celebrities?) and fairly tipsy by the time we'd got talking so it was a bit of a shock when he called the next day and clearly remembered my name. I thought it was quite cool to be going on a date with a star even if he was a very 'minor' one, and a good few inches smaller than me. However, in his head, he might as well have been an Oscar winner! I'm surprised he didn't hire a pack of bodyguards, as he seemed to be so concerned by all his invisible 'fans'.

He suggested going to an exclusive club that I'd never been to but had read about in the back pages of the society magazines. Admittedly my heart began beating a bit quicker than normal as we approached the door and Mr-Almost-Famous bypassed the queue. However as we reached the door, he leaned over and whispered in my ear, 'Listen I get in for free here so I'll meet you inside. Okay?'

Looking back I should have turned on my heel there and then and gone home but as I deliberated on what I was going to do next, one of the bouncers recognised me (he'd done security work for a company I used to work for) and ushered me in free of charge.

Once I was inside my wide-eyed date said, 'How the hell did you manage that?' Of course I was so insulted, I didn't honour him with an answer. Then he proceeded to chat up every unsuspecting woman in the place. Not many were interested but he didn't seem to notice. Still, it was fairly humiliating sitting there nursing my drink alone like Billy-No-Mates. At the end of the night, I decided that things were obviously not going to work out between us and told him as much.

'Just because I'm famous and you're NOT!' he spluttered, his spiteful little face contorted with rage. And to make matters worse a bit of his spittle flew from his mouth and hit me in the eye.

We never met up again.

Anyway I'm sorry for going off on a tangent there but you know going to that fortune-teller got me thinking. I mean, I wonder how you do meet the perfect man? Is there such a thing as fate? Or is it just a load of old crap, meeting your soul mate and stuff? People say they 'just know' when they meet their partner. But what about all those people who get divorced? Did they not know? And how come everybody finds the right person just before they hit thirty these days? It's just too much of a coincidence if you ask me. There's got to be a lot of compromising going on.

I wonder how Ellie met Connor. She never told me very much about him. I've a fair idea they met on a press trip in Tunisia but the exact details have never been clear. I wonder who made the first move and whether it was love at first sight etc? Now I suppose I'll never know. After all, I've had absolutely no contact with Ellie since she moved out. She hasn't returned my calls and although I've tried explaining to her via her message minder, that absolutely nothing happened between Connor and myself, she still hasn't replied.

Maybe I should just write a long letter and explain everything. The thing is though, it's going to be pretty hard to explain how myself and Connor ended up in my room wearing practically nothing. Especially when Ellie was in hospital looking after an injured friend. I still feel sick even thinking about it. My God, the girl must think I'm the biggest creep in the world. I would if I were her. I would absolutely hate me.

The doorbell rings. It's Dervala. She wants to tell me all about her night of passion with the Peter Andre look-alike. I don't particularly want to listen to the sordid story but I do anyway. She says she shagged him and hasn't heard from him since. She wants to know if I think this is a bad sign.

I pretend to put a lot of thought into my answer. 'I think you should learn how to play hard to get, Derv,' I offer eventually. 'It works most of the time.'

'I suppose.' She lights a Marlboro Red, takes a deep puff and blows smoke all around my kitchen. With a discreet cough I stand up to open a window.

'Have you tried getting anyone for the flat yet?' she suddenly enquires, reaching for an empty mug to flick her ashes into.

'Um yeah, well sort of. At least I've made out a list of requirements.'

'A list?' Dervala looks intrigued. 'Go on, show us.'

I show her the list I made earlier. Dervala studies it and then nearly chokes on her cigarette. 'You're not being too fussy or anything, are you?'

'How do you mean?'

'You are asking for a lot, aren't you?

'Yeah, well I'll have to share my life with this person for the best part of the year so I can't be ending up with a nutcase. You have to be so careful these days. Did you never see the film *Single White Female?*'

'Now you're being dramatic. Why are you putting yourself under so much pressure anyway? Can't you manage the rent on your own?'

'On my salary? No, I bloody well can't. Do you have any idea how much I get paid? It's all right for you 'cos you're still living with your folks. I urgently need someone to share the bills with, but I also want someone, you know, decent.'

'Don't you think Ellie will want to move back though? She might you know, after this whole thing blows over.'

'Dervala,' I say in a serious voice, 'this *thing* will never blow over. Ellie will never forgive me for what happened.'

'Well, I think that's a real pity. Anyway, you could

put an ad up in the local supermarket but I'd advise putting something in the local press too. You'll get more of a choice that way.'

'I s'pose. If I have a lot of people queuing it'll make people more interested, right?'

'Right. People always want what others want. Like when you're going out with someone, other men always express an interest.'

'Do you know something? You're so right. When you're single, men don't tend to bang down your front door and you tend to remain single for a very long time 'cos people think there's something wrong with you. But when you're taken all these other men suddenly seem to come out of the woodwork proclaiming their undying love for you.'

'You said it.'

'Well, do you know something? From now on, I'm going to tell everyone I've a boyfriend so that I'll seem more attractive.'

'That's the spirit. Hey, you're not looking for anyone at the moment though, are you?'

'Well, not actively, no. But I wouldn't say no to Brad Pitt.'

'Or Peter Andre.'

'Yeah, well whatever . . .'

At 6.55 the following evening I peep out the window and my heart gives a little flutter when I see the length of the queue. It's pretty exciting seeing all those people waiting outside to get into my humble abode. After all, one of those people might be the perfect flatmate and we'll hit it off and live happily ever after. Wouldn't that be fantastic? Then again, I don't want to get my hopes up too much. After all, if I'm overly eager, potential flatmates might be put off.

They seem to be mostly women in the queue, which is good. I specifically asked for females in my ad, as I don't fancy hairy men walking around butt naked in the kitchen, putting me off my Kellogg's Cheerios or Special K (depending on how fat I feel). I'd love to get a better look but I don't want to be spotted peering out at the queue, like some old biddy.

I just take another quick peek outside and to my amazement I see somebody in the middle of it all, holding a big bunch of flowers. Wow! I have to say I *am* impressed. I mean talk about making an effort! But I wouldn't pick some girl just because she brought me flowers though. No. I'm not as shallow as all that. Of *course* not. For all I know she might have robbed them from the next-door neighbour's garden! I can't resist another little look however. I squint through a crack in the curtains to see what the flower-carrying woman looks like. But hang on a minute, it's not a woman at all. It's a bloke. A tall, handsome . . . it's, wait a minute . . . what the fuck is Connor doing in the queue?

I wake up this morning feeling pretty low. At first I can't think why but then it dawns on me. Yes. Or rather it hits me like a slap in the face. I'm thirty today. Yes, thirty. The big three O! So that means I can no longer call myself a 'twentysomething'. Not truthfully anyway.

I don't mind being thirty of course – it doesn't bother me *that* much. After all, it's got to be better than being twenty, and infinitely better than being an angst-ridden spotty teenager with more issues than you could shake a twig at. But the thing is, and this is the really horrible part, I'm not a millionaire yet. And not only am I not a millionaire, I'm not even any-where near it. And that's the real problem. You see, like most people I always thought I'd be a millionaire before I hit thirty, but not only have I not got zillions in the bank, I am actually overdrawn. And to make matters much, much worse, when I switch on my mobile phone to see if anybody has called to wish me a Happy Birthday, I realise that the only person who has left a message is a guy called Edwin. He says he's from the credit-card company and that he would like me to ring him back at my earliest convenience. Right. Well, obviously it will not be at all convenient to ring somebody called Edwin about my drastic lack of funds on my thirtieth birthday so he'll just have to wait until tomorrow. Bloody Edwin. What kind of name is that anyway?

I sit up, rest my back against a small hill of comfy pillows and yawn. I've the day off today. Yes, I requested the day off to celebrate my birthday. A few weeks ago when I was filling in my holiday roster it seemed like a good idea. Now though I'm wondering why I even bothered. After all, nobody knows it's my birthday except my family (and knowing them they've probably forgotten). Maybe I should have organised something. Perhaps I should have arranged for a big gang of us to meet up. Then again, I'd be kind of embarrassed doing that. As if I only contacted people to get them to buy me presents. Or ply me with cheap booze for the night or something.

I wander into the kitchen, which seems kind of bare since Ellie left and took all her cheerful-looking pots and plants with her. At least Connor's roses are nice, although they're already beginning to wilt. Half of them hang their heads in shame as if to remind me why Connor gave them to me in the first place.

He said he wanted to apologise last night, as he stood in the doorway, looking even more handsome than I'd remembered him. I felt my face burn with embarrassment as he pressed the bunch into my arms.

'Not now,' I said through gritted teeth. 'I'm interviewing people for the flat.'

'Okay, so my timing isn't great. I won't stick around, but I want you to take them anyway,' he insisted. 'It's the least I can do after all the trouble I caused.'

I could see all the women in the queue staring with awe and admiration. But they were obviously just judging him by his looks. Of course they didn't know the full story and never will, thank God. If they did they might not have been too impressed. Connor just stood there, his soulful eyes penetrating my gaze. I could feel myself going ten shades of red and just wanted to die.

'Thanks,' I muttered. 'But seriously you'd better go now. I'm not putting on a comedy show for a bunch of curious strangers. Otherwise I'll never manage to get a new flatmate.'

'Listen, as I said, I know the timing's pretty bad. I didn't realise you were . . . you were . . . listen I'll call around again tomorrow maybe?' Connor stared at me with his dark-blue film-star eyes and it took all my willpower not to let my knees give from under me.

'I really don't think that's necessary,' I said, feeling more and more uncomfortable by the second. 'After all I lost my flatmate 'cos of you.'

'Well . . . I could have said I lost my girlfriend because of you,' he said after a slight pause, 'but I didn't.'

He gave me one long last searching look and then

slowly walked away, oblivious to the stares of the remaining women in the queue.

But now as I sit in my little flat, alone on my thirtieth birthday, I wonder how I let a guy that good-looking walk down the garden path and out of my life forever. After all, it's not like anyone decent ever fancies me. It's not like they're beating down my door to take me out. And the only text messages I get these days are from Dervala telling me to ring her as she's no credit left in her ready-to-go phone. Imagine being thirty and knowing that nobody in the whole wide world fancies you. It's so depressing. In fact the only men who ever seem to express interest in me bear an uncanny resemblance to Mr Bean. Except that they're not funny of course. And not on TV.

I stare out the window now, at the grey Dublin sky. It's the end of September and I'm already dreading facing the long winter months ahead. I despise the short dark days and the dreary daily commute into town in my little banger, which doesn't even have a radio. Everything about winter depresses me except for Christmas. I like Christmas except for the actual day of course. That is always a hell of an anticlimax due to our annual family fight. And the fact that nobody is ever happy with their presents. Why do I always end up getting a book I've already read and the same CD from two different people?

Last year after a blazing row, I stormed out of the house and went over to Ellie's family. They were all sitting around the fire chatting politely. Somebody was playing the piano and nobody was even drunk. It was so nice and civilised. I wanted to stay there forever. I didn't need my own family members to remind me how shit my life was because I already knew that. But after a while Ellie convinced me to go home and make up with my folks instead of going back to the cold empty flat to stuff my face with Christmas cake and Quality Street. She said that next year I might not have a chance to celebrate with the people I love. She was right. My grandfather died the following spring. That Christmas was his last, and when Ellie dropped me back later, we ended up watching *Only Fools and Horses* together and laughing our heads off.

Right. No more moping about, thinking of birthdays and Christmas and my poor late granddad. I need to see about getting a new tenant to help me pay the bills before my phone and electricity is cut off. Every time I open the post now, I seem to be screwed for more money. And every time I seem to pay a bill, a fresh one pops through my letterbox. I almost need a full-time secretary to deal with all my bill admin at this stage.

Now then, I've already written out a list of candidates for the flat. From that list I must choose somebody who appears sane; who will not try and stab me in the middle of the night, leave out-of-date milk in the fridge or write my name on the bathroom mirror with blood-red lipstick.

Okay so let's weigh up the options. Ten people called last night, as well as Connor. And he doesn't count of course. One woman asked if it was okay if her boyfriend stayed over a few nights a week.

'No problem,' I assured her, mentally crossing her off my list of potentials. If I'd wanted to share with an amorous couple, I'd have advertised for one. I will absolutely NOT have couples getting up to high jinks in my flat.

A very young girl with wild dark curly hair and a nose ring said she was just about to start Economics and Politics in UCD and couldn't wait to go 'absolutely mad'. She didn't make the grade either. 'Going mad' is something you do in your teens and twenties. In your thirties it's definitely time to slow down. Or at least share a flat with somebody who is slowing down instead of just getting revved up.

A divorced man in his mid-forties told me he had just quit his job to write 'the great Irish novel', and another guy with greasy hair tied back in a long thin plait said he was crazy about yoga and would I mind if he meditated in the kitchen. Honest to God; did these people not read my ad? I want a young professional female flatmate, not some hippy loony looking for the meaning of life in between my fridge and the microwave!

One woman asked was I a vegetarian, explaining that she couldn't possibly put her food in the same fridge as decaying carcasses of fish, birds and animals. Now, I'm a veggie myself but I reckon this woman was a bit over the top. I could picture her sitting chained to railings outside government buildings, and hanging about unwashed in a forest for weeks in a bid to save a single branch, never mind a tree!

A woman called Alice also asked how long the place was available for.

'The lease is up in nine months,' I said. That didn't suit her. She said she was looking for something a bit more long term. Something more *permanent*. She was looking to settle down, she stressed and didn't even ask to be shown around. What? Was she looking for us to get married or something?

A guy with dreadlocks and a guitar asked if he could move in immediately as his girlfriend and himself were having a few problems. Apparently she had kicked him out that morning, and therefore he was technically homeless.

'I'm afraid that's not possible,' I told him firmly. 'I like to see everybody and then sleep on it.'

'Rightio,' he shrugged and ambled off down the path as if in a daze. I knew I wouldn't hear from him again. The following evening he'd probably be in Oz. Or another planet even.

The last potential flatmate was a slim, very good-looking blonde who thought the place was a bit small and wondered was there ample parking for her BMW. When she found the answer to be negative she clickety-clicked down the path, talking loudly into her mobile phone and I could hear her saying, 'Ah no, Gabrielle, definitely *not*. It was a bit of a dump really. Horrible green flowery wallpaper. Reminded me of vomit. And the girl wasn't really our type.'

I stood rooted to the spot in shock. Not our type? What on earth was she talking about, the snooty bitch! And anyway my place is NOT a dump. I mean, it's not exactly the most modern place ever but it's really homely and warm in the winter when you light a fire and there's a lovely . . . hang on, why am I even thinking about what that cow said? Good luck to her. I hope a rat bites her in the next place she visits. I hope her BMW breaks down on her way home. Okay, okay, deep breath, I need to calm down. Maybe I'm a bit stressed. It's just that I've had a long day and suddenly don't feel like interviewing anyone else.

I hovered in the doorway for a little longer and looked around to see if I could see anybody else. I couldn't, even though at least twenty-five more people had phoned earlier asking for directions. Why do they do that, I wondered. Are people in offices really that bored nowadays? Wouldn't it be more fun to ring sex lines or something?

I retreated into my flat and washed an old, slightly chipped vase to put Connor's roses into. They looked so pretty. Ellie would have loved them. She loves flowers. Then I went to bed hoping that I'd be inspired in the middle of the night. I woke up this morning however and realised I was no nearer to finding the perfect flatmate. Dammit.

The phone rings suddenly. It's my sister Gemma calling from Cardiff. She says my birthday card is in the post, which of course means that she is about to go to the post office and then pretend the delay is all the Royal Mail's fault again. Imagine. Yet another year and I receive absolutely zilch from her. No wonder birthdays are so depressing.

'So, what do you think of being thirty?' she quizzes. 'Not too bad, eh?'

'It's amazing,' I say sarcastically. 'I feel like a completely different person. I thoroughly recommend middle age.'

'Haha. Seriously though, thirty does seem quite old, doesn't it? You'd need to get a move on now. Time's running out.'

'Running out? Running out for what?'

'Well, everyone your age will be getting hitched now. You'd need to get moving or only the duds will be left. Once men enter their thirties the hair-lines rapidly recede, the beer bellies rapidly expand and the good-looking ones are all locked away by wily females who have clasped a gold band around their finger.'

'Hmm. Feck that, I don't have time to be out chasing potential husbands. I'd find that all a bit exhausting. But I do need to get myself a decent job though.'

'Where?'

'I don't know. As long as it's in a building with lots of men I can have flings with. The only single man in my office wears Fair Isle jumpers, is saving for a house and only drinks at company events where the booze is free. I want to start working in a job I really enjoy. Somewhere with lots of talent.'

'Don't we all want that? How do you think I feel about looking at willies all day? At least you get to sit on your arse and surf the net.'

Just to explain quickly, my sister is a urologist,

which means that she really *does* examine willies for a living, when she's not giving out about the long hours she works, of course. Gemma is the world's greatest moan. She also complains about all the extra marital sex going on between the doctors but I reckon she's just jealous 'cos she's not getting any action herself. However, at least she gets a lot of money to do what she does, and she lives in a really cool apartment beside Charlotte Church or somebody and is a member of the luxury gym at St David's Hotel.

I, on the other hand, earn shag-all money, live in Booterstown in a seriously small flat with horrible green wallpaper on the walls. And now I unfortunately must share it with a complete stranger, whom I might or might not get along with. I dislike my job so much that I start dreading Monday morning as early as Saturday afternoon and I spend my life looking at the calendar and counting the days before the next bank holiday weekend. Also, nobody in my office shows anybody any respect. Not even the Portuguese porter. He still asks me to show him my ID even though I've been working in the building for almost a year!

I'm sick of being treated like a nobody. At least people respect my sister Gemma. She's saving lives and therefore is worthy in the eyes of society. People want to know her and invite her to dinner parties and things. But what about me? I just put stamps on letters, photocopy documents I can't make head nor tail of, and speak to clients who rudely slam down phones mid conversation. Plus I cannot even *remember* the last party I was at. Apart from the one we had recently in the flat. And inviting oneself to one's own party doesn't really count, does it?

Suddenly I feel very sad. Like the kid who never gets picked for the hockey team. Or the fat girl who really hopes the sleazebag in the local nightclub will ask her to dance. Just because he has asked everybody else and it will look really bad if he leaves her out. Yes, it's crap living my life. From now on I want to be in the fun set. In the swing of things. I'd like to be one of those people who is *forced* to turn down invitations instead of being pathetically grateful to random girlfriends who phone for last minute drinks. Just so they can chew my ear while analysing their own relationship.

'Surfing the net becomes boring after a few hours though,' I tell Gemma, suddenly remembering that I'm still on the phone. 'Being in an office job isn't all it's cracked up to be. And I'm putting on so much weight. Any time anyone goes to the shop I ask them to get me some chocolate, crisps or a cheese and coleslaw sambo just to relieve the boredom. I'm always craving things.'

'You need to nip that in the bud.'

'I know, I know, but how? At the moment I'm going through a white chocolate Maltesers phase. Last week it was cheese and onion Taytos. Next week, please God, it'll be celery sticks or something.'

'What weight are you now?'

'Ten and a half stone.'

'I'm nine stone two. I'm a disgrace!'

'Thanks, Gemma, you've just brightened up my day.'

'You know what to do, cut out the crap, stop drinking and walk for two hours every night. And I mean power walk, not just strolling around listening to love songs on your Walkman. Tell you what, I'll be in Dublin in a month's time. If you've lost a stone by then I'll give you a two hundred euro shopping voucher.'

'God, Gemma, that's pretty generous of you. Are you sure?'

'I'm not being generous at all,' Gemma says. 'I don't want people saying they saw that fat sister of mine. You need to pull yourself together. Have you anything to look forward to at the moment?'

'No.'

'See, that's the problem. You *must* have something to look forward to. You're not seeing anyone, are you?'

'You know I'm not.'

'Well that's a pity 'cos if you were and he broke it off, you'd drop the weight effortlessly.'

'Don't I know it? I lost a stone after Greg without even noticing. It was brilliant. They should actually hire out bastards in the local slimming club. They usually help women lose weight more than any silly charts and exercise programmes.'

'And you need to start going out more,' Gemma continues in her 'helpful' manner. 'Go dancing, it's great for the figure. Is Ellie still seeing that gorgeous guy by the way? Maybe he had some friends?'

'How do you know about him?'

'Oh, last time I phoned, she was yapping on and

on about some hunk she'd just met. She said you lot were having a party and he was bringing his friends round. How did that go? Did you score at all?'

'Er, no . . . not exactly. Listen, Gemma, I'd better let you go, this must be costing you a fortune.'

'Nah, I'm phoning from the hospital. Don't worry, I can talk for a bit longer.'

'Yes but *I* can't. If I don't reach a toilet in the next two minutes, my bladder will burst. Sorry for being so blunt but I'll talk to you later, okay?'

'God, you're so *rude*, Fiona. Maybe if you were a bit more polite you'd have better luck with men, you know? I'm only saying that to you 'cos you're my little sister, and I'm always looking out for you. Anyway, Happy Birthday again. Don't go too mad, do you hear me?'

'Yeah, yeah, bye.'

I put down the phone. Don't go too mad? Jesus, I wish I bloody well had a choice!

I feel kind of depressed after talking to Gemma. If she's supposed to be looking out for me, why don't I feel safe? There's something a bit miserable about one's birthday, isn't there? When you were younger everybody seemed to make a huge fuss and you were treated like a princess for the day. Now nobody really gives a curse, and you end up telling complete strangers that it's your birthday just so that they'll look at you blankly and go 'Oh Happy Birthday.'

There's a knock on the door. Great. It's my mum. She's armed with a stinking piece of fish for my cat Timmy, who has incidentally been missing for the last few days. Hmm. I wonder where he is. He moves in with the people next door every now and then, until they get sick of him and he comes crawling back with his tail between his legs.

'What do you want for your birthday?' Mum barks, stuffing the smelly piece of fish in among some beer cans. 'Ughh, how can you live like this, dearest? You've no food in the flat and what's this?' She opens an out-of-date jar of tomato sauce with a layer of grey fluff sitting on the top.

'Well I'm on a kind of a diet,' I tell her.

Mum lifts up her sunglasses and looks me up and down. 'Well *that's* good anyway. Men don't fancy fat girls, never did. When I was your age I was a slender seven and a half stone and that was after having three children.'

'Mmm.'

'Anyway, if you're not doing anything, you can hop in the car now and we can go to Dunnes Stores and see if we can get you something nice for your birthday. Maybe you could get something cheerful for the flat. I always think it's very dark in here with that dreadful green wallpaper. By the way, where's Ellie?'

'At work.'

It's not a lie. I mean, the probability is that Ellie *is* indeed at work – where else would she be? But obviously I don't want to tell Mum that Ellie has moved out. Not yet. Not until I've thought of a bloody excuse anyway. My mother thinks there's nobody like Ellie. If I say we've fallen out Mum will think it's all my fault. Which it isn't. Connor is to blame. We were all happy until he came along.

'Nice roses.' Mum's beady eyes catch sight of the bunch. 'Have you flower food for them? Who gave them to you? Anybody nice?'

'No. Listen, I'll just grab my coat and we'll go to Dunnes.'

We pick out two nice cream-coloured chairs and two chocolate-coloured cushions and then go for coffee and carrot cake. As soon as I get home my mobile phone rings.

'What are we doing for your birthday?' Dervala screeches down the line.

'Um, I don't fancy doing much,' I mumble unenthusiastically. 'I'm too old to be bopping around now and anyway I don't want to go to a loud club where I'll end up not being able to get a seat and fighting off randy young men at the bar.'

'Nonsense, you have to go out,' she insists. 'Anyway thirty is the new twenty. I read that somewhere recently.'

'Yeah right. No honestly, Derv, I'm not up for a mad session. Not tonight anyway. I've work tomorrow.'

'Since when did that ever make any difference?'

'Well, now that I'm thirty I'm going to start taking work seriously,' I tell her.

'Okay, so will I call over with a bottle of wine then?'

I think about it for a moment. I really shouldn't . . .

'Okay, you're on. Actually, make that two bottles.'

*

'To middle age!' Dervala enthuses as she cracks open bottle number two. 'And to the future. May life give you everything you deserve. You're wasted in that poxy job, you know. Have you thought about moving on yet?'

'Yeah, all the time. I'm just not sure what I want to do though. It's so depressing. I mean I'm thirty and I have absolutely no money in the bank. It's just really hit home today. I'm broke. Isn't that just crap?'

'Very.'

'And what's worse is that everybody I seem to meet is in a brilliant job, making stacks of money, has miraculously fallen in love with the right person, is deliriously happy, tells everybody how much their house has increased in value since they bought it, is in the process of starting a family and trades their car in every two years.'

'Gosh. You must be meeting the exact same people as me. So where did we both go so wrong? Why don't we have a house and an ageing balding boastful fella to go with it?'

'Not all property owners are bald, Derv.'

'Look on the bright side. At least you don't have a crazy car loan like I do. Mine's a crippler.'

'I know, but my old banger breaks down so often, I usually have to get the bus everywhere instead. How embarrassing is that? I still feel like a student for God's sake.'

'But what do you really, really want to do though?' Dervala says, refilling our glasses but still managing to spill half on the table. 'I mean you didn't like working as a nanny or a hotel receptionist, did you?'

'Ah come on now,' I giggle. 'I did those kind of jobs when I left school. But realistically I couldn't go back to doing anything like that now.'

'Well you didn't like teaching English as a foreign language either.'

'No, that was exhausting,' I admit. 'And I never met anybody normal doing that either. All my pupils wanted to marry me so they could get visas and live in Ireland.'

'At least you've been proposed to though. Sadly I think I've more chance of being run over by the LUAS than getting a marriage proposal. But enough about me. Back to your job prospects. You liked working for *Gloss* magazine when you were there.'

'Yeah I did, kind of, didn't I?'

'You were very enthusiastic about the magazine world.'

'Well, working in *Gloss* was probably my best job so far. Yes, I did like that, apart from the fact that Faith, my editor, kept all the free make-up and went to all the celeb parties herself. In the end I got sick of being an agony aunt, and writing the horoscopes and monthly sex tips. I mean the only celebrity I ever got to interview was Daniel O'Donnell for God's sake!'

'Maybe, if you'd stuck at it, they would have eventually let you interview more interesting people. Like . . . oh I dunno . . .'

'Yeah, but I'll never know now though, will I? I

suppose I shouldn't have got so drunk at the Christmas party . . .'

'. . . and snogged Father Christmas.'

'Yes, that wasn't the cleverest move I ever made but sure how was I to know he was Faith's man? He looked completely different with a white beard.'

'Never trust a man with a red hat and a white beard . . .' Dervala advises and knocks back the rest of our wine.

'Hey, is it all gone?'

'What?'

'The wine, there's hardly any left! This is a disaster!'

'Don't worry.' Dervala fishes out her mobile and starts punching in digits.

'Who are you ringing?' I feel a moment of panic coming on. 'You'd better not be ringing Peter Andre. It's best not to drink and dial.'

'Who's drunk? I'm just ringing a taxi to go down to Spar and get us another bottle of wine. And a birthday cake, haha! We never got a birthday cake! Anyway I don't think we're drunk *enough*. I mean, think about it, you're never going to be thirty again.'

'Dervala, as far as I know, I'll be thirty for a whole year.'

When the taxi arrives Dervala toddles off to the local Spar to get 'all we need when we need it' for our little late-night feast. We've suddenly decided that you only live once. Within minutes the doorbell rings again. Hey, that was quick!

For a laugh I open the letterbox from the inside

and shout, 'you're not coming in ya bitch ya,' in a funny voice. Actually it probably isn't funny at all but you know when you're drunk everything seems so hilarious. The doorbell rings again.

'Get lost, ya drunken whore,' I giggle.

Dervala doesn't answer and simply gives the doorbell another very long ring. Ah for God's sake, she isn't playing this game at all! I open up. And freeze with mortification. It's not Dervala at all. It's a young, frighteningly thin girl with long damp brown hair and steamed-up glasses. Jesus, how did I not notice the rain? It's bloody lashing out there.

The girl stares at me way too intensely for my liking.

'Am I too late?'

I peer at the scrawny thing standing drenched in my doorway.

'Too late for what?'

'Am I not at the right address? Do you not have a room to rent?'

'Huh? No, I mean, I showed it last night.'

The girl's face falls. 'I don't believe it,' she says suddenly looking devastated. 'I must have read the notice wrong. I presume it's gone and all.'

'Well, actually, it's . . .'

Shit, what am I going to do? Am I going to show her in and let her see the empty wine bottles on the table? She'll think I've a major fecking drink problem, if I do. Then again, if I explain that it's my birthday, will she think I'm a sad case for not going out to celebrate? God, someone help me out here.

Now.

'It's still available,' I say suddenly.

Her face breaks into a huge smile. 'Oh thank *God* for that,' she gives a sigh of relief. 'I've been trudging around all day and you should see the state of some of the places I've visited. I wouldn't let animals into some of them. So, do you live here by yourself?'

'Ye . . . es, I do indeed. It's in a bit of a mess right now 'cos I wasn't expecting anybody tonight you know. My friend is over with me now. Well . . . actually she has just popped out for a minute to get some er . . . some er, groceries.'

'Would I be able to see the room now?'

'Sure. Come on in.' I stand back and hope she can't smell the fumes of alcohol off me. I don't want her thinking I'm a wino or anything.

'Oh it's really nice,' she says enthusiastically, admiring the living room. 'It's very homely, isn't it?'

I like her immediately. She's obviously easily pleased and not even put off by the green wallpaper. Not like that other horrible woman with the BMW. Good luck to *her*.

'Come on, I'll show you the bedroom.'

I lead the way. I notice she hasn't mentioned the empty wine bottles. Maybe she hasn't seen them. Or maybe she thinks I just use them as vases or something.

'Do you have a cat?' she asks, almost tripping over a small toy mouse at the bedroom door.

'Kind of. I share him with the neighbours. He only calls in every now and then when he's bored.'

'What age is he?

'He's about two. I've had him since he was a kitten. Someone threw him over a friend's wall and the poor little thing was badly injured. I'd been saving to go away to a luxury spa for a night and ended up giving my money to the local vet instead. I spend more on him than I do on myself.'

'Gosh, some people can be so cruel, can't they?'

'Yes, anybody who abuses an animal should be shot.'

'I love cats,' she tells me. 'They're so clever, aren't they?'

Another bonus point! If she loves cats she can feed Timmy when I go holidays.

'Clever yes, but not at all faithful.'

'Like men.'

'Exactly.'

God, this girl is great!

I show her the spare room. It's tiny and there are marks on the wall where Ellie's photos used to be. But she loves it.

'It's perfect. It's just great. I'll definitely take it. When can I move in? What's the rent? I've plenty of cash on me so I could give you the deposit now.'

'I . . . well . . .'

'Oh God, I'm being very presumptuous. You need time to think about it, don't you? Maybe I could give you a call tomorrow? I don't want to be putting you under any pressure or anything. How about I go and look at a few more places while you're thinking about it?'

Suddenly I have this vision of this lovely country

girl leaving here, finding another flat and roommate and never ever darkening my doorstep again. If this happens, where will that leave me? I'll end up having to interview another bunch of fruit and nuts all over again next week.

'No, you can have the room,' I say like lightning. 'The rent is four hundred euro and the deposit is the same.'

'That's very reasonable. I can give you all the money now if you want. Do I have to sign a lease or anything?'

'No, if you want to move out, you can give me four weeks' notice and vice versa. Em, do you have any other questions?'

The doorbell rings and my heart sinks. Jesus, I don't really want my new flatmate to meet Dervala just this minute. She might change her mind about moving in. Then again, I can't just leave Dervala standing on the doorstep in the pouring rain either, can I? Oh fuck it.

I answer the door and Dervala, laden down with plastic bags, starts singing Happy Birthday in a really loud voice. She stops immediately when she sees we've company.

'Hi there,' she looks appropriately embarrassed. 'Fiona didn't tell me she was inviting anyone else to the party.'

'*Is* this a party?'

'This is my friend Dervala,' I cut in. 'And, Dervala, this is er . . .' Christ what the hell is her name? '. . . my new flatmate.'

Dervala looks as astonished as I feel ridiculous.

'I'm Bunny,' the girl introduces herself.

Bunny? OHMIGOD!

'Nice to meet you, Bunny,' Dervala says with a half smile. 'Fiona never told me you were moving in.'

'That's because I didn't know,' I say with false gaiety followed by a silly laugh. I must say I'm beginning to feel like a complete tool. I've just realised I don't know the first thing about this Bunny creature.

'Do you work near here?' Dervala asks curiously.

'Oh no,' Bunny beams enthusiastically. 'Not at all.'

'So where do you work?'

'Well, haha, as a matter of fact, I don't.'

'You don't work at all?' I cut in anxiously.

'No, actually. I'm unemployed.'

I've been in an ambulance once before. And that was years ago. It was the time when my finger got stuck in the wheel of a bike. And even though the pain was absolutely horrendous, and my finger was all cut and mangled, I remember thinking it was quite exciting with the siren going off and everyone making a fuss and everything. This time around however, it is so, so different. Yes, this is nothing short of a nightmare.

The three of us, Bunny, Dervala and I, are in the back of the ambulance, along with two paramedics. Bunny is on a stretcher because she passed out in the toilets of a nightculb and hit her head against the stone floor. And Dervala is crying because she is drunk. I, however, am feeling frighteningly sober and am frantically praying that Bunny isn't going to die.

At the hospital I'm gravely informed that I must complete a form for Bunny as she is drifting in and out of consciousness and unable to give details herself. I read through the questions in complete panic. How the hell can I fill this out? I don't even know Bunny's real name, never mind her religion or medical history! How can I possibly answer all these questions about somebody I only met a couple of hours ago?

The administration woman behind the desk finds this all very strange.

'What do you mean you don't know your friend's name?'

'She's not my friend, she's my flatmate,' I explain helplessly.

The woman just stares coldly and waits for me to continue.

'She only just moved in tonight.'

'Excuse me?'

The expression on the woman's face is now a mixture of disbelief and distrust. She clearly thinks I'm still drunk, which I most definitely am not. I may have had a few but . . .

'It was my birthday, see? And myself and my friend here were having a few glasses of wine. And Bunny came to see the flat and decided she wanted to move in. Then she had a few glasses of wine with us to celebrate and we ended up in a nightclub. It all happened so fast. One minute we were all dancing and having fun and the next minute she just disappeared. We thought she'd gone to the bathroom. When I went looking for her, she'd passed out on the floor and hit her head.'

'She's not used to alcohol?'

'I don't know,' I answer miserably. 'Well, obviously *not*. But as I said I don't know the first thing about her. I don't know where she's from nor do I have any contact details for her. I'm really sorry.'

Dervala starts snivelling again as the woman purses her lips and shakes her head, displaying her utter contempt.

A nurse appears then and says she thinks Bunny is going to be okay but she'll need to stay the night and be kept under observation.

'Is she on medication?' the nurse wants to know.

'I haven't a clue,' I say, my voice beginning to crack now. 'I don't know anything about the girl except that she's twenty-four years old and came to Dublin to look for a job after she split up with her boyfriend. I know that might sound mad but truthfully, it's all we know about her.'

'It's the truth, we shwear to God,' Dervala adds, making us look even more idiotic than we already do. I shoot her a warning look but she doesn't even notice.

'Okay,' the nurse says in a more serious voice. 'I need you girls to do something for me now. I need you to go home and look in Bunny's room for any pills, no matter how innocent they might look, and phone me back with the information written on the bottles. It's very important that you do that.'

'But she hasn't even moved in,' I explain. 'She didn't bring any stuff.'

The nurse remains remarkably calm. 'Did she have a handbag?'

'Oh . . . actually yes she did,' I suddenly remember.

'She decided to leave it in the flat in case it got stolen. Isn't that right, Dervala?'

But Dervala doesn't look as if she could tell you her own name, never mind whether Bunny left a handbag in somebody's flat.

'I'll ring you in about ten minutes,' I promise the nurse, so grateful that she isn't making us out to be two psychopaths trying to murder an innocent country girl by ramming booze down her throat.

'Is she going to be all right?' I ask, because honestly if anything happened to Bunny, I would never ever forgive myself and besides, who would I ring? How would I tell her folks? The police would need to get involved and the media would undoubtedly come looking for us. Maybe they'd camp out on the doorstep trying to get a photo.

Jesus, how the hell did we get ourselves in to this mess? Dervala was just supposed to be calling over for a drink to cheer me up on my thirtieth birthday. Instead I feel like a bold fifteen-year-old schoolgirl who has just raided my parents' drinks cabinet, and got the girl next door drunk. Only Bunny *isn't* the girl next door. She's my new flatmate. What's more she doesn't have a job and she's probably a drug addict. Christ!

Back at the flat, I open Bunny's handbag and my eyes nearly pop out of my head. Bunny's bag is like a mobile bloody pharmacy. What in the name of God is all this? I count at least five small white bottles of tablets. Dervala says she's too tired to do anything except go to bed. Then she plonks her generously built frame onto the sofa and closes her eyes. Some bloody help she is! I ring the nurse in the hospital and call out the prescription numbers on all the bottles. She then explains to me that one of the bottles contains strong diet pills, which are not supposed to be taken with alcohol.

'That's probably the reason why Bunny passed out,' she adds gently.

I breathe a huge sigh of relief. 'So she's not going to die?'

'No,' the nurse explains, 'but we'll keep her here for a few more hours and then you can bring her home. By the way, are you sure Bunny is no longer in a relationship?'

'Not any more, no. Not as far as I'm aware anyway.'

'Good.'

Hmm. Why does the nurse think that's good?

'So anyway, as I said, you can bring her home in a few hours,' the nurse then continues in a professional tone of voice.

Home? Oh yeah, I forgot. Bunny lives here now, doesn't she? God, this is nuts! I'm supposed to be in work in just over three hours' time and instead I'll have to take another day off to look after a sick pill-popping stranger. Dervala is now snoring loudly on the sofa and looks like she won't be waking any time soon.

Christ. I feel wretched. Was it really only yesterday that I sat in my kitchen, promising to get a proper grip on my life?

'Is she still not up yet?'

'No, Dervala, she's not budging. I've put my head around the door a few times but she's just so out of it. I wish there was somebody I could ring. She's *got* to have some sort of family. Maybe they're worried about her. She doesn't even have a phone with her. Just a wallet.'

'At least she's going to be okay.'

'Yeah but I'm really worried now. I mean she's obviously a bit mad and I can't just go off to work and leave her here in the flat by herself now, can I?'

'No, I suppose not. Did work ring you?'

'No, but *I* rang *them* to say I wouldn't be coming in. Needless to say they weren't too impressed. I suppose they reckon I've just got a hangover from last night.'

'I rang in sick too. They were pretty suspicious all right, but fuck them.'

That's Derv for you. Always looking on the bright side of life!

The phone rings. It's a man looking for Ellie.

'Ellie has moved out,' I explain wearily. God, I'm getting a bit sick of this. He's about the hundredth person to phone for her in the last few days. Where is she? How the hell am I supposed to know?

'No, no I don't have another telephone number for her except her mobile. Have you tried that? Oh I see. All right then. Just hang on 'til I get a pen.'

I carefully write down the message although I'm not sure why I'm even helping out here. It's not as if Ellie will ever be calling to see who phoned. It's weird. It's like she has just vanished or something. Can you believe she was once my best friend?

The man on the other end of the phone is from some travel company in Birmingham. He wants to know if Ellie can go to Birmingham in a couple of days on a press trip. The first-class tickets can be couriered out, and Ellie will be picked up from the airport by limousine and brought to the luxury Malmaison Hotel where she'll enjoy a gourmet meal with some travel industry heads.

I'm writing all this frantically on the back of an envelope. The next morning she will be brought around Birmingham with a personal guide to visit the sights, and then lunch in an exclusive restaurant before being flown back to Dublin. As I write I can feel more than a pang of jealousy coming on. While Ellie swans around Birmingham for a couple of days being wined and dined, I'll be in work receiving a bollicking from my boss Joe or his annoying assistant Cynthia. Yes, not too exciting really, is it? I will have to sit there and take it too, because if I don't I'll be fired and have no money at all. And if that wasn't bad enough, some strange bird is still conked out in the spare room, sleeping off the mother of all hangovers.

'Who was that?' Dervala asks when I've put down the phone.

'Some guy offering Ellie a jammy press trip. Depressing isn't it? I know it's Birmingham and not Barbados but Jesus, it sounds great. I'd love to go on a trip where I'm wined and dined and brought around to see a bunch of stuff.'

'God yeah, I wouldn't mind it myself. Where else does Ellie go?'

'Where *doesn't* she go? Australia for ten days, a week in Thailand at some spa resort, five days wine tasting in the South of France – and that's only in the last few months. I believe the pay isn't great though. Ellie says that although you get to stay in five-star hotels and eat in the best restaurants all over the world, you don't end up with a lot of money in the bank really.'

'But hang on a sec, you could work for most of the year in an office just to save for your annual holidays. This way you get to go for free.'

'Mmm. Never thought about it like that. I've a good mind to ring that guy back and say I'll go myself.'

'You're right,' Dervala agrees lighting up a cigarette.

'I *am* joking by the way,' I laugh.

'Are you? But why? Why wouldn't you go? I mean if Ellie can't go the trip's going to be wasted anyway.'

'Do you think her editor would mind? I've met

him before. His name's Stuart. I chatted to him briefly at a party one night when he asked me to dance. Don't think I made a good impression though.'

'Didn't you?'

'Well after the first song, someone else cut in and I ended up snogging that other person.'

'Oh well, he's not going to hold that against you. As long as you can write a decent piece.'

'Um, maybe. I wrote a bit for the *College Tribune* in UCD, and of course I have my badly paid sex column for *Gloss* to add to my CV. Sometimes I also write press releases in work on the few occasions when I'm allowed. So I think a four hundred word piece on Birmingham would be quite within my grasp. In fact as far as I remember Stuart even asked me about my writing experience at the party. He said that they're always kinda stuck in the office.'

'Well there you go, give him a ring. What's stopping you?'

'But what about work?'

'Resign.'

'Just like that?'

'You hate your job, don't you?'

'Yeah, but what'll I do about money and stuff?'

'You'll be all right. Feel the fear and all that, why don't you?'

'Hang on, why don't *you* resign and go off to Birmingham for one night on the piss? It's not rational thinking, is it? Anyway I don't know if Stuart would even agree to let me write a piece, and Ellie would probably go ballistic for trespassing on her territory.'

'I'm sure she wouldn't. Ellie's very laid back.'

'Not exactly where I'm concerned though. I mean she already thinks I took her man so can you imagine what she'd think if I started doing her job? No, Dervala, it's not worth it.'

A knock on the kitchen door makes us jump.

We both swing around.

It's Bunny.

'How's your head?' Dervala enquires.

Bunny slowly puts a hand to her forehead and then examines it as if she's checking for signs of blood. She looks like she did several rounds in a boxing ring and then went back for more. She's also wearing one of my old nighties, which doesn't quite manage to conceal the numerous bruises on her arms and legs. Jesus, where did they come from? She doesn't answer Dervala. Maybe she didn't hear her.

'Good-morning,' I try cheerfully. 'Would you like a cup of coffee or would you prefer tea? Did you drink the pint of water I left by the bed?'

Dazed, Bunny looks from me to Dervala and then back to me again. Then she coughs loudly for about five minutes. I'm convinced she's going to throw up but she doesn't. Then she looks at us again.

Eventually she speaks.

'Forgive me for being ignorant,' she says in a very slow, very hoarse tone of voice. 'You girls seem very nice and all, and I'm very grateful for your concern. But,' she pauses and her eyes suddenly take on a wild, frightened look, 'if you don't mind me asking . . . who the hell are you?'

'**I**'d like a word with you in the boardroom, Fiona.'
That dreaded sentence. We all know what that
means. This is it, isn't it? I'm for the chop. I know I
am. My heart has taken a sudden dive. I've heard that
tone of voice before from Cynthia. And music to the
ear, it ain't!

Cynthia, as I may or may not have told you, is PA
to Joe, and my immediate boss. Yes, yes I know, I'm
not even a *real* PA. I'm just a PA to another PA, which
is really embarrassing, but anyway . . .

Cynthia doesn't want a word. Even *I* know that.
No. She wants to give me an earful of words, nasty
condescending words that I don't want to hear. I
follow her skinny frame into the boardroom and on
my way there I think to myself, do you know what?
I'm way too old for this kind of shit. In school I'd have
to follow the nuns around when I misbehaved. And
write out a hundred times that 'I was a bold girl and
it will never happen again'. I'm thirty now however. A

big girl, in more ways than one. In fact I've officially been an adult for more than twelve years. And Cynthia, despite her superiority complex, is probably not more than a year or two older than I am. So, I'm wondering why on earth I should listen to any crap that she decides to spew out at me.

We sit down and she starts off in a whiny voice, enquiring about my recent absenteeism.

'Listen, save your breath, Cynthia,' I cut her off mid-sentence. 'I'm not in the mood for a warning. And let's face it; I'm not happy with this set-up and even *less* happy with your attitude towards me since I started as an employee here. In fact I'm almost *sure* that if I read my "Bullying in the Workplace", pamphlet again carefully, I'd have grounds to take action. But luckily for you I couldn't even be bothered doing that. In fact,' I pause for a bit of dramatic effect. 'In fact, I am going to offer you my resignation right this minute.'

Whohoo, I don't know where the hell that came from but I think it sounded pretty cool, don't you? I mean, considering I hadn't even got anything rehearsed. I'd like to repeat myself but there's no need. Cynthia has clearly got the message. She also seems really pissed off when I add, 'So was there anything else you wanted?'

I clear my desk immediately. Cynthia and I have mutually decided it's for the best. I'm to get two weeks' holiday pay 'cos I'm owed time off. And then . . . well then I'm not really sure what I'm going to do with all my time off because I haven't really thought about it properly.

On my way home, as I'm walking along aimlessly, it suddenly hits me that not only do I not have a man, a normal flatmate or a job to pay the bills, but I still haven't even lost that half stone I've been going on about for ages. No. Nor have I even taken time out to enjoy life either. Like when was the last time I sat in the park and simply enjoyed the surroundings? See? I can't even remember, can I? I've been so busy doing work I hate and chasing men who don't fancy me that I haven't had time to appreciate the little things in my life.

With this new-founded interest in all things wonderful, I decide to go to Herbert Park and just sit there and take in a bit of nature. Imagine being able to do that in the middle of the afternoon when everybody else is in work! Isn't that just great? Suddenly I feel sorry for all those office workers pretending to be busy on their computers when in fact all they do is email pals and check out porn sites. Thank God, I'm not one of those sad cases any more. I have moved on. Yes! I am no longer just a cog in the work mill. The park beckons.

At the park, the ducks aren't too pleased as I fire pieces of my sandwich into the pond. I don't get it. Don't they realise I just spent nearly €4.50 on my sun-dried tomato and basil sandwich with goat's cheese? I'm not just some mad old woman with a blue mould loaf, thank you very much. But they don't seem to know the difference, do they?

The pieces of my expensive sambo float miserably on top of scum on the dirty green water. The ducks around here have an unpleasant superiority complex, I think. I mean they're not like the ducks in UCD who seem to seriously appreciate your efforts. Huh! Who do they think they are? It must be something to do with living in one of the most expensive areas in the city, and the ridiculous prices people pay to live in properties the size of a shoebox. Well, I won't be coming back here, I vow, and try to get up, only to discover that somebody has left a chewed piece of gum on the seat. Jesus, well, that's just great! I try to prise it off the back of my skirt. And then, just to top things off, a thick raindrop hits me hard on the nose and I look up to see a threatening thunderous grey sky.

Oh well, so much for a nice day in the park. I hear the distant rumble of thunder and run like hell to the Herbert Park Hotel for shelter. Sitting in the hotel bar with the rain crashing down outside I send Ellie a text. I tell her to ring me urgently. Otherwise she probably won't bother replying. Then again, if she doesn't reply, then maybe I can go to Birmingham myself and live it up a bit! I live in hope . . .

One cup of coffee and a flick of *Glamour* magazine later, I decide that Ellie has no intention of ringing me back so I ring her instead. 'This number is out of service,' says the haughty female voice at the other end. I'm gobsmacked. Moreover, I'm insulted. And I'm *so* taking it personally that Ellie has obviously changed her mobile number because of me. Does she really hate me that much? What can I do about it? I can't do *nothing*, can I? I mean I can't have her going around thinking I'm a scumbag for the rest of my life.

I feel really upset and sort of hysterical now as I make my way down to the DART station to get the train to Booterstown. The rain seems to have stopped for the moment but I can't sit down because everything is wet. I've nowhere to go now except my flat, which I feel I don't even like any more since Bunny moved in. I have no job to go to, no purpose in life, and I don't even have a dull unimaginative boyfriend wondering whether I want to catch some action flick tonight. Or a spouse wondering what we'll have for dinner. Spouse. Hmm. What a nasty sound-ing word. I far prefer 'companion'. It's more soothing. Anyway since I don't have a spouse, companion, husband, fiancé, partner, date, 'special friend', or hang on, what's the male equivalent of a mistress? Isn't there a word for that? Come to think of it, I don't think there is. Isn't that ridiculous? Anyway since I don't have anything that could pass for a second half, I'll have to think of a way to amuse myself for the rest of the day. The worst thing I can do is sit looking at blank walls wondering where my life goes from here.

I walk slowly towards Lansdowne station, feeling sad. Every second car that passes is a BMW or a Merc with some overweight 'suit' yelling on a mobile phone, or one of those space wagons driven by a sour-looking blonde with huge sunglasses and an unhappy one-year-old strapped into the back seat. Women who spend all day driving their kids around in people carriers perplex me. I don't get it at all. Do their husbands find them interesting? Or do their other halves only half listen to the fact that Jilly and Pete are pregnant again, or that Ronnie and Sally have just bought a second home in the South of France. Or that Mary and Jack have just got planning permission for their conservatory. Does hubby find it all so tedious that he'd prefer not to come home at all on a Friday night? So much so that he'd rather get hammered in the Ice Bar in the Four Seasons Hotel. And buy drinks for the likes of Dervala and her friends, who are almost half his age and secretly think he's a sad bastard?

God forgive me but I'd rather be dead than live a life like that. You wouldn't *believe* the amount of married men who openly accuse their wives of making them miserable. They're the same men however who refuse to bring their wives to dinner, preferring instead to treat a young one who 'looks after herself'.

Dervala recently went through a self-destructive period of dating deadbeat husbands. She found they all had something in common. They all drank too much, were overweight, jealous of some guy in the office who was *apparently* jealous of him, and accused their wives of 'letting themselves go'. Dervala said it was like going out with the same man all the time. Only the names changed.

I asked her why she bothered. 'They'll never leave their wives for you,' I pointed out.

She was highly insulted. 'As if I'd *want* them to leave their wives! God forbid I'm too young to be a stepmother. And even if I did, in a moment of madness, marry any of them, in a couple of years *I'd* be the one accused of letting myself go.'

I didn't approve of her silly 'married men merry-go-around' that she seemed incapable of coming off, but that didn't bother her. She liked been wined and dined and was busy amassing an impressive jewellery and handbag collection. But everything suddenly came to a head when she fell for the last married guy. One afternoon she spotted him in town with another woman and realised he was two-timing her, well three-timing her, if you included his wife.

She was gutted and utterly inconsolable. And then spent weeks plotting revenge against the man who had taken her for a ride, quite literally. I found it all very hard to understand. After all, Dervala had been *quite* understanding when her slime ball seducer said he couldn't leave his wife because of the kids. She had listened to him patiently when he told her how his wife had 'trapped' him by getting pregnant all those years ago. She had nodded sympathetically when he told her with puppy-dog eyes, that he had never known true love, but that if he left home his wife would be very vindictive, make his life hell and turn his kids against him. All that was fine apparently. What destroyed her was finding out that Mr Slime Ball was seeing another pretty young plaything like herself!

Anyway, you'll be glad to know that Dervala has now moved on from dirty dads to flirty lads and is going through toy boys like nobody's business. She had a good run of them in the last fortnight and although she's pretty pissed off that the Peter Andre look-alike didn't send so much as a 'c u around' text, the others are still meeting her for the odd shag.

She's a funny creature. A highly sexed, foul-mouthed girl, she has no shame in showing off a mid-riff that would be far better covered up, and thighs that have contradicted the promises of every cellulite cream on the market. Yes, Dervala is typical of that new breed of chain-smoking, vodka-swilling Dublin girl, who play men at their own game of 'snakes and ladders' and seem to win. In some ways, I admire her lack of morals, utter selfishness and complete disregard for middle-class society nonsense as we once knew it, but sometimes I think it's a lot less complicated being me. I'm all for an easy life. I like my head to be man free. I couldn't be arsed texting all those losers I meet outside kebab shops in the small hours of the morning. What's the point? Why would I spend hours analysing their nonsensical messages? Why should I regularly get off my head on coke and wake up a couple of mornings a week covered in unexplained cuts and bruises? That kind of 'fun' just doesn't do it for me, and although now and again I do crave excitement and wish I were where it was 'all happening', most of the time I just like to chill out and let it 'all happen' to other people.

So that's why I've decided to take things easy for the next few days. I'm going to think about my life although not too much in case I start wondering why we are all here. I'm sure you've done that haven't you? It's a pretty depressing game to play. 'Cos there's no satisfactory answer, and sooner or later the thought of it just drives you mad! I guess my motto is to keep fairly busy but not to the point of distraction. I decide all this walking along the coast.

When I get back to the flat I can already hear the television blaring from an upstairs window. Bunny must still be up there. What has she done all day? I wonder has she even got dressed yet.

Last night she explained the bruising (ex-boyfriend), the loss of memory (she'd gone on the batter after their last punch-up) and the move to Dublin (because she'd know nobody here and nobody would know her). At one stage she started crying while telling me that her mother and father had been killed in a tragic car crash, and that she'd also miscarried the baby she'd been expecting with the abusive ex.

I remember thinking that maybe my life wasn't so bad after all, and maybe God had sent me Bunny to put my own silly uneventful existence into perspective. But I had kind of hoped that Bunny might have ventured outside the flat today. I'm tired now and all I want to do is chill for a bit.

I mount the stairs and hear *The Ricki Lake Show* on the TV. God, I didn't even know they still showed Ricki on TV. Don't the unemployed and stay-at-home mums deserve better? Honestly you'd have more fun at work!

As I enter the flat, I'm surprised to see Bunny lying on the sofa wearing my new D&G tracksuit like an old pair of pyjamas. Instead of accusing her of going uninvited into my room though, I simply take a deep breath, smile and ask her how she is feeling.

'Much better,' she says, 'thanks.'

'I see you've been out shopping,' I nod at the tray of cream and jam doughnuts on her knee.

'Oh no, I haven't been out yet. Some woman called over with them. I ate two and gave one to Timmy who was here earlier. He didn't stay long though and neither did the woman. It's a pity 'cos she was nice and all.'

Oh my God, Mum will kill me for not telling her about my new flatmate. And as for Timmy, how dare he not wait around to say hello!

'So did Mum leave a message, did she ask me to give her a bell?'

'Huh?'

Bunny's eyes are glued to the man in the middle of the two women who is saying 'I don't want either of these two bitches, Ricki.'

I repeat my question a bit louder.

Bunny turns around looking confused. 'Your mother? I haven't met your mother yet, have I? Did I meet her that first night I called? I don't remember now.'

'You *said* you were talking to her earlier.'

'Did I? No I didn't. No, I never said I met your mother. I said some woman . . .'

'What woman? What was her name?'

'Um . . . God, I can't think of it now.'

'What did she look like?'

Jesus, who is this frigging woman who lets herself

into my flat just like that and brings fresh doughnuts for Bunny and Timmy? Have I some kind of Fairy flipping Godmother that I don't know about?

'Kind of pretty, thinner than you . . .'

I smile rigidly as if I haven't quite understood the insult.

'Long curly hair, light blue jacket . . .'

My heart suddenly bungee jumps. I can feel the blood drain from my face.

'Ellie?' I whispered, the word catching somewhere in my throat as I repeated it. 'Ellie was here?'

'Yeah, that's it, that was her name. At least I *think* it was her name.'

I pause for a moment feeling slightly awkward, but then manage to find my voice again. 'What did she want?'

Bunny stops gobbling her doughnut for a second, wipes some cream off her mouth and frowns. 'Well would you believe it?' she says, as if in deep thought. 'I don't actually know.'

'But she *must* have said something,' I say beginning to lose patience now.

'She asked Timmy if he had been a good boy,' Bunny says in a rather serious voice. 'But he didn't bother answering. You know Timmy.'

I just look at her in disbelief. Is this girl for real?

Then Bunny starts to laugh and laugh and laughs so much that she has to cover her mouth to smother the uncontrollable hooting. I lean against the doorway, patiently waiting for her to finish. Although I felt very, very sorry for Bunny last night, I've got to admit that at this very minute my good intentions are slowly draining away.

Eventually she calms down.

'Sorry about that,' she says. 'Sometimes I've a weird sense of humour. I just keep laughing for no reason. Yeah the woman who was here was just asking if you were around, left in these doughnuts and asked who I was and I said my name was Bunny. Then I asked who *she* was and she said her name was Ellie and that she wanted to talk to you.'

Oh my God! Ellie called? Thank God, she has forgiven me. Everything can go back to the way it was. I am so so delighted. I have been lost without Ellie. But hang on, Bunny is still rattling on and I'm not even listening!

'I think she probably wants to move back in again but I was like, "smell you later, sister, the room's mine now . . ."'

And Bunny starts laughing again.

'Hi, is that Stuart? Hi Stuart, sorry for disturbing you, my name is Fiona Lemon. I met you recently at a party and I'm just wondering if you have a number for Ellie?'

'Fiona Lemon! Speak of the devil, I was just talking about you!'

'You were?' I ask in astonishment.

'Yeah, I was out for a long liquid lunch with some pals, and we ended up discussing our most embarrassing moment, of all things.'

'Oh yes?' I say bewildered, wondering what on earth this has to do with me.

'And one of them said he passed out at his Christmas Party after head butting a Santa Claus on roller blades.'

'I see.'

'So I thought this was hilarious and said I thought I had the perfect woman for him.'

'Yes? And who might that be?'

'Well *you* of course, Fiona. Ellie was telling me about you shagging Santa at your Christmas Party so I thought . . .'

'Excuse me, I did NOT, absolutely not shag Santa Claus,' I say highly indignantly. 'I just kissed him briefly. Anyway I didn't call to discuss my most embarrassing moment ever, but to see if you had Ellie's mobile.'

I feel like slamming down the phone. What an unbelievably ignorant man. I remember Ellie saying something about Stuart having a big mouth, but honestly, he should learn some manners! Come to think of it, I have a feeling Ellie used to fancy Stuart. God only knows why!

'I haven't been in touch with Ellie for the past couple of days,' Stuart says grumpily. 'Is she not answering her phone or something?'

'Well I can't get a signal. She called over to the flat this afternoon but I missed her. I really need to get in touch with her 'cos some guy rang wanting her to go to Birmingham on a press trip.'

'Oh yeah, I know, he rang here too but Ellie wasn't in the office. She works from home mostly these days, as you know. Has she moved out of your flat or something?'

He seems very keen to know the 'ins' and 'outs' of everything. God, he isn't half nosy, is he? Maybe he fancies Ellie or something. I wonder if he's married. Ellie rarely talked about him. Except to say that he was a great skier. Apparently he gave her a few skiing lessons in the Alps when they were on a trip together.

But apart from that I know very little.

'Yeah, it's a long story,' I mutter, deeply regretting the call now. I certainly do not intend discussing the 'big fight' or whatever you might call it, with Ellie's boss.

'Anyway it's important that Ellie gets the message so she can go on the trip.'

'To be honest, Fiona, I doubt she'd even go at this stage. It's only a one-nighter and Ellie has gone on so many city breaks she doesn't want to go on any more now. Anyway she's not returning my calls either at the moment for some strange reason.'

'So the trip will be wasted?'

'Why? Would *you* be interested in going?'

I swallow hard. Then take a deep breath. I can actually hear my heart beating a little faster. This is *exactly* what I wanted to hear. Wow! I didn't think it would be this easy.

'Well, I wouldn't say no. But . . . but are you *sure* you wouldn't mind if I went?'

'It's nothing to me. Hey, as long as you behave yourself and aren't thrown out of the hotel for being drunk and disorderly, haha . . .'

I squirm. Is that really the impression he has of me? Good God, how terribly embarrassing!

'I'd write a glowing piece about Birmingham,' I promise. 'I've written stuff before for various publications.'

But Stuart doesn't seem to give a rat's behind what I've written. He says I'm to ring that man back straight away, tell him I can't get in touch with Ellie, but that I also write for *Travelling About* and will be replacing Ellie.

Replacing Ellie. Hmmm. That's sounds a bit harsh, doesn't it? I'm not sure I'm comfortable with that choice of words but I say nothing. After all, this is a chance in a lifetime, an opportunity to be treated like a star in a foreign country (even if it is only 40 minutes across the water!). And as Stuart said himself, Ellie is sick of city breaks anyway – is she mad? She should try working in an office that's always either too hot or too cold. And one where you can't swivel your chair around in case one of your colleague's kitchen knives ends up firmly entrenched in your spine!

I put down the phone and shout for joy. Bunny pops her head into the kitchen.

'Are you okay?'

'Yeah, no I'm fine,' I beam.

'Your eyes are shining,' she says in a deadpan voice.

'Are they? Well, that's good, considering I just lost my job today.'

'You did?'

'Well actually I resigned. I was sick of working in that dump anyway. It's for the best.'

'You're better off. I resigned my job too you know. I was working in a funfair but I was exhausted.'

'In a funfair?'

'Yeah, I was working on a stall called Hook the Duck, where people paid for five sticks with little hooks at the end of them. There was a number written on the ducks' arses so the punters would lift up the ducks and I'd check to see if the duck had an odd number on its arse. Odd numbers won you a prize.'

'No way, really?' I'm intrigued. What a colourful life Bunny has led!

'Why would I lie?' her dark eyes suddenly flash accusingly.

'Er . . . well you wouldn't, would you? I believe you and everything but . . . was that fun?'

'Of course it wasn't.' Bunny looks disgusted. 'It was just a summer job while I was waiting for my exams. The people who used to come into the fair were pretty ignorant. Especially the men. You'd ask them to hook the duck and they'd go, "no, but I wouldn't mind fucking you". Imagine! With their kids beside them and all! The sleazy bastards!'

'Men,' I shake my head.

'Yeah men, who'd have them, eh?'

'Mmm. So did you get your exams then? What were you studying?'

'Travel and tourism.'

'Very good.'

'What's good about it? It was a load of crap if you ask me.'

'Was it? So you're not going to pursue a travel career?'

'Well I wouldn't mind the *travel*, it's the career bit I don't want.'

'But you have to do something,' I point out. 'I mean most of us would love to do nothing but amuse ourselves, but we've no choice.'

'I just want to have some fun though,' says Bunny with a pout. 'I don't want to sit in a travel agency telling people which Irish bars they should or shouldn't visit in Mallorca. Or answer phones to people wondering if it's safe to visit Egypt.'

I know exactly what she means. Answering annoying questions on the phone all day can be very boring. I don't want to encourage her though. I definitely don't want a flatmate who just sits around wondering how to amuse herself.

'I'm going to Birmingham tomorrow night,' I announce, deciding to change the subject.

Bunny looks surprised. 'Really? How come?'

'It's work,' I feign a sigh as if it's all a bit boring. 'I don't really want to go but . . .'

'But I thought you said you'd resigned? What'll you do over there?'

'Oh, non-stop meetings and God knows what else . . . to be honest I'm not particularly looking forward to it.'

Bunny, nevertheless, looks seriously impressed.

'Will you be going on a plane?'

'No, I'll be cycling,' I laugh.

But Bunny doesn't laugh. She doesn't even smile. 'I've never been on a plane,' she says wistfully. 'I'm sure it's really exciting.'

'You've never been on a plane?'

'No.'

'I don't believe it!'

'Seriously. When my uncle in Manchester died the whole family was supposed to go over to the funeral but then it was too expensive so just Mam, Dad and my brother went.'

'Oh,' I say sombrely.

'Yes . . . still it's very exciting for you, isn't it?'

I don't like to tell Bunny that taking a plane for me is only mildly more exciting than taking the train. And that the flight to Birmingham will not be showing a film and the airhostesses will NOT be ramming mini bottles of champagne down my throat. But I don't want to be condescending. Bunny might come across as a strange fish, and has an annoying habit of shouting out the first thing that comes into her head, but I reckon her heart is in exactly the right place.

'So are you going to pack now?' Bunny enquires.

'Oh, I'll do it later. I won't need much, just an overnight case. I'm not going too mad or anything. Oh thank you,' I say, gratefully accepting a mug of steaming black coffee. 'God I needed that. It's really weird to be going on this trip. It was supposed to be Ellie's gig but I wasn't able to contact her. It's a pity she didn't leave me a number or anything.'

'Oh I remember now,' Bunny suddenly blurts out. 'She said she'd lost her mobile phone or something but said she'd be in touch again.'

'Ah Jesus, Bunny, you should have got her new number off her!'

'Sorry I just completely didn't think. Oh well, when you see her you can explain. I don't think it's such a big deal anyway.'

Maybe she's right. I look at my watch. It's late.

Even if I *had* Ellie's new mobile number it'd be too late to call her to tell her I'm off to Birmingham first thing in the morning. Maybe Stuart was telling the truth though. Perhaps Ellie couldn't actually give a hoot. I decide not too think about it any more 'cos everything's arranged now. I ask Bunny what her plans are for the next few days. She shrugs and says she hasn't the faintest idea.

'But what about your clothes?' I enquire. 'You'll need to get all your stuff.'

'My stuff is all back in my ex-boyfriend's house though. I'm not contacting him 'cos I don't want him to know where I am.'

'Don't you think he'll ring the guards or something wondering where you are?'

Bunny gives a bitter-sounding laugh and pulls back her sleeves to remind me of her colourful bruises. 'Do you honestly think he wants to be involved with the guards?'

'But why don't you report him? I mean, he has all your stuff. You can't let him get away with this. And you can't just hide forever either. What are you going to do for money? I mean, don't get me wrong, I'm not trying to give you a hard time, but you've got to live.'

'Oh, money is not a problem,' Bunny says confidently. 'My problem is Shaney, my ex. He would kill to get his hands on my money.'

I am intrigued here. Why is Bunny so mysterious and always talking in riddles? What is she hiding? How has she all this money? Did she steal it? Is she involved in something illegal? I don't like to accuse her but I'll be damned if I'll hide some sort of criminal in my flat.

'Bunny,' I say, 'look me straight in the eye, and tell me where you got all this so-called money.'

She does look me straight in the eye, her steely-grey eyes penetrating mine. 'I haven't told anyone, so why should I tell you?'

'Where did you get the money?' I'm not going to back down. She either tells me now or I'm phoning the police.

'Okay, tell anyone and you're dead, but . . .'

I wait patiently, but there is a surge of annoyance rising within me. Jesus, would she ever spit it out?

'Well,' she says, in a far-away kind of voice. 'Would you believe it? I've won the lottery!'

Oh my God, I am so, so nervous. My stomach is tied up in a painful knot. Sweat beads are gathering at the base of my neck and my cotton T-shirt is sticking to me uncomfortably.

I'm in the departures lounge, looking out for Irish journalists who look like they might be going to Birmingham. But I'm terrified that I'm going to stand out as being a fake. I mean, they're probably all seasoned hacks with buckets of confidence whereas I am (or *was*) basically a PA to another PA and couldn't even manage that!

I walk around pretending I know exactly where I'm going but the reality is I'm just as lost as half the people milling around here looking completely confused. What is it about airport terminals that manages to turn perfectly normal people into headless chickens?

Eventually I see the desk for MyTravelLite. I check myself in but there's no sign of any other journalists and nobody is waiting at the desk with a sign or anything. But I'm not panicking yet. No. I have to remain calm and realise that somebody somewhere must be expecting little old me.

I sincerely hope nobody from *Gloss* is coming on this trip. I mean I would *die* if say, Faith, my old editor, turned up. But Faith probably wouldn't be that interested in a cultural trip to Birmingham. She only turns up to top-notch events like London Fashion Week or spa weekends in trendy hotels. She has no interest in actually doing any work. I only managed to last about two months in *Gloss* before quitting in frustration. Instead of swanning around A list events meeting A list celebs and leading an A list existence during my time there, I found myself stuck answering the phones to PR people who were anxious to get free publicity for their Z list clients.

You quickly learn to distinguish the good PR companies from the tricky dickies. The decent firms send over crates of champagne or the latest perfume ranges. Unfortunately though, all the good stuff was usually nabbed by Faith, leaving me to scramble around the floor like a street urchin gathering left-overs. Still, I was *more* than a little grateful with my collection of electric-blue mascaras, perfumed coat hangers, orange nail varnish and gold body glitter. I mean I knew I'd never actually *use* any of this junk but it was *free* and that was the main thing.

Looking back at the behaviour of the *Gloss* girls, I realise how bloody immoral their behaviour was. I mean, they would have begged, borrowed or stolen to look good and wouldn't have dreamed of stepping into a chemist or beauty salon to actually *pay* for anything. If they were going to a wedding, they wouldn't splash out on a dress. No sister! Instead they'd have top designers courier over some samples. And what did the publicity-hungry designers get in return? Well, the editor would stick in a brief mention of their latest product in the next issue of *Gloss*. And say that their latest designs were *apparently* loved by Jennifer Lopez or somebody. And everybody would be happy. Except for Jennifer Lopez obviously, because she wouldn't know anything about it.

There's still no sign of anyone. I might as well go through the security gates so. Normally when I take a flight I'm always running in a sweat 'cos somebody is announcing 'Final departure call for passenger Lemon.' But today, thank God, I'm here in time so I'll browse through the perfumes. I wander among the rows and rows of glorious glass bottles, unable to make my mind up, because they all smell so, *so* nice. Also I'm never really sure if they're good value because I never buy myself perfumes at full price anyway.

I must say I'm beginning to envy Bunny with her lottery win. All I ever won was a bottle of whiskey when I was a little girl. I won it at the raffle at my annual school 'Bring and Buy' sale. Dad gave out blue murder at the time, saying it was so irresponsible of the school to allow a child win a bottle of whiskey, then he confiscated it and we found him the next morning, stocious drunk on the couch, the empty bottle on the floor beside him. But apart from that I've never won a thing.

Bunny says it hasn't quite sunk in yet and she doesn't know if it ever will. She says she's terrified that the money could ruin her life so she wants to stay as normal as possible. I think it's all pretty bloody amazing. I've been working all my life and have never even been in credit. If I got a grand to spend I'd be over the moon.

Sometimes when we're out in an expensive bar, Dervala will ask for the cocktail menu and order something fancy without even looking at the price. That's the main advantage of living at home, isn't it? I, however, must always check if I've enough for the taxi home. A 'Sex on the Beach' is all very glamorous but not if that means my having to walk home several hours later in torrential rain, my feet numb with the cold.

Bunny told me that when she'd initially cashed in her winnings she'd gone pretty crazy, but had decided not to go public. She said the people in her village would go mad if she got her picture taken in the papers. And besides every village idiot in the vicinity would be suddenly proclaiming their undying love for her. But she stressed that one of the main reasons she'd fled to Dublin was so that her boyfriend wouldn't find out. He'd only be demanding half the money, she said, and she'd be damned if she'd let him have it. He was a very violent man, apparently. She didn't have to convince me too much on that one. One look at Bunny's bruises and nobody could possibly doubt this man was anything other than a vicious thug. No wonder the hospital nurse had been so interested in Bunny's love life. Everything was beginning to make sense now.

At first she'd thought she would go on a cruise but then decided she didn't really want to be stuck on a big ship for weeks with a bunch of geriatrics doing aqua aerobics in the ship's pool. And having surfed through some property sites on the Internet, she'd realised that she didn't have a clue where she wanted to buy and decided she'd rent in Dublin first to get to know the different areas in the city.

She could have got a car, but didn't know how to drive, nor did she know the first thing about designer clothes. I nodded sympathetically, all the time thinking what a bizarre conversation it was. After all, I've had these 'lottery ticket' conversations many many times with the likes of Ellie, Dervala and my sister Gemma, but those conversations are usually full of 'what ifs' and 'buts'. And of course when none of us ever win, it's always a bit of an anticlimax. However now I actually *know* somebody who has won the Lotto. Before this, winning vast sums of money only happened to anonymous people smiling in the newspapers.

'So what made you pick my flat to live in?' I'd wanted to know. 'I mean you could have lived any-where! You could have checked yourself into a five-star hotel for a month!'

'Well I thought you sounded fun in your ad! I also wanted to make new friends and go out. Sure what would I be doing in a posh place with nobody to talk to except hotel staff? The minute I came here and saw the empty wine bottles scattered around the table, I reckoned you'd be a party animal!'

I shuddered at the memory of that night. It was horrible ending up in the hospital and everything. I've hardly touched a drop of alcohol since. Anyone thinking of giving up the booze should spend a night in A&E with someone like Bunny. Believe me, they wouldn't be going back in a mad hurry!

Suddenly my flight is announced. And being the typical worrier that I am I hurry along to Area C where I take a seat and pretend to read *B* magazine. Every now and then I look up in case they've started boarding. And also to see if I can spot a group of rowdy Irish journos. I can't. They must all be in the bar. Typical. Ellie once told me that all journalists want to do on press trips is drink themselves stupid.

Bearing this useful piece of info in mind, I scan the boarding area for a crowd of people who look like they're well on their way to being hammered, but the only people I see in this state are a family who appear to be going to a funeral.

'He was a wonderful man,' they all agree. 'One of the nicest people you could have met.'

Okay then, that lot are *definitely* going to a funeral!

Right. It's time to board. I'm so glad I have an aisle seat. Because I arrived early I was given a choice between an aisle or a window. As a child of course I always wanted the window to look at the view. But now I'm older I prefer the aisle so I don't have to disturb people going to and from the toilet. Anyway, as long as I'm not stuck between two large sweaty men hogging the armrests, I'm happy enough.

I'm one of the first on the plane and the rest of my row is empty. I wonder have they put all the journalists sitting together or what? I watch the passengers spill slowly onto the plane. It's interesting watching them. There's some really ignorant guy like the man standing around row six just now. He's holding everybody up while painstakingly placing his laptop in the overhead bin. Of course it's quite apparent that he doesn't give a damn that half the passengers are still waiting on the steps outside in the freezing cold. The next minute he slowly takes off his jacket and carefully folds it, so it doesn't crease. Then, wait for it, he is now removing his jumper . . . Good God, is he going to strip entirely? One of the airhostesses approaches him and asks him to kindly take his seat so that everybody else can embark. Visibly irritated, the man sits down and finally everybody else gets a chance to find their seat. I spot a very tall, very striking, thin girl, heading towards the back of the plane where I am seated. She is so tall in fact, that her dark-haired head almost touches the airplane ceiling. She has defined aristocratic-looking features but her face is hard, as if she is the type of woman who is always on the defence. I sincerely hope she isn't going to sit beside me. She doesn't. Instead she takes the seat behind and I can feel her knees dig into the back of my seat. A strong overbearing smell of her perfume soon wafts over our row of seats. I don't recognise it but it's enough to make me gag.

I hope that the two seats beside me will be left free so that I'll have the row to myself. But no such luck however. The last couple to board the plane just happen to be seated beside me and from the minute they sit down, they start bickering. At first they couldn't decide who was going to sit at the window and who was going to take the middle seat. Now they're fighting over a copy of the *Irish Examiner*, would you believe! The missus has bought a torn copy and the husband is giving out about it.

'What can I do about it?' she barks. 'It's too late to bring it back now. Or do you want them to delay the flight?'

'I just don't understand,' he says refusing to let it go. 'Did you just take the first copy? How many times have I told you never to take the first copy but to take the second one, the one underneath?'

'Right, tell you what, we'll ask the airhostess for some Sellotape and we can fix up the page then, would that shut you up?'

I squirm away from them, pretending to study the safety manual. Why do they bother? I wonder. Why do couples stay together long after the love has gone? And why do spouses get away with abusing each other in a way that nobody else would? It's baffling! And to think people feel sorry for me being single!

We're off now and the plane thunders down the runway. I still get terribly excited every time I take off somewhere for some reason. Even if the plane is just going to Birmingham I feel as excited as if I were heading off to space! I don't even know how to explain it, but when those wheels leave the ground, it's like you're leaving everything behind. And in my case that's the unpleasant business of losing my job, my best friend and almost my reason (thanks to Bunny) all in a matter of days. But it's all going to be plain sailing from now on, I convince myself, and order a quarter bottle of wine from the airhostess.

Now we're landing. That was quick, wasn't it? No sooner had I started to enjoy my wine than the airhostess was whipping the empty bottle off me. I now feel kind of warm with a fuzzy happiness. I'm almost sorry we're landing. Why aren't there traffic control restrictions when you need them? I wouldn't mind doing another few laps of the Birmingham area while sipping another bottle of wine.

The plane thunders down the runway and then eventually slows down as we're all welcomed to Birmingham and reminded that the airport is strictly a no smoking zone etc., etc., etc. Nobody claps. Then again, we haven't just landed in Faro or Palma so there's no reason for everybody to get over excited, is there?

Then we seem to be driving around for ages to find our parking spot. As soon as the fasten seatbelt sign switches off, everybody stands up immediately. Now, why do they do this? I mean it's not like anybody can get out until the doors open. And after you get out you usually have to wait on a feeder bus for everybody else anyway. Why are some people always rushing?

I just sit in my seat and watch everybody else fight

for standing space. Thankfully the 'happy' pair beside me also remain sitting down and don't pressurise me to stand up, the way some fellow passengers sometimes do. They haven't exchanged a word during the flight. I wonder why they're going to Birmingham. Hopefully not for a romantic break!

Inside the terminal I spot my name on a placard and my heart gives a little leap. For years, going through various airports, I'd see people waiting patiently holding cardboard signs with names. Especially at Heathrow. But the only people ever meeting me are usually my mother or sister and they're rarely on time. So not only does nobody ever hold up my name, they never even give me a 'welcome home' hug. All I ever get is an abusive tirade about the traffic and a warning to hurry along due to the car being parked in the ridiculously expensive short-term Aer Rianta car park.

In fact, believe it or not, the heartiest welcome I ever got was from a jolly middle-aged woman who shouted with joy as I came through the doors. When I looked at her in astonishment, she quickly explained that she didn't know me but had seen 'Australia Airlines' on my case. 'It's such a long way from home, isn't it?' she said wistfully. 'I'm the only one in my family living on this side of the world.'

'Well actually, I've only been skiing in Salzburg.' I pointed apologetically to the label. 'See? It's actually Austrian Airlines I'm afraid.'

I don't know which one of us was more embarrassed!

So anyway, I approach the man with the cardboard sign and tell him I'm Fiona Lemon.

'Are you one of the journalists?' he smiles, extending a hand for me to shake.

'Yes, that's right,' I tell him, my chest swelling with pride. 'I am one of the journalists. I'm with *Travelling About*.'

It's the first time in my life that anybody has actually called me a 'journalist' and I must say I think it sounds rather important. I mean, don't forget, only yesterday morning I was a mere PA to another pain-in-the-ass PA. I still feel like pinching myself.

The man tells me his name is Terry and he's wondering whether I have bumped into any of the other journalists yet.

'Er . . . no, I haven't met anybody yet,' I explain. 'Are there many of us?'

'Just yourself, Angela-Jean Murray and Killian Toolin.'

Killian Toolin. Hmm. I know that name from somewhere. I definitely know that name. Sugar, how do I know it? This is very annoying.

'Hi, I'm Angela-Jean.'

The girl's voice is crystal clear, if a tad bit haughty. I look around and am not too surprised to see the very tall girl who was sitting behind me on the flight.

'Welcome to Birmingham, Angela-Jean,' says Terry. 'Have you met Fiona Lemon?'

'Fiona Lemon. From where?' Angela-Jean slips a hand limply into mine. It feels like a wet fish.

'From Booterstown in Dublin,' I say awkwardly.

'I meant from which publication,' she says rather condescendingly.

'*Travelling About.*'

'I can't say I've ever heard of it,' she says as she roots for something in her Burberry bag (it's a real one – I can tell!).

'Did you have a nice flight?' Terry enquires politely, looking at me.

'It was very pleasant,' I tell him.

'Maybe for you,' Angela-Jean cuts in, 'because you're so short. But I have very very long legs. Unless I'm sitting at row one or an emergency exit I tend to get cramps.'

'You *are* very tall,' Terry says, looking up at her with more than a hint of admiration. 'You could have been a model.'

'Indeed I could,' Angela-Jean says wearily as if people point that fact out all the time. 'But I'm *way* too intelligent for that.'

'So who do you work for?' I ask just to fill the silence.

'I work for *Irish Femme.*'

'Really?'

Angela-Jean just gives me a bored withered look. 'Don't you read my stuff?'

'Um . . . no, I mean I've flicked through the magazine once or twice in the hairdressers but I think *Irish Femme* is for a, er . . . I dunno, a more mature audience?'

From the look on her face I might as well have suggested that she works for the *Geriatric Gazette*.

She seems absolutely incensed. Two purple spots suddenly appear on her high cheekbones. 'Excuse me,' she says dismissively. 'I want to pop outside for some fresh air and a cigarette.'

'Oh no, I hope I didn't offend her,' I say to Terry as she storms off. But he doesn't even hear. Instead he is busy welcoming some tall . . . pretty cute . . . hmm, has potential . . . dark . . . very nice, turn around now . . . Jesus! It's that guy I snogged at the party in our flat! Oh no. Oh *God* no!

Once I'm safely on the mini bus I rush to the back to make sure I don't have to sit beside Killian. Everybody else fills up the first six or seven rows so I end up looking really silly in the back row all to myself. Because I'm so far back, Terry must use a microphone especially so that I can hear.

I am so so mortified about bumping into Killian though. After all, what are the chances of being on a trip with the one guy you snogged at a party before passing out? Why do things like that always happen to me? Am I jinxed or what? Of course, mutual recognition was immediate as we shook hands awkwardly. In fact I don't know whose face was redder as Terry asked us if we'd met yet, but it was probably a draw.

Of course, Terry, being a complete professional, didn't bat an eyelid.

'What's your name?' I asked feeling pretty foolish. 'I don't think I got your name the first time.'

'Killian, and you're right I don't think we got

around to exchanging names the last time we er . . .
bumped into each other.'

He gave me a knowing wink. Oh the embarrassment of it all! Imagine! Although we exchanged
plenty of saliva, no actual conversation took place. I
wonder why? Ah yes, I remember now. I think I
collapsed *before* he could ask me my hobbies and
what kind of music I was into. Good God, I'd need to
grow up, wouldn't I? I'm not seventeen any more.
Mentally I blame the punch. It'll never happen again.

There are only eight journalists in the coach,
besides myself, two skinny oul' lads from different
broadsheets, three UK journos who have flown in
from various destinations and a fairly big-boned but
pleasant-looking Irish tabloid hack with glasses, a
beer belly and a funny cap on his head. Then there's
Angela-Jean who is trying to poison us with the fumes
of her nail polish – I can even smell it down the back
here. And Killian.

I reckon the oul' lads will probably hit the sack
when we hit the hotel. They're probably tired. And I
will have just one drink with my meal before going to
bed with my book. Angela-Jean will probably put on
a mud face pack and relax with a cup of herbal tea, by
the looks of her. Anyway I doubt anyone will go too
mad, because of course, we all need to be up early
tomorrow to visit the sights.

I wonder whose room I'll have to share. I'll
probably be stuck with Angela-Jean. I mean, surely
they won't stick me in a room with one of the men,
will they?

*

Am I the most naïve girl on the planet? I am, aren't I? It's so obvious I'm not a proper journo. Okay, so first of all, everybody had their own room. When I suggested to Angela-Jean that we'd probably be sharing a room, she looked at me like I was some sort of closet lesbian. Well, how was I to know that on press trips, journalists always get their own rooms?

And secondly, nobody had an early night. Not one single person. When I stupidly asked if anybody else was taking it easy later on, they looked at me like I'd suddenly grown a second nose.

It soon became perfectly clear to me that if I dodged out of joining them on a major drink-fest, my antisocial behaviour would be frowned upon. So I just kind of accepted that I was in for an all nighter. Talk about peer pressure, eh?

Everybody went crazy with the free drink. You'd swear alcohol was banned in Ireland the way everybody was carrying on. Even Angela-Jean fairly lashed into the wine at the ultra-hip restaurant where we had dinner. In fact she knocked it back faster than anybody and because she refused to eat a morsel, the booze went to her head faster. In fact the more wine she drank, the louder she talked about her important job as social editor of *Irish Femme* and how PR people were always on the phone pestering her for free publicity. And how she hated interviewing common celebrities with zero breeding for her weekly social column, 'A-J About Town'.

Then she stopped talking for a while, as she had to

leave the table to go to the Ladies and puke her guts out. However she came back fifteen minutes later, having cleaned herself up, and re-applied full make-up (though not, admittedly, as perfectly this time around) to sample the liquors that had been laid out for us. Instead of being absolutely dying with shame, A-J seemed most relieved that she had vomited. Immediately I suspected a serious case of bulimia.

The food was top class – too good to puke up really. And the company wasn't bad either. I didn't really speak to Killian because thankfully we weren't sitting near each other. And besides, he was locked before we even got to the restaurant. He said he'd had a couple in Dublin airport, a couple on the plane, a couple in the bar of the Malmaison and of course, *more* than a couple at the restaurant. In fact all of the Irish journos were fairly hammered at the restaurant. So much so that I was a bit worried about how it might look to the other nationalities. However, the English, Welsh, and Scottish journalists who'd hooked up with us at the airport, didn't even notice. And when one of them fell off his chair after hearing a joke that wasn't even that funny, I remember thinking there was no need to worry about the Irish contingent.

We ended up going to a trendy nightclub, except for the two oul' lads who said they'd prefer to go back to the hotel for a nightcap. The nightclub was very hip and we were treated like mini stars with our own reserved seating area and complimentary drinks. We were sitting behind a little red rope and people kept looking over to see if they recognised us and looked pretty disappointed when they realised we weren't famous. Not that I cared. This is the life, I thought, knocking back the bubbly and relaxing. A-J was still going strong. 'I'm used to all this,' she kept saying, trying to sound bored but I could tell she was secretly loving it all. 'I meet celebrities ALL the time. It's SO boring. I don't give a flying FUCK if they've got a new album coming out and I CERTAINLY don't want a signed copy. I don't have the space in my apartment for any of it.'

Thank God, the music in the club was so loud that nobody could actually hear A-J's bizarre ranting. At first I thought she was being exceptionally pretentious. After all, meeting celebrities and getting paid to do it, *must* be exciting. Being invited to top fashion shows and being handed goody bags on your way out has *got* to be a load of fun. How can you not like being invited to constant champagne launches and the openings of this that and the other? I mean, how can you complain? Doesn't A-J know how the other half live?

'But you're lucky,' I tell her. 'I mean, obviously work isn't supposed to be a bundle of laughs. But you have an audience who reads your column every week . . .'

'*You* don't read it,' she accuses spitefully.

'No, but I will from now on,' I say, trying to humour her. 'Look on the bright side, Angela-Jean. You go to places people in offices can only dream about. You travel the world on press trips, you get to sample all the ranges of make-up before they hit the shelves, you meet the kind of people the rest of us only see on television. Think about it . . .'

'I don't WANT to think about it,' A-J wails, knocking over her vodka and soda and then sucking the spilt contents from the shiny table with a straw. 'I *hate* my life. I just want to have fun. I want to travel. Not on press trips with you lot or whatever, but by myself. And I don't want to meet another self-obsessed celebrity for as long as I goddamn live. They're all so bloody short and uninteresting.'

With that, Angela-Jean bursts into incontrollable tears, leaving me absolutely stunned. I try to put a comforting arm around her but she pushes me away. I don't know what to do now. I'm very, very worried. How can someone go from being an ultra-cool sophisticated babe into a slobbering mess within hours?

'Leave her alone,' I hear someone say. 'She's just looking for attention.'

It's Killian. He is sitting beside me now, drinking something that looks like whiskey. How do these journalists keep going, I wonder. I have thankfully switched to Sprite to limit the damage. To be honest I'm a bit wary of misbehaving in case Terry phones Stuart at *Travelling About* to complain, and I never get to go on another press trip again.

'I can't just leave her like this, she's very upset,' I say to Killian, and then look back over my shoulder at Angela-Jean who is stooped forward with her face in her hands.

Killian, on the other hand, isn't remotely worried.

'She's *always* like this,' he says raising his eyes to the ceiling.

'She is?' I ask, wide-eyed.

'Yeah, she's got a reputation for being a major fucking drama queen. A friend of mine went out with her and said she was really high maintenance. He couldn't wait to get rid of her!'

'No way. Are you serious?'

''Course I'm serious. Yeah okay, she's not the worst-looking bird in the world but no normal bloke would put up with her. She expected my pal to drive around the city while she drank champagne in the back seat of his car with all her silly pals on a regular basis. All he needed was a navy cap and people would have definitely thought he was her chauffeur. Anyway that one would sell her granny for a story.'

Suddenly A-J takes her head out of her hands. 'Hey,' she says looking up at us with bleary eyes. 'Are you talking about me?'

I freeze. Uh oh. I hadn't realised Killian was talking so loud.

'No,' he says. 'We're talking about somebody else. Some bitch.'

'Who?'

'Amy Whittle.'

'Oh, that's all right. Yeah. She's a whore.'

A-J puts her head back in her hands.

'Who's Amy Whittle?' I ask.

'Amy? Oh she's a social diarist for a rival magazine. Herself and A-J are arch enemies, everyone knows that. But sure they're as bad as each other.'

I'm intrigued. 'How do you know all this?'

'Ah sure the scene in Dublin is so incestuous, it only takes a few weeks to find out everybody's business.'

'Is it really that small?'

' 'Course it is. Like a goldfish bowl. Why do you think A-J is cracking up? There are so few celebs in Ireland that it gets boring interviewing the same people week in, week out. That's why they have those programmes like *You're a Star* so that we have a fresh bunch of disposable celebs to write about every few months.'

'How depressing!'

'You're telling me.'

'So what kind of stuff do *you* write about?' I ask, curiosity taking over.

'A mixture of news and features. It suits me. I'd hate to be stuck on the news desk answering the phone. And if I only wrote showbiz I'd go out of my mind. Nobody ever sticks it for very long. They all end up losing it like Angela-Jean at some time or another. But hey, let's stop talking about work anyway. I hate the way hacks always talk shop on these things. Come on, let's dance.'

He grabs my arm more than a little forcefully and gives me a long hard look. I return it in surprise. Where on earth did *that* come from? Has he been hitting on me all night without me realising it? Am I really slow or something? Does he expect us to carry on where we left off at the party? Help!

'Angela-Jean can mind our drinks and stuff,' he suggests.

I glance at A-J, whose head is now resting on the marble table, not budging. She doesn't look like she's fit to look after herself, never mind anybody's 'stuff'.

'Come on,' Killian takes my hand, obviously determined not to take no for an answer.

My head spinning somewhat, I follow him onto the dance floor where he wraps his arms around me. I'm wondering if he's going to make a move. I'm *fairly* sure of his intentions, but what I'm *not* sure about is what I'm going to do about them. Okay, so he's cute and I wouldn't *mind* snogging him, but I'm just a bit worried about the consequences. What would the other journalists think? Would they be shocked? I'm only new to this game and don't want to be out before I'm in, if you know what I mean?

Suddenly I feel Killian's hand caressing my hair. It feels nice. His body feels warm and it's very toned. I'm feeling pretty turned on by his body pressed against mine.

When I look up our eyes lock. He bends down and his full lips brush mine. I can't resist and soon we're snogging passionately. What do I care about the people around us? We know nobody here except for A-J who's practically out cold. And anyway, we're not doing any harm, are we?

Mmm. Killian's a good kisser. That's important. Yes, it's *extremely* important. I just hate it when they slobber all over you. Is there anything more gross than a really wet kisser? I mean snogging some men is like sticking your tongue into a big bowl of jelly that hasn't set properly – ugh! Thankfully Killian has passed my kissing test though. I give him at least an eight or a nine. Mmm. Eventually we pause for a breather.

'Wow,' Killian murmurs in my ear. 'You're a really good kisser, you know that?'

'Thanks, so are you,' I say 'cos I'm pretty tipsy at this stage. Normally, when I'm sober I don't go in for that kind of mush.

'The only thing is . . .' he begins. 'The only thing . . .'

'The only thing is what?'

'Nothing.'

'What? What's the only thing? Come on, you can't do that to me. Don't be so annoying. What were you going to say? Spit it out.'

'Well, the thing is . . . the thing *is*, Connor's probably going to kill me when he hears about this.'

'Connor?' My heart gives a small leap at the mention of his name. 'As in my friend Ellie's boyfriend? Connor Kinnerty?'

'Of course. Unless there's some other Connor I don't know about.'

Oh no, what have I done? This is a really, really bad idea. Why did I drink tonight? Why did I snog Killian? He's going to go running back to Connor to gloat and then he won't have anything to do with me ever again. Then again, why should I care? Yeah, why should I indeed! After all, it's not like Connor and I . . . Connor and I . . . oh God, I'm so confused now. I need to get a glass of water and sober up so I can think straight.

'But why would Connor kill *you*?' I ask suspiciously.

'Oh you know, 'cos I think he really liked you.'

'Yeah?' My heart gives another kind of flutter.

'Well, he didn't say much but he was moping about the place for a few days after he called around to you and you showed him the door. I know him better than anyone, I could tell he was gutted.'

'I *didn't* show him the door,' I argue. 'I had people coming to see the flat. The last thing I needed was a public showdown on my own doorstep. I thought he understood.'

'Oh well it doesn't matter whether he did or not. Let's not talk about Connor any more,' Killian says cheerfully. 'It's all about you and me now, sweetheart. Anyway, I'm sure he's over you by now, haha.'

I'm not sure I'm too thrilled to hear that. Mind you, I don't want to give Killian the impression I'm really interested in Connor either. I mean, I barely know Connor. Yeah, he's unbelievably cute, and sexy and . . . hang on a minute, maybe I *am* into him. Maybe I've secretly liked him all along but didn't want anyone to get hurt, especially not me.

'I'm sure he *is* over me,' I say defiantly, anxious not to give Killian anything to read into. 'I mean, he hardly knows me. I only ever met him once. And that was at the party I'd rather forget.'

'Exactly. So even if he's pissed off about us at first, he'll come round to it.'

Us? *Us*? Oh my God!

'Anyway,' Killian continues. 'I don't think we should talk about Connor any more. He's back with

Ellie now so he can't complain.'

'He is?' I say suddenly, the words getting stuck in my throat. I feel the walls of the nightclub closing in on me.

'Yeah, she's moved in with him now and everything. Next thing, we'll hear they're getting married or something. It's a pain in the ass all this settling down lark. Loads of my friends are being all sensible and boring and stuff at the moment.'

I don't answer. I can't.

'I mean, *I* wouldn't be into that just yet. Hell no, I've a few more years of partying left in me, I reckon, haha. I might move in with someone though. If you live with someone and it doesn't work out, you can move on. If you've married them though, you're pretty much fucked.'

I still can't speak. My mouth has gone completely dry. I'm trying to digest all of this somehow. I start chewing on my thumbnail.

'Say,' continues Killian, obviously not noticing that I still haven't answered him back. 'How about us going back to the hotel and getting to know each other a bit better, eh?'

It's a bit of a pain trying to get A-J to leave the club. 'I'll be all right here,' she keeps saying over and over again. 'I promish. You go on, I'm jush having a resht.'

'You are NOT having a rest and you're not staying here by yourself,' I say crossly, gripping her bony arm to keep her from falling.

'Don't worry about me. I'll go home with the others,' A-J insists, her eyes beginning to roll in her head. 'Honesshtly I'll be fine.'

'Everyone else has gone back to the hotel,' I try to explain. 'There are no *others* here.'

'She needs a slap in the face,' Killian whispers in my ear. 'Come on, let's go. That one is well able to look after herself. Leave her be.'

I look at him in complete shock. Is he for real? Does he honestly think I would leave A-J in a foreign city in the state that she's in? I wouldn't do that to *anyone*, especially not a woman who's had far too much to drink.

'And anyway,' Killian continues, completely oblivious to the shock on my face, 'I'm dying to get you back to the hotel. I bet you've got a beautiful body. I'm getting horny just thinking of the two of us writhing about in that big luxury double bed.'

The tone of his voice repels me. Have you ever gone from finding somebody fairly attractive to finding them completely and utterly repulsive within minutes? Well, as far as Killian is concerned, this is exactly what is happening to me and suddenly I cannot wait to leave this club and get a taxi back to the hotel where I intend getting into my own luxury double bed all by myself. Already I deeply regret having played tonsil tennis with this selfish piece of work and cannot wait to get away from him. Bizarrely, he is so caught up in himself, that he doesn't even realise he's being ignored. I help a reluctant A-J to her feet, which is no mean feat considering she's at least six foot.

Back in the hotel, I spot the two older journalists who left us hours ago for a quick nightcap. By the looks of them they've had quite a *few* nightcaps and are practically bouncing off the walls of the lobby.

I say 'hello'. They stare back blankly. It takes them a moment to register. Then they smile and it's drunken hugs all around. But just as I'm about to announce I'm off to bed, the Scottish guy (I'll be damned if I can remember his name now), suggests we play some drinking games.

'You cannot be serious,' I shout in protest.

Accidentally I catch Killian's eye and he raises an eyebrow as if to say 'you coming?'

When I don't respond, he whispers in my ear and suggests I follow him up to his room. I nod in agreement and once he's safely out of the way, I sit down in the residents' bar to join in the drinking games.

A-J goes outside to throw up again, and when she comes back in she announces that she'll just have a Diet Coke because she's going to take it easy for the rest of the night. I nearly choke on my straw. Take it easy? Am I hearing things? What planet are these people living on? I'd thought I'd seen it all, but I, Fiona Lemon, in fact, seem to know nothing about anything!

I begin to relax and start having some fun. Simon the Scotsman is a bit of a hoot actually and is entertaining us all with ridiculous card jokes. We're all falling around laughing but the real reason *I* am laughing *particularly* loudly is because I am imagining silly Killy upstairs getting ready for a lurve session that just ain't going to happen!

11

OHMIGOD. MY flipping head. Get it out of this cement mixer now! The roof of my mouth tastes like a filthy carpet. I'm dying, I honestly am. Where am I anyway? This isn't my bed. Actually it's much nicer than mine. Why am I in this beautiful room? Frantically I glance at the space beside me in the bed. It's empty, thank *God*. For a moment there I thought I might have . . . oh yes, I remember now. Birmingham. That's right. That's where I am. Jesus, did we really only arrive last night? I feel like I've been here for at least a week!

I sit up in bed, and rest my head idly against the headrest. It feels like it's being crushed. I rub my eyes vigorously, leaving an unhealthy streak of black mascara on the back of my hand. Well now you *surely* didn't think I'd cleansed, toned and moisturised at 5.00 this morning, did you? Christ, was it really five? So much for having just the one glass, eh? 'Just the one' has to be the most overused abused phrase in the

English language. Oh, in addition to 'I'll call you,' and 'It's in the post' of course.

I glance at my watch. It's 9.00 a.m. No wonder I feel like shit. I've only had four hours' sleep. And drunken sleep doesn't really count anyway 'cos your body goes into shock and works overtime trying to digest all the poison. Why do we do it to ourselves, eh?

Right, I'd better get a move on. Terry said yesterday that we had to be down in the lobby for 9.30. From there a minibus will pick us up and give us a guided tour of the city. Thank God I brought my sunglasses. I can tell you now I won't be taking them off until I get on that plane back to Dublin this evening. I haul my poor dehydrated body out of the bed and stick my head into the mini-bar to grab some water. The sight of all the mini bottles of gin, whiskies and liqueurs makes me feel queasy, but hang on . . . is that a bar of chocolate I see in there? Hmm, I'd better take that too. The sugar will be good for me. Yes indeed. I hop into the shower. By the way you should *see* the bathroom here! It's so cool and retro and I can't really describe it – you'd have to be here, but thank God you're not 'cos I'm not looking the best. I lather myself in the complimentary shower gel. Already I feel better. So what if I'm a bit hungover? It's only a once off, isn't it? I'll have a good night's sleep tonight when I get home and will then feel normal again.

By the time I'm ready it's 9.40. Oh Jesus, the others will all be waiting patiently in the lobby now.

They'll be furious at me for keeping them waiting. I shove everything into my overnight bag and give the room a quick search to see if I've left anything behind. Then I take the lift down to the lobby. It's empty, except for an American couple checking out. Panic rises within me. Where the hell is everybody? Would they have left without me? Oh no! How could they do this? Couldn't somebody have rung my room to check where I was?

Okay, Fiona, relax. You should have Terry's number somewhere in that overstuffed night bag of yours. And even if the worst comes to the worst, you can get a taxi to the airport and meet the others later.

I take a deep breath but feel deeply disappointed with myself. They'll think I'm very rude. They'll think I wasn't able to hack the pace. Oh yes, I can drink all night, but when it comes to getting up and doing some actual work (i.e. seeing the sights, so I can pass on all the valuable information to the readers of *Travelling About*) I just lie on in bed, with no consideration to any of my fellow journalists. I give a deep melodramatic sigh.

'Hello!' I hear a cheerful familiar English accent. 'Are you the first down?'

Oh thank God, it's Terry. They haven't left without me after all! What a relief! I feel like giving our Birmingham rep a big bear hug but I don't. After last night, he probably thinks we're all slightly unhinged anyway.

'Yes, I'm first!' I beam. 'I can't think where the

others are though. Do you think they got the time wrong?'

Terry shakes his head and looks at his watch. 'I'll give them until ten before I start ringing around the rooms. I take it you had a late night?'

Oh no, did the hotel staff complain about our behaviour or something? I'm afraid to ask. How much does he know? Is he shocked that we stayed up so late?

'Er . . . it was pretty late, I guess.' I don't tell him it was so bright the birds were probably singing!

'And did you enjoy yourself?'

'Oh yes, very much so,' I say enthusiastically. *Apart from the fact that Killian tried his damndest to get into my knickers and that A-J insulted me about . . . oh at least ten times!*

The two older journalists show their faces within five minutes of each other. They seem remarkably fresh-faced considering only a few hours ago they were stumbling around this very foyer. They pleasantly ask me how my head is.

I reckon it's probably better than both of theirs put together.

Ten minutes later, we're all gathered around, waiting on our two 'no-shows', A-J and Killian. There's some quiet nudging about their whereabouts, but I assure the rest of the group, in no uncertain terms, that my two colleagues went to their rooms separately. Terry rings Killian's room at least three times without getting a response. If he's feeling pissed off (and nobody could blame him if he is), he doesn't show it. Simon has kindly offered to go and knock on Killian's hotel room to ascertain his whereabouts so that the rest of us can get moving. Within minutes Angela-Jean is with us, and gives us a curt apology. Her eyes are hidden behind large Chanel sunglasses and if I hadn't witnessed her throwing up at least twice last night I'd never have believed it!

Simon is soon back, explaining that Killian *won't* be accompanying us on the tour of the city but *will* join us for lunch later.

Terry and the rest of the journalists don't seem that bothered. I'm flabbergasted though. What is he going to write about if he doesn't experience all Birmingham has to offer? Oh well, it's not my problem and in a way, I'm fairly relieved I won't have to spend the morning avoiding eye contact.

We're off. At least we think we're off but the heavy traffic around the city centre means we don't get very far. Our second guide (a young woman with a microphone at the top of the bus) apologises profusely for the delay. But hey, I'm used to it anyway, coming from Dublin. I notice the Welsh guy is asleep.

Great, we're moving now and the bubbly guide is pointing out lots of interesting buildings. I'm wondering should I be writing this stuff down. Nobody else is, so I don't want to be the only enthusiastic person, like the school swot who sits under the teacher's nose scribbling away. I decide I'm just going to sit back and enjoy the ride and hope to God I remember all of this stuff later.

I notice Angela-Jean is clutching a bottle of water and her skin has gone a curious shade of green. I hope she's not going to be sick or anything. After all it's not highly unlikely due to her performances last night. The guide rambles on pleasantly only pausing now and again to ask if anybody wants to ask any questions. Nobody does.

The first stop is Birmingham's famous jewellery quarter, where we all get out to visit a small museum where they used to make jewellery by hand. It's fascinating seeing all the old machinery in it. Really, it's just like stepping back in time. The museum has been left just as it was the day the last of the employees finished working there. Even the kettle and some mugs and a box of tea bags have been left in the tiny kitchen area. Wow, this is pretty interesting stuff. Adjacent, there's a little shop where you can buy authentic handmade jewellery. I buy a charming little bracelet.

Back in the bus my stomach starts to grumble. I'm dying for lunch now since I didn't have time to grab breakfast this morning. A-J is sitting in front of me texting someone on her mobile phone. I lean forward to ask her if she's hungry but she answers in the negative. No wonder the girl is so thin. If she's that disciplined with a raging hangover, what must she be like normally?

The bus starts up again and everybody is either talking into their mobile phone or texting people. Is it always like this when you stick a crowd of journos on a bus? Are they actually interviewing people or chasing some hot story? Can't they relax for just five minutes? Suddenly I feel left out because I'm the only one not glued to my mobile. Maybe I should just text my mum to let her know how much I'm enjoying the trip. But then I remember that I haven't even told Mum I'm here, so I decide to leave it.

Okay, now *this* is impressive. Our guide points out the fabulous Bullring Shopping Centre. We all get out of the bus for a browse. Birmingham is hopping and everybody is carrying shopping bags. God, my dad wouldn't be able to believe this place. He worked in Birmingham for a few years in the sixties but doesn't really like talking about his time there. Dad is an intelligent man but all Birmingham offered him was site work. And he had an Irish landlady who was a thundering bitch. I think he might have started drinking while he was there but thank God he met my mum, who was working for an insurance firm and dragged him back to Ireland. They set up a corner shop with the money he had earned in Birmingham but to be honest, it was my mother who ran it and still does.

Right, back in the bus again. I would have loved more time browsing around the shops but we haven't time, the guide explains. It's probably just as well 'cos when you convert euro into sterling, shopping in the UK is pretty expensive. Bunny would have a good time here, I suddenly think feeling more than a hint of jealousy. Imagine being let loose in the Bullring with thousands of pounds in cash!

We're going to lunch now. Good. The walls of my

stomach are caving in. I hope the rest of the bus can't hear my loud tummy rumbles. The restaurant is very chic and modern with a cool nightclub feel to it. Lots of really good-looking men are standing by the bar. I'm impressed. In fact since I've arrived in Birmingham I've noticed how handsome some of the men here are. They dress better than Dublin men too. Most Irish men don't bother with designer clothes, preferring to get by on the much 'cheaper' Irish charm.

We're shown to our table at the back near the glass doors. The place is bright and airy and there's a terrific buzz about it. I order goat's cheese salad for starters, and spinach tortellini for the main course. A choice of red and white wine arrives immediately at our table. Oh what a waste, I think. Our crowd is so hungover that nobody will be able to touch it. Wrong, wrong, and wrong again. Not one person refuses, not even me! The first sip of ice cool Chablis goes down a treat. There, I feel better already. God this is great. I'm so glad I'm here instead of my poxy old office eating my homemade soggy sandwiches!

Suddenly I picture Joe and Cynthia sitting opposite each other in the tiny, unbelievably dreary canteen, reading out bits of newspaper articles. I have to stifle a laugh. They probably think I'm down at the local job centre with my CV and a long face. God, if only they knew! Already I feel I'm a high-flying journo sitting in a top-notch restaurant.

'Look over there,' Simon nudges me.

I turn around. I can't see anything out of the ordinary.

What?'

'Do you recognise him?'

'Who?'

'The guy in the cap, that's that bloke who won the first *Big Brother*.'

'Oh yeah.' I recognise him now. 'What's his name again?'

None of us can think of it straight away.

'Craig,' Angela-Jean says in a bored tone of voice. 'His name's Craig. Big deal.'

'You must be a big *Big Brother* fan,' teases John, the Welsh journalist.

'I certainly am not.'

'Well you know a lot more than the rest of us.'

Angela-Jean impatiently chases a piece of asparagus around her plate with a fork. 'I was forced to report on the last four *Big Brother* programmes. I didn't have a choice. I didn't really mind at first but the last one was the pits. The contestants were complete savages. And who cares that Michelle and Stu are still together?'

'*Are* they still together?' I pipe up.

A-J gives me a withering look and doesn't answer back. She's made one thing clear though. Under no circumstances does she want to start a conversation about reality TV.

Suddenly we're interrupted. Killian has made his grand appearance. He looks like he has slept well. *Bastard!* He says hello to everyone as if he has just happened to bump into us. He doesn't apologise however, and manages to successfully avoid eye contact with me. Hmm, as if I care! He's already missed the starters but makes up for it by ordering a steak for his main course and saying 'yes, please' to a large glass of white as well as a Jack and coke.

Thankfully I'm not seated beside or opposite him. I don't think I could honestly put up with him. I try to resume a conversation with A-J.

'So are you looking forward to going back to work tomorrow?' I venture.

'Of course I'm not,' she snaps. 'What kind of a silly question is that?'

'Listen, there's no need to be so defensive, I'm only trying to talk. If you don't want to talk to me, well that's just fine.'

I resume eating, my face feeling fairly flushed. Oh dear, I certainly don't want to go home having made a load of enemies on this trip. That wasn't the plan at all, but honestly what is that sourpuss's problem? I continue to concentrate on my plate, feeling pretty pleased with myself for making a stand all the same. She deserved it. And anyway, it's not like I made a scene because nobody else is listening.

'Sorry,' A-J says quietly. 'I didn't mean to upset you. I'm going through a bit of a rough patch at the moment. I'm not myself.'

'Oh. Oh right. Well, don't worry about it. We all had a late night last night so . . .'

'That's no excuse though,' A-J takes a swig of her wine. 'The truth is I've a lot on my mind.'

'Do you want to talk about it?' I ask tentatively.

'No, not really.'

'That's fine.'

'Well,' she continues regardless, 'I'm kind of stuck in a rut. My boyfriend, sorry *ex*-boyfriend, thinks he's too young to settle down even though he's thirty-seven years old. I'm not getting any younger and time is marching on with my biological clock. We had a talk before this trip.'

'A talk?'

'Yes, you know one of those activities that men enjoy as much as a trip to the dentist. Anyway the talk didn't go well, surprise, surprise. Naturally I had to give him the boot. It's all over now.'

'Oh. I'm sorry to hear that. Break-ups are always painful, aren't they?'

'Yes. And very inconvenient. We were going to buy a house together because I can't possibly afford a decent house on my own pitiful salary. Now all my plans are out the window. I'm at a loss to know what to do.'

'Oh dear.'

'Yes, not great, is it?'

'Um . . . I don't know what to say.'

'So anyway I'm having a bit of a mini crisis. I'm sick to death of my job. I know nobody believes me but I swear to God, I cannot stand meeting the same five or six silly celebrities who show up to random events, hang around VIP clubs and sit behind velvet ropes. And I'll strangle the next PR company who hassles me to attend the launch of some bloody bathroom product. Glamorous, huh? It's a crap, CRAP job and I'm not doing it any more.'

A-J's slightly raised voice causes a few people at the next table to look up.

She ignores the sudden interest, but when they go back to their food, A-J continues her rant. 'I mean, sometimes you get invited to so many things but no celebrities turn up, right?'

'Right,' I nod even though I don't have the faintest idea what she's talking about. I mean, what do I know about meeting celebrities for a living? The only one I ever talked to was Daniel O'Donnell and that was over the phone. Nobody I told got excited about it. Even my mother kept saying to me 'If *only* you could have interviewed Sean Connery instead.' Like I had a choice in the matter!

'And then,' A-J continues dramatically, 'you rack your brains trying to think of something to write about and you can't think of anything at all. Then you start ringing all the contacts in your book. But even Louis Walsh sometimes can't think of a quote for you and when *that* happens you're in big trouble!'

'Oh my God,' I look up from my dessert menu. 'I know you were complaining about your job a lot last night, but I didn't realise how *serious* you were. Hey, what are you having for dessert? Do you fancy sharing one?'

The fleeting look of horror that passes over A-J's face says it all. I go ahead and order chocolate cake anyway. I know I'm supposed to be starting my diet some time soon but I'm hungover so I have an excuse. And anyway it would be rude not to accept all this lovely hospitality.

*

Later, at the Aston Villa Club Grounds we are led on to the pitch. The stadium is huge and very impressive even though I'm not a football fan. We get to see the huge Jacuzzi in the changing rooms that fits about twelve footballers at the same time. Phew ... I'm getting hot just thinking about it.

Upstairs, in the hospitality area, we are treated to coffee and biscuits and somebody from the club is telling us all about the club and the team members and stuff. The lads are all interested but Angela-Jean and myself just sit by the window looking out onto the pitch.

'So,' she sighs dramatically. 'I feel a weight has been lifted off my shoulders talking to you, you know?'

'Well, I did work for *Gloss* so I know how embarrassing it was having to make up the horoscopes and stuff. But even *that* was simple compared to being the agony aunt. I just didn't feel qualified to do it. Some of the letters would make me burst into tears they were so sad.'

'Really?'

'Yes, they were heartbreaking and I wanted *Gloss* to get a professional psychologist to deal with the more harrowing stories but they said they didn't have a budget for it. In the end, I just couldn't take any more.'

'It's all down to money at the end of the day isn't it? Everyone thinks working in a magazine is so glamorous, but what's glamour? That's what I'd like to know! Anyway I'm calling it quits now. I'm off to New Zealand to find myself.'

I wait for A-J to laugh but the expression on her face remains motionless. Only then do I realise she's quite serious. Suddenly I have a comical image of A-J standing in a tropical rainforest shouting out her own name.

'Do you think you *will* find yourself over there?' I eventually ask.

A-J shrugs. 'Who knows? But I'll have a lot of fun looking, that's for sure.'

'So when are you going to resign?'

'I'm not sure, maybe tomorrow?'

'That soon? No way!'

'Why wait? I mean I've made my mind up. There's no point humming and hawing about it. If I think about it too much I'll end up not going. That's what people always do. They get a great idea and then talk themselves out of it.'

'But isn't this a big decision? I mean I know I've just jacked in my own job but I was just a glorified skivvy so that wasn't much of a risk but *you* . . . you know, you've built up quite a profile for yourself. And that takes years. Surely to God, you should think about it. You're probably not thinking straight 'cos of the way that guy . . .

'. . . that *prick*!'

'Well, you shouldn't just run away, that's all I'm saying. Why don't you just take six weeks off to get your head together and then make your decision when you're feeling better?'

'You know, maybe you've a point.' A-J frowns, pulling at a button on her sleeve. 'But I'd have to get somebody to fill in for me. I mean, if I don't, they'll replace me before my plane takes off.'

'I'm sure it won't be too difficult,' I say reassuringly. 'Lots of people would love to hobnob with the stars and get front row seats at fashion shows.'

Then Angela-Jean looks me straight in the eye. And all of a sudden I'm wondering if . . . if . . .

She's not going to ask me. Nooooo. She's not. She can't. But . . . but she is. I can almost see the light bulb flashing on top of her head.

'I don't suppose *you* would be interested in a temping position, Fiona?'

'**B**unny!' I almost drop my overnight case in shock. 'Oh Bunny, Bunny, Bunny, what on earth have you done to yourself?'

My new flatmate just looks at me with startled wide eyes, opens her mouth as if to say something, but then closes it again just as quickly.

'Don't you like my new look?' she asks, her lower lip trembling slightly.

'God, Bunny I don't know what to say, I . . . God, what have you done to yourself?'

Bunny's face crumples, and to my horror her eyes fill with tears and one enormous teardrop slides down her appallingly made-up face and onto the revolting brown and orange knitted poncho that some pushy Dublin shop assistant must have unsuspectedly forced on her.

'Now, listen, Bunny, I didn't mean . . .'

'Oh yes you did,' Bunny gulps accusingly. 'You really *did* mean it. And anyway you didn't have to say anything. The look on your face said it all. You think I look like a right mess. You think I'm a joke. Doncha?'

With that, she stands up, turns on her spiky high heels (oh Christ, where did she get those?), runs clumsily to her room and slams the door loudly. Only then do I notice everything else in the room. Oh my God, what has happened to the living room?

First of all, there is an enormous top-of-the-range Fuck-off TV/DVD player. Like something you'd often see on the top floor of Brown Thomas and think to yourself 'very nice but who the hell can afford it?' There's also a seriously cool-looking hi-fi system and a treadmill by the window with loads of sophisticated-looking buttons on the panel. Jesus, all we need now is the built-in sauna and Jacuzzi!

My eyes are literally popping out of their sockets! I feel like a kid let loose in the adult equivalent of Charlie's chocolate factory. Seriously, I've never seen so many gadgets. And oh my God, she's gone and bought one of those trendy little mini fridges too. She has plugged it into the far corner and when I open it up I find a bottle of Bollinger standing proudly by itself. Ooooh. Somebody around here intends celebrating!

Over in the teeny weeny kitchen area, I spot a juice maker, a cappuccino maker and one of those ultra-hip weighing scales that screws into the wall (does Bunny intend baking or what?).

God, Bunny must have gone a bit nuts when I was away! But although all these gadgets are pretty cool, I am horrified by what she has done to her appearance. Her hair, whoever she let at it, has been vandalised with bright red streaks. It's too naff to be trendy! That particular hairstyle never did anybody any favours. Her make-up looks like a crazy little kid was experimenting on it after finding some of her mum's old make-up.

Then something quite beautiful catches my eye. A simple bouquet of long white lilies are laid out on the kitchen counter and tied in a huge white ribbon. There's a little card attached. It reads:

> *'Thanks for making me so welcome, Fiona, and for helping me get through the last few days. I cannot thank you enough. And by the way, the treadmill is yours to keep. Love Bunny X.'*

My heart sinks. Oh no. I feel like a more evil version of Cruella de Ville. I can't believe I have insulted Bunny. She obviously thinks, or at least *thought*, that I was a nice person. Now that illusion is shattered. And I'm embarrassed now. Mortified actually. I mean, I can't accept such expensive gifts from a girl I barely know. What kind of a person would that make me?

I put the lilies in a vase and place them on the windowsill so they can catch the rays of sunshine in the morning. They look so dainty and perfect and the smell from them is divine. I'm almost more touched by the gift of flowers than the treadmill. And not being ungrateful or anything, but is Bunny trying to tell me something?

After about ten minutes sitting in the armchair

watching some boring programme about finding a second home in the South of France, I realise that Bunny probably isn't going to make an appearance again tonight, unless I make amends. So I take a deep breath, brace myself for a tirade of abuse and knock gently on Bunny's door.

Instead of yelling and throwing a tantrum though, Bunny quietly calls 'come in'. I push open her door, and she is lying on the bed wearing a simple pair of cotton pyjamas. Her hair is pulled back in a ponytail, she has removed every trace of the 'drag queen' make-up and appears to be flicking through American *Vogue*. She holds up the magazine, and then gives a sad sort of smile.

'See, I'm only trying to learn,' she says quietly.

'Listen, I have to apologise,' I say hovering in the doorway. 'I was completely out of order earlier. And I want to thank you for the lilies – what a beautiful surprise! You shouldn't have, but thanks a million.'

'Don't mention it. You're welcome. I really wanted to do something.'

'But the treadmill, I can't possibly accept that. It's too much.'

'Now listen here,' Bunny sits up straight in the bed. '*You* need it more than I do, right?'

'Um . . .'

It's hard to tell if Bunny's insulting me or not,

'We can *both* use it,' she continues practically. 'The man in the shop told me that it's top of the range and tells you how many kilometres you've run and how many calories you've lost.'

'Oh er . . . great. Gosh, you really went on a bit of a shopping spree this afternoon, didn't you?'

Bunny shrugs. 'Well you can't win the lottery and not go a tiny bit mad, can you?'

'I suppose so. I've never won it so maybe I'm not the best person to . . .'

'But the hair has to go . . .' Bunny interrupts. 'Even I know that. The hairdresser asked me what I wanted and I said I didn't really know. She said she had a great idea . . .'

'Oh no. God, no.'

'Oh yes,' Bunny starts to laugh now, to my utter relief. 'She said she'd make me look like a model.'

'Modelling what? The American flag? Your hair is full of red stripes!'

'I know, I know. It'll have to be fixed tomorrow. You'll have to recommend a good hairdresser.'

'No problem. By the way, who did your make-up?'

'Some guy in a department store said he'd make me over for free.'

'But I bet he got you to buy a lot of products afterwards . . .'

'Well, yes, God, I'm really embarrassed now. They saw me coming didn't they?'

'Listen, not to worry. They catch everybody sometime. The hair can all be fixed but that poncho you bought is going straight back to the shop tomorrow.'

'Is it really that bad?'

'Worse,' I say adamantly. 'I suppose the shop assistant told you it looked amazing on you.'

'Well, as a matter of fact . . .'

'I *knew* it,' I groan. 'Those sales people have no morals. Anyway we're going to go shopping tomorrow, but you'll need your own personal shopper.'

'Really? Do they like, exist in Ireland?'

'Well I may know somebody who knows exactly where to shop, and where to get nails, hair and make-up done. She's not exactly a personal shopper but I'll do my best to get her to help you. Believe me, when this girl is finished with you, you won't know yourself.'

'Wow! My own personal shopper! I'll be like J-Lo.'

'No, no, no,' I say quickly. 'I'm not thinking J-Lo or Beyoncé or anything – too horribly bling, bling for Ireland. Yes indeed. You need to be different. You're skinny and Irish with pale white skin and grey eyes. A subtle classical look would suit you. Think Jennifer Aniston, Di, Gwyneth Paltrow before she became a bit scruffy. Or a young Kiera Knightley type, do you get my drift?'

Bunny's eyes widen excitedly as she nods in agreement.

'And Bunny, what happened to your glasses?'

'I got rid of them,' she says blinking. 'I'm just getting used to these contact lenses. So anyway, what's my fairy-godmother's name?'

'Angela-Jean.'

'She sounds really glamorous,' Bunny says dreamily.

'Yeah well I can tell you this much,' I warn. 'She has a particularly short fuse so you'd better be on your best behaviour.'

13

Phew! Just finished writing up my piece on Birmingham. Hope Stu likes it! Now I'm feeling highly organised. All I need to do now is finalise everything with Angela-Jean. I pick up the phone whilst admiring my vase of lilies and at the same time ignoring my unused treadmill.

'Yes, it's all sorted now,' Angela-Jean says calmly over the phone. 'You're to start on Tuesday and I'll spend four days training you in.'

'Thank you, thank you, you're so kind. Oh my God, I can't believe I'm actually going to be doing this job. Last week I was unemployed!'

'Think positively. Anyway, I'm not kind at all,' A-J says bluntly. 'If it were up to me I'd be on the first flight to New Zealand, but Cecille, my editor insists that I show you the ropes before I head off. Those are the conditions.'

'She doesn't mind me stepping in, does she?'

'Of course not,' says A-J. 'I told her you were an

experienced travel writer who had also written for *Gloss*. To be honest, I think she was pretty impressed with all your experience.'

'Oh my God,' I say panicking somewhat. 'Why did you say I was experienced? I mean, come on, I've only been on one press trip to Birmingham!'

'So what? How many press trips do you think you need to go on? One is enough. Anyway that's my story and you'd better stick to it.'

'Right. If you say so then . . . so er, what do we have to do during the week?'

'Well I've a pile of poxy invites to things. Places I don't want to go to, people I don't want to meet . . . that sort of thing. . . . Let's see, there's a fashion show, the launch of a car, the launch of a new mascara range, the launch of a deli, the launch of a CD, the launch of a street festival, and the launch of a new breakfast cereal.'

'You are joking!'

'Of course I'm not joking, babes. All I do is attend bloody launches. It's the same old shite day in day out. I can't bear it. Why do you think I want to get the hell out of here?'

'Bu . . . ut,' I say dubiously. If it's that bad then what on earth am I getting myself into?

'Oh, you'll be fine. At first it's all a bit of a novelty and you'll have fun. I know I did, but believe me, it wears off pretty quickly.'

'Listen, Angela-Jean,' I say with some hesitation. 'I . . . er, I've a favour to ask.'

'Shoot.'

'Well see, you might think this is a bit strange but hear me out anyway. I . . . I have this friend. And this friend has a lot of money but no taste if you know what I mean.'

'Like so many women in this city,' adds A-J.

'Well, see she needs a personal shopper, and I was thinking that you'd be perfect. I mean, I know it's a lot to ask to give up a whole day but . . . she's prepared to pay.'

Angela-Jean gives a dramatic sigh. 'Who is this rich bitch anyway? Does she expect me to follow her around like a panting lap dog while she swans around Brown Thomas looking down on everybody? Is that what she's looking for 'cos I don't think I'm the right woman for the job.'

'Oh it's not like that,' I stress. 'She's anything but a rich bitch. In fact she's pathetically grateful. She desperately needs some help. Please? Can you help out?'

I know I'm cornering her. And I also know that she'll find it hard to refuse, because if it weren't for me, she wouldn't be able to head off in the secure knowledge that her job will still be here on her return. So I remain silent at the other end of the phone and wait for her to agree.

'How much help does she need exactly? How long will it take?' she asks cagily.

'Oh, just a day or so. We could go around the shops on Monday and get her some new things for her wardrobe. Then you can advise her on where to get her hair done and all that.'

'Okay,' A-J agrees heavily. 'But the minute she starts bossing me around, I'm out of there.'

I smile to myself. The idea of poor Bunny bossing anybody about is laughable.

'So are you looking forward to your new post anyway?' A-J asks, almost as an afterthought.

'I'm scared,' I admit. 'I mean, I keep thinking all these celebrities will realise I'm a novice.'

'Don't you worry about any of those idiots,' A-J scoffs. 'Remember you're doing *them* a favour by giving them publicity. Never forget that. They should be licking *your* ass.'

'I see,' I say, although I'm not terribly convinced.

'By the way, do you know a girl called Ellie Dunney?'

I suddenly freeze. Oh my God, does she know Ellie? What has Ellie been saying about me? Does she know I went to Birmingham instead of her? Then again, she *must* know by now. Stuart would have got in contact with her.

'Yes, I know her well,' I tell Angela-Jean. 'Er . . . why?'

'Oh, I was just curious. I saw her CV on our editor's desk this morning so I was wondering if you knew her. She's a travel writer and you travel writers are constantly bumping into each other, aren't you?'

'Er . . .'

'But the only vacancy we have is the temporary post you're getting.'

'I see.'

'So she won't be getting it.'

Jesus, I can't believe Ellie applied for this job too!

'Anyway, a pregnant woman wouldn't be suitable for your job.'

I freeze. Pregnant? What on earth is A-J talking about?

'You need to be tough to do this kind of work. After all, being a showbiz correspondent is no joke with all the long nights and hanging around waiting for interviews . . .'

I start to feel queasy. Surely, surely Ellie isn't . . . can't be . . . expecting a baby.

14

'And she doesn't mind doing this?' Bunny asks as we wait for Angela-Jean to call around.

'No, she's delighted to be of service,' I lie. Of course there's no *way* I'm going to admit I practically blackmailed A-J to do this. I'm trying my best to muster up some enthusiasm for Bunny's sake. Alas, that hasn't been very easy. I've barely slept since finding out about Ellie's pregnancy. It's hard to get my head around the whole thing. I mean I can't believe herself and Connor are going to be parents! I wonder if Ellie knew she was pregnant at the party. Oh God, I feel sick even thinking about it. Did Connor know? He couldn't have, could he?

Is that why Ellie called around the other day? Did she want to tell me her good news? How did she feel about seeing Bunny here? Was she devastated to see how quickly I had installed somebody else in her place? Or would she have understood my panic? Understood that I couldn't possibly have been able to

pay the rent alone? Oh God, my head's just spinning.
I'm desperate for some answers here.

Bunny is looking out the window like a child
looking out for Santa's sleigh on Christmas Eve. I
have never seen anybody so excited about anything in
my life. I really hope Angela-Jean doesn't burst her
bubble. I hope she goes easy on Bunny, because
despite her recent winnings, she's still very vulnerable and a bit lost. Only last night she confided in me
that her Lotto win still hasn't sunk in yet. She still
thinks it's all a dream and fears that at any moment
her rough ex-boyfriend is going to reappear and give
her a good beating.

Bunny suddenly gives a little gasp as a shiny black
Golf pulls up outside. 'Is that her?'

'Yep,' I answer as A-J opens the door and swings
her impossibly long legs out of the car, then she
spends a few minutes checking her make-up in her
little compact mirror.

'She's stunning, isn't she?' Bunny says in a quiet
awed whisper.

'Well, she's a good-looking girl all right, thin
enough to be a top model and as for attitude? The
girl's got buckets of it!'

The doorbell rings loudly.

'You answer it,' says Bunny quickly and runs to the
mirror to check herself out one more time. 'I don't
look too awful, do I?'

'Listen, relax, will you?' I laugh as I run towards
the front door. 'A-J is here to help out not to judge, do
you hear?'

A-J gives me two air kisses before sauntering in to the room, a strong smell of perfume wafting after her.

'You must be Bunny, I'm delighted to meet you.' She extends a leather-gloved hand to Bunny who accepts it shyly. 'Fiona has been telling me all about you'

'She has? What has she been saying?'

A-J doesn't answer. Instead she has a good look around the living room.

'You've got a lot of stuff here,' she comments. 'The treadmill is yours, I suppose.'

She looks directly at me. 'When are you going to start using it?'

'Soon, soon,' I mutter, feeling myself go slightly red. I'm getting paranoid now. A-J is the fourth person in the last week or so to make a snide comment about my weight. If only there was an easy way to slim down!

'Right then.' Angela-Jean claps her hands as if she's about to train Bunny for the army. 'Let's take a look at your wardrobe then, shall we?'

'Mine?' Bunny looks scared.

'Come on now, hurry up, we've no time to lose,' says A-J barging into Bunny's room and throwing open her wardrobe doors. Confusion quickly takes over. 'What's going on here? Where's all your stuff?'

'I don't have any of my clothes here. I left them all back in my home town.'

'Okay, so we're starting from scratch here. Good, good, no need to worry. I just wanted to establish exactly where we stood. Do you know something?

I'm going to make you look like a star. In fact I'm going to make everybody think you are a star. And why not? Wouldn't that be fun? Think about it! You can be my little social experiment!'

Soon we're all bundling excitedly into A-J's car.

'One of you better sit in the front,' she barks. 'I'm not a taxi driver, girls.'

I dutifully sit in the passenger seat as A-J sticks on the Scissor Sisters and we head for the city centre. A-J decides to park in the Brown Thomas car park and 'take it from there'. The first stop is Fitzpatrick's on Grafton Street where staff greet A-J like an old friend.

A-J picks out a pair of brown suede high-heels, a pair of black patent low heels, a chocolate-coloured pair of knee-high boots and the same pair in black. Next stop is BT2, which Bunny finds a tad confusing as the men and women's clothes are all mixed in together so you have to really search for what you want. After about an hour of dressing and undressing Bunny, I feel like one of those bored boyfriends that gets dragged around shops on a Saturday afternoon. I sit on the floor and cross my legs as A-J continues to order Bunny into jeans, and mix and match different colours until we're both perfectly satisfied that Bunny looks like Ireland's answer to Sienna Miller.

'I look completely . . . oh what's the word?' Bunny looks in the full-length mirror before giving a satisfied little whirl.

'Boho,' A-J says in a dead-pan voice.

'But wasn't she supposed to be going for a classical look?' I wonder aloud.

A flash of annoyance clouds A-J's face. It's the first time today she's let the guard down, if only momentarily.

'We don't want Bunny to be labelled,' she says firmly. 'She'll need to try out a few different looks to see which one suits best. The most important thing is that she doesn't look cheap. Too many women have too much cash but not enough taste. We want the whole of Dublin to wonder who on earth Bunny is. And to achieve that she must stand out from the crowd.'

I hold my tongue. Bunny looks happy enough so we bring the purchases to the cash register and the credit card is handed over.

'Right,' says A-J, 'next stop is the first floor of Brown Thomas, you can't go too far wrong there.'

We trot across the road, laden with bags. Bunny is on a high and it's great to see her with some colour in her cheeks. I feel like we're kids with a real life Barbie. In fact it's hard to believe Bunny is a real person with real money. And that this isn't some kind of pretend game.

We follow A-J up the stairs. Again, all the shop assistants seem to know her. She tells them exactly what she's looking for. One hour later, Bunny is the proud owner of a classic cream-coloured Louise Kennedy suit, two pairs of Paul Costello trousers and a plain black Gucci skirt, which looks nothing remarkable on the hanger yet a million dollars on

Bunny. Before we leave the store, we also acquire a Prada and two Gucci handbags. A-J reveals that big bags are back, which is great because as she points out, tiny bags may look cute but can't fit a mobile phone *and* a decent hairbrush!

After all that shopping, we need a break. We head over to the Westbury Hotel for a coffee. I'd love something to eat but feel too guilty ordering in the presence of A-J.

'I think we're doing great,' I announce happily as we wait for our coffees. You really are an expert, A-J.'

'Thanks,' she shrugs, 'but it's nothing really. I've been to so many fashion shows in my life time I could pick out flattering outfits in my sleep.'

'If they could see me back in my hometown . . .' Bunny says wistfully.

'Oh they will see you, that's for sure,' A-J says.

'But how?'

'If we can sort Bunny's hair out we can go to a fashion show tonight, all three of us. Bunny is sure to have her photo taken.'

'Oh but I *couldn't*,' Bunny says going a deep scarlet colour. 'I'd be way too shy for all that kind of stuff.'

'You can and you bloody well will. I haven't kitted you out like a starlet for nothing.'

'Do I look like a starlet?' Bunny looks secretly delighted.

'Absolutely. Actually you look better than a starlet. You look like a real star. All you need now is a good measure of attitude.' Angela-Jean gives her arm a reassuring squeeze as Bunny winces slightly. Oh dear, I think, Bunny is obviously still in pain. Her bruises haven't gone away yet. In fact I'm surprised A-J hasn't noticed them.

Coffee drunk and paid for, our next stop is Roccoco in the Westbury Mall to buy Bunny an evening dress. She tries on many and yet again cannot decide on any particular one. Angela-Jean decides she must buy two because she points out 'you can't wear the same evening dress twice in one season'.

I'm quite enjoying Bunny's crash course in shopping! Even *I* am beginning to know my Gucci from my Prada at this stage! Ellie would be so proud. She'd love all this. Oh no, there I go reminding myself of Ellie again. A wave of sadness washes over me. It's so upsetting that we're no longer in contact. I want to see her more than ever now and wish herself and Connor all the happiness in the world . . . only . . . only I'm not sure that I could say it sincerely from the bottom of my heart. God, what kind of a monster does that make me?

Why can't I be happy for her? Why can't I shake off that horrible niggling feeling I'm carrying around? The feeling that Connor is *completely* unsuitable. I know he doesn't love her. At least I'm pretty sure he doesn't love her. I mean I saw the look in his eyes when he stood on my doorstep. And I felt the attraction between us that night when we were alone, half-dressed in Ellie's bedroom. I wouldn't admit it to myself back then, but . . .

'Wakey wakey! Calling Fiona, over and out.' A-J snaps her fingers impatiently in my face, bringing me back to earth with a bang. I'm grateful to be honest. I mean I don't know why I am thinking about Connor and Ellie at all. They have moved on, so I must too. In fact even the mere mention of my name must embarrass them.

'Where to now?' Bunny asks, like a kid at the fairground who hasn't had a go on the roller-coaster yet.

'Patience, my pet,' A-J pats Bunny's head affectionately. God, she really does seem to have taken a shine to her young protégée. I hope she doesn't get so fond of Bunny that she decides not to go to New Zealand after all. Because in a way I'm looking forward to getting stuck into my new role as a celebrity gossip columnist (or should I call myself a social diarist?). I mean, it'll be pretty exciting to see my name printed at the top of the page, won't it? In *Gloss* my name never appeared. There were good reasons for that actually. Obviously I couldn't stick my name on the horoscope page; my 'agony aunt' readers only knew me as 'Fi-Fi'. My editor said it was for the best. She said there were a lot of freaks out there. Apparently the last agony aunt had had this forty-five-year-old nut writing her love letters, sending flowers and really freaky poems. He wrote that the two of them were destined to be together.

'Oh my God,' I said, my blood beginning to chill.

'Yes,' Faith continued, obviously enjoying the look of horror on my face, 'and then on my advice, she stopped all contact with him and he started sending really abusive emails. Or he'd ring her and just breathe heavily.'

'Good Jesus, what happened to her in the end? How did she get rid of him?'

'Well, it was very, very difficult. I mean this guy tried to follow poor Marie home one evening but thankfully she noticed him and called the police. They gave him a warning to stay away from her but she was so upset about the whole thing, she felt she couldn't work here any more. It was very sad.'

Funny the way Faith looked anything but sad telling me the story. In fact she looked positively thrilled to be scaring the flipping daylights out of me.

'So that's why I wouldn't recommend putting your full name or photo on the page,' said Faith with an evil smile. 'But of course you're *more* than welcome to stick your name above the sex tips.'

I declined the generous offer, however, as by then I'd already decided to hand in my notice.

I ended up leaving the magazine after a few weeks. After all there was no point in writing for a magazine unless you got some credit for it. A couple of times my mother, or my sister had bought the magazine but when they couldn't see my name, they'd been very disappointed.

I could hardly tell them that I wrote the sex tips now, could I? I could just imagine my parents giving out about all the money spent on my education. While Gemma had gone on to be a surgeon, I, Fiona had gone on to be some kind of literary slag.

They'd always had high hopes for me. God knows why. I was really crap in school. Oh I'll never forget the boredom. Sitting in geography class learning about rock formation somewhere I knew I'd never visit, like the North Pole or the Equator. What use was that? I would have taught geography differently.

Yes, I would have taught students all about Greece because most of them head there in September straight after they get their Leaving Cert results. I think a crash course about how to survive the islands would be more beneficial than learning how long a river in Africa is.

The youngsters should be given useful tips like why you shouldn't drink and drive a moped with or without a helmet. Or why you shouldn't drink yourself into a near coma night after night just because the drink is cheaper. And why, no matter how much you think you don't need it, anything less than factor 12 is a big no no for Irish people. And that smothering yourself in oil and baking in the sun for twelve hours, can lead to sunstroke, or at least severe sunburn. And that no, lemon juice in your hair will NOT turn it blonde. And that Gary from Manchester who proclaimed his undying love in the Greek Taverna under the purple electric thingy for the purpose of electrocuting flies, will NOT keep in touch.

God, I'd better hurry up. Bunny and A-J are walking well ahead, nattering away like old friends. You wouldn't think they had just met. As I catch up with them, A-J is ushering Bunny into the hair salon. She asks for the head stylist, whom she knows personally and shows off Bunny's poor stripy head. Everyone agrees that her hairstyle is absolutely appalling and I'm relieved that I'm not the only one who thinks so. Her appointment is made for first thing tomorrow afternoon. Bunny, we are assured, will undergo a magnificent transformation. But it looks like she won't be able to make it to the fashion show after all.

Next minute, we're back out on the street again and A-J says we need a couple of pieces of jewellery for Bunny.

'I know where we can pick up some fabulous pieces of costume jewellery,' A-J advises. 'I sometimes plug the designer in my column so we'll get a great discount.'

'Yeah?' Bunny and myself speak in unison.

'Absolutely, I'll call her on the mobile and get her to come over to your place with a few choice pieces, so you can pick out what you want.'

'Cool.' Bunny almost does a little dance on the spot.

We lug all the bags back to the Brown Thomas car park as A-J makes yet another call to a . . . wait-for-it . . . mobile beautician who will be over tonight with her lotions and potions for Bunny, who will indulge in a massage, a leg wax and bikini wax, an eye-lash tint, an eyebrow tint and a mini facial. The following morning the same beautician will apply St Tropez fake tan, and then give her a professional make-up lesson.

'God, I'm jealous,' I can't help saying. 'I'll be

sitting in the next room applying my own nail varnish as a treat.'

'Of course you won't, missus,' says A-J. 'You're coming out to the fashion show with me tonight, remember?'

'Does that mean I won't be going?' asks Bunny.

A-J grimaces. 'Not tonight I'm afraid. This beautician is very, very busy and can only fit you in tonight. Don't worry, it'll be worth it.'

Later, as we head for the fancy hotel where the fashion show is taking place, A-J confides in me that we couldn't have possibly invited Bunny along.

'Why not?'

'Not with that hairstyle, I'm afraid. I'll have to get *Toni and Guy* to sort her out. At the moment she looks like a cartoon character. The society photographers wouldn't touch us with a bargepole.'

'What society photographers?' I ask, astonished.

'Oh you know, you often get your picture taken at these things, but the lads can be really picky. It often really depends on whom you're standing next to. Like if you're standing with a man, they usually won't bother 'cos they don't put pictures of men who aren't famous in magazines.'

'Oh yeah?'

This is news to me. I just presumed they took photos of the first ten people they saw so they could hurry on to the next event.

'Yeah. They take pictures of people they think their readers will be interested in. Or good-looking women who are well dressed. It helps if you're wearing something colourful too. Black doesn't look good on the printed page.'

'I'd never have thought of that.'

'You have to think of all these things now, Fiona. The same people always appear in all the magazines. Haven't you noticed that?'

'Er . . . yeah. I've never really thought about it but I suppose it *is* always the same old faces peering out.'

'Well, see the photographers do that on purpose. They know if they get familiar faces, they've a better chance of getting the photos published.'

'I suppose it makes sense then.'

'But if you're standing with some clown, who looks like they've just had a scrap with a tin of paint and lost, they'll just ignore you.'

'The photographers?'

'Yeah.'

'So how do you become someone who gets photographed all the time?'

'It's simple,' A-J explains, as we hand our coats to the timid-looking young girl at the door. 'You turn up to the opening of an envelope dressed like you're going to the Oscars, you hang around near the entrance trying not to look too desperate, and you don't get drunk until the last photographer has left the building.'

'Oh, I see, I'm getting the gist of it now,' I say with a giggle. With that I spot three bottle blondes with brown faces and identical short skirts, pretending to look interested in each other's conversations but scanning the room every few seconds for the photographers. A-J notices them too.

'A typical example if ever you needed one,' she mutters, nodding in their direction.

'Are they sisters?'

'Mmm. The Pointer Sisters.'

'Why are they called that?'

''Cos they're always pointing at people and whispering about them. I don't know what they actually *do* for a living. But they turn up to every cockfight. I reckon they're racing each other to find a suitable husband. Pathetic, if you ask me. Oh hi, Jason, how are *you*? How was South Africa? Wow, what a tan!'

'Thanks doll. Yeah South Africa was cool man; it's a bit of a bummer being back though. Listen, would you two ladies mind if I took a quick photo?'

'Not at all,' says A-J oozing charm I never knew she even possessed.

The photographer, a strange-looking guy with spiky red hair and tongue piercing, flashes his bulb as A-J slips an arm around my waist. God, I feel a bit cheesy and slightly uncomfortable too. The Pointer Sisters are glaring over but thankfully only one of them is pointing – they must take it in turns!

Eventually Jason puts down his camera and fishes out a little notebook from his breast pocket.

'Can I take your name?' he says, looking at me.

'Fiona Lemon.'

'Oh yeah, I've taken your picture before, haven't I?'

'Uh . . .'

'Yes, loads of times,' A-J says quickly. 'By the way

Jase, Fiona is taking over from me for a while at *Irish Femme* so you two will probably be bumping into each other quite a lot on the social scene over the next few weeks.'

'Cool,' says Jason. 'Where are you off to, man?'

'I'm off to New Zealand to find myself,' A-J grins.

'Wow, I went to India once to do that.'

'And did you?' I ask him.

'Did I what?'

'Find yourself?'

'Yeah I think I did but then I lost me again. Got to get outta these gigs though. I can't stand this kind of bullshit.'

'Tell me about it,' A-J throws her eyes to heaven. 'Any heads here?'

Jason shakes his spiky red head. 'Nah, just the usual suspects. No VIPs yet. I see the Pointer Sisters over there, they've been eyeing me since I arrived. I don't want to take their photo if I can help it though. They'll break the damn camera on me again. Anyway,' he gives the weariest sigh, 'I'd better scoot off and look like I'm doing a bit of work. Go in and get some free champagne before it all runs out. Catch yiz later, right?'

'He seems nice,' I comment as Jason disappears into the crowd with the Pointer Sisters looking wistfully after him.

'He's okay, a bit of a dope head really, I suppose he's not the worst though. Come on now, let's go get ourselves some bubbly.'

A couple of *very* made-up, twenty-something girls

look at me suspiciously as I approach the desk where everybody must sign in. Then they spot A-J and their hostile looks evaporate.

'Hi girls,' A-J says with false gaiety. This is followed by a bit of air kissing until A-J finally introduces me as her stand-in for *Irish Femme*.

'Hello,' I say shyly. These girls are so made-up and stylish that they make me feel quite small and insignificant in comparison.

'Remember what I said?' A-J whispers in my ear, after we say good-bye and head towards the table full of chilled quarter bottles of champagne. 'They need you more than you need them.'

I can't help laughing at A-J's attitude. She's a total pro at this. Nobody and nothing fazes her. It's baffling that she wants to give all this up to trek around forests and climb mountains in a country more populated by sheep than people.

The champagne goes down a treat. We're sipping it from straws like true IT girls. I am so, so excited to be here. I still can't believe I'm part of this very glamorous crowd. Everybody here seems to know everybody else though. And I'm half afraid somebody is going to see me, realise that I don't belong here at all, and arrange to have me removed.

'God, this is so boring,' Angela-Jean says in a sour tone of voice. 'There's nobody here, nobody at all, sure there isn't?'

'Er . . . no, I dunno,' I find myself floundering. I mean, I think this is pretty great! Free champagne and oooh . . . they look nice . . .

'Would you like a cocktail sausage?' says the young waitress in the black T-shirt with a quiet smile.

'Um, I'd much prefer one of these,' I reach out. 'They look gorgeous. What are they?'

'They're mini vegetarian quiches. Would you like one?'

'Yum, yes please,' I say eagerly.

The waitress then sticks her tray under A-J's upturned nose. 'Would you . . .?'

'No, thank you,' she snaps.

'Are you not hungry?' I ask as the poor girl slinks away.

'No,' A-J insists, 'and even if I was I wouldn't eat mini quiches, sausage rolls, vegetable samosas, chicken wings or any of the usual calorie-ridden rubbish they try to force on you at these things. Believe me, after a week at this game, you won't be able to face another sizzly thing on a stick ever again.'

'Going to these things must save a fortune on grocery bills though.'

But A-J doesn't seem to think so. 'You can't eat this junk all the time. You really need to live healthily in this job,' she says before gulping down the rest of her champagne and picking another glass off the pristine white linen table.

'Are you *really* not enjoying this?' I ask A-J tentatively. I'm never sure if she's serious or not. I know I'm having the time of my life. Imagine, little old me at something as glamorous as this!

'It's okay,' she shrugs. 'I've been to worse I suppose. But there's nobody here.'

I look around the place feeling slightly confused. How can she say there's nobody here? Sure, isn't the place swarming with well-dressed women?'

'Do you . . . do you mean there are no men here?'

That must be it. A-J must be looking for a date. I don't know if she still has anything to do with the man who didn't want to settle down. Maybe she's actively searching for somebody else.

'Of *course* I'm not,' she gives a hollow laugh. 'Looking for love? In a place like this? Hetero men don't usually turn up at fashion shows. I'm not looking for anyone. This is work, not a school disco. I need names, names, and more names. There are no names here, you know?'

I don't have a clue what she's going on about. A-J suddenly launches into detailed explanation.

'You see, Fiona,' she begins. 'I have to fill a full page every week, and you will have to do it while I'm away. It's not the easiest gig in the world, although most people think otherwise.'

'I s'pose you're right. Everyone thinks it's all fun and games.'

'Yeah but this is just a fecking rent-a-crowd here tonight. I can't just write about the Foxrock fannies and women from the arse end of nowhere who pretend they're from D4. These people do nothing but turn up to these events, you know? I've got to get *stories*, and entertaining ones at that. You can't simply trot out the PR guff that's rammed down your throat at these things.'

'Right. But how do you know who's worth writing about?'

'Oh, you get to know the names and faces. I mean you'll recognise a lot of people from TV. The casts of Irish soaps will usually turn up to absolutely anything, you know?'

'Yeah? Gosh. I don't really watch any of them.'

'Well you should start . . . just so you'll recognise their faces.'

'I will,' I promise. 'What else should I watch?'

'Ah that's about it. You know all the RTE people already: Gerry Ryan, Joe Duffy, Ryan Tubridy, Mary Kennedy, Anne Doyle, Marty Whelan, Pat from the Late Late . . .'

'Of course, I haven't been living under a hedge all my life, you know. Who else?'

'Well there's an annual Rose of Tralee and an annual Miss Ireland both of whom are slightly famous for about a year until they're replaced and they fade back into oblivion. Of course a few of them *do* hang around, unwilling to let go of their snatched crown, but I'm not sure why they bother . . .'

'Oh my God!'

'Yeah, it's embarrassing isn't it? People should know when to move on. Especially former beauty queens.'

'No, no, I'm not talking about that at all,' I say in a very low voice. 'I've just seen my ex-editor Faith.'

'Oh *that* old cow! I'd forgotten that you worked with her.'

'Well I haven't.'

'Doesn't she write some kind of gossip page as well?'

'Yeah, she guards it with her life. She wouldn't let anybody get that gig.'

'Well, her column is shite,' Angela-Jean says with more than a hint of venom. 'It's just full of regurgitated press releases and blatant plugs. What a load of crap!'

I smile in spite of myself. Nobody gets off lightly where A-J is concerned. One thing is sure here, though, there's some fierce competition among the gossip columnists for scoops. Seems to me they'd claw each other's eyes out for the sake of a story!

'Well hello!'

Oh good Jesus. It's Faith. Right in my face! Her beady eyes are flashing like a lunatic's and I'm sure she's wondering what the hell I'm doing drinking champagne with her rival. I'm not going to tell her though, Hell, no! Let her sweat.

'Faith, how are you?' To my surprise A-J automatically air kisses the woman she has just unashamedly slated. 'It's good to see you.'

'And you,' Faith coos. Then she looks me directly in the eye and for a moment I'm terrified she's going to kiss me too, but she doesn't. Instead she clasps one of my warm hands in her very cold ones. 'You look really great,' she says insincerely.

The sound of her voice sends an involuntary shudder down my spine. How I hate it! It reminds me of how she used to boss me around. *Fiona, run out to the post office and post this,' 'Fiona, did you jam the photocopier and forget to tell somebody?' 'Have you not got a boyfriend, Fiona? You're great at coming up with the sex tips, considering . . .' 'I'm organising the Christmas party this year, Fiona, so I'll just put you down for one, will I?'*

'Thank you.' I don't return the compliment. She can get lost if she thinks I'm going to be nice to her after the hell she put me through.

'Anyone here?' Faith asks nobody in particular and scans the room with eagle eyes.

'Not a soul,' A-J tells her triumphantly. 'But that's not very surprising really. I mean everybody is at the opening of Danny Devine's new hairdressing salon over on the Northside.'

'No way! Are you serious? I didn't think *anybody* would bother going to that,' Faith says, looking like she has swallowed a saucer of sour milk.

'Mmm, well there you go now, apparently Bono is a good friend of Danny's and is making a surprise guest appearance, but . . .' A-J's hand suddenly flies to her mouth. '. . . oooh I dunno if I should have told you that. It's like top information, I just got a tip off.'

Faith is trying her best to hide her gloating smile. My heart sinks. I'd thought A-J was really clued in, but maybe I had underestimated her. I can't believe she's given that piece of vital information to a rival gossip. Why? I wonder. I mean, she didn't even tell *me* about this secret event! And I'd have loved to have met Bono in the flesh!

Faith suddenly looks at her watch. 'Goodness, is that the time? Where does it fly to? Listen, I don't think I'll stick around for the show after all. I'm all fashioned out these days, hee hee. I think I'd better head. Will you text me to let me know if anybody decent shows up after I'm gone?'

'Of course we will, won't we, Fiona?'

I nod foolishly.

'You should pop into the salon on your way home, Faith,' adds A-J. 'It'd be well worth your while.'

'Yes . . . well, I might just pop in for a minute . . .' Faith says hurriedly, looking more than a little flustered now.

A-J gives another saccharine smile as she air kisses Faith once again. This time there's no escape for me. I find myself being air kissed too and nearly pass out with the stink of free promotional perfume. Faith then toddles off into the crowd.

'See ya,' A-J calls as I turn to look at her in amazement.

'Was all that stuff about Bono true?'

'Of course not,' she answers with a wicked smile. 'Now then, let's get ourselves some more champagne.'

15

'And were the models really stunning?' Bunny is all agog.

'Stunning! And they were really skinny. *Too* skinny though if you ask me.'

'And did you get to see the whole show?'

We're waiting for Bunny's beautician to arrive to apply her fake tan. Her skin is glowing after yesterday's facial. She says it was embarrassing taking off her clothes to have the massage because she was afraid the beautician would comment on her bruises.

'And did she?'

'No,' Bunny hung her head, 'but she started telling me about a friend of hers who had been abused. And gave me the name of the place her friend had gone to for help and . . .'

Bunny is silent for a moment, then two heavy teardrops slide down her fragile face. Soon she's sobbing uncontrollably. I cradle her in my arms until her slight body stops heaving. I feel like my heart is about to break. Bunny has more money now than she knows what to do with, but she has no parents, and no real friends.

'You're going to be okay, pet.' I stroke Bunny's stripy red head gently. 'After you get your hair fixed this afternoon, you won't know yourself.'

Bunny wipes her eyes. 'You're very kind,' she sniffs. 'Yourself and A-J have been absolute angels to me.'

I think of A-J at that fashion show last night, glaring at all the models because they were skinnier than her, and how she followed a coked-out-of-her-head high society princess into the bathroom to see if she could hear her snorting her husband's nouveau riche cash.

'Well she *does* have her good points,' I agree softly. 'But I wouldn't go so far as using the word angel.'

'She *is* an angel though,' Bunny is adamant.

Whatever, I think. It's not worth having a debate about.

'I rang her this morning,' Bunny continues.

'You did?' I ask in surprise. 'I doubt she was too thrilled to get the early morning call. She was fairly lashing back the champers last night.'

'Well funnily enough she didn't seem to mind at all. She was up anyway doing bits and bobs, she told me.'

I must say I'm impressed. I honestly hadn't thought A-J would surface until this afternoon. Where does she get her energy?

'But what did you ring her for?' I ask, curiosity getting the better of me.

'I wanted to settle with her.'

'Settle?'

'Yes, I wanted to know her fee so I could write a cheque for all her hard work yesterday.'

'Oh, I see.'

'But she wouldn't hear of it,' says Bunny, looking slightly worried.

'She wouldn't?'

I'm shocked. I really am. I honestly didn't think A-J would refuse her fee.

'No, she said it was her good deed for the week and that I was to forget about it.'

'Did she indeed?' I say thoughtfully.

Gosh. I really have underestimated A-J, haven't I?

My phone rings and startles me. 'Excuse me, Bunny, I'll just get this.'

'Hi, it's Gemma,' my sister's familiar voice booms down the line.

'Hey Gemma, well, stranger, no time long hear!'

She laughs. 'Listen,' she says excitedly, 'my pal Corrine just passed her Botox exams. She's doing me this weekend and says if you come over to Cardiff she'll give you your injection at a hefty discount.'

'Oh,' I say, feeling a bit subdued. Surely I'm not old enough to start injecting my forehead yet, am I? I mean, I don't want to look permanently surprised.

'Well, you know, it's nothing, just a prick. Loads of women get it done in their lunch break. Anyway, all I'm saying is that if you want to get it done give me a shout and I'll have it arranged.'

'Okay.'

'Any other news?'

'I got a job.'

'Another one? Jesus, I can't keep up with you these days.'

'I'm a social diarist for *Irish Femme*.'

'Good on you. Haha, it's hilarious though, isn't it? I can't imagine *you* of all people mingling with the stars.'

'Why not?' I ask, feeling mildly insulted.

'I dunno, you're too ordinary.'

'Ah leave me alone, ya silly cow.'

'No, I mean, you're too down to earth to be hanging around with those "society" people. God forgive me but they haven't a brain cell among them. But if you get any cool invitations anywhere will you let me know and I'll fly back to Dublin for the night? I'm getting a bit tired of going out to the Hilton every single weekend. I need a change of scenery.'

'Ah but Cardiff's good craic.'

'You're just saying that because you're only here on rugby and Bank Holiday weekends. It's too small sometimes though, a bit like Dublin. I feel like I know everybody here and I've only been here for a year. I need to move, maybe go to London.'

'The grass is always greener . . .' I warn.

'I know, I know. I'm just going through a "is this all there is?" phase in my life. If I was in London I'd probably be dying to get back here again. Who knows? So anyway, does this mean you'll be meeting the likes of Pierce Brosnan and Liam Neeson?'

'Nah, sure those people don't really hang around VIP bars, you know? They're too busy making a living in Hollywood or wherever. I mean if I meet the odd C-lister, I'll be doing all right. The top letters of the celeb alphabet rarely turn up to things. If they do, it's major news.'

'Well that's a bit of a bummer. I was hoping you might introduce me to a wealthy rock star!'

'No chance. Sure why would any A-list star turn up anywhere for a glass of warm champagne which loses its fizz once the corks pop? The stars lead busy lives you know. They're not going to turn up to something for a free bottle of moisturiser and a T-shirt bearing some company slogan.'

'Yeah, I s'pose you're right. Oh no, there goes my bleeper. Talk to you soon, right?'

'Sure, thanks for calling.'

As I put down the phone, I thank the Lord she didn't ask me how my diet was going. I'd need to do something about my spare tyre once and for all, I think, pinching more than an inch around my mid riff. I wish I could be as skinny as A-J but then again all that starving must be a pain in the butt. I mean, where's the fun in that?

The doorbell rings. Gosh, everybody's busy this morning. Whatever happened to lie-ins? I open the door and A-J is standing outside with her hair scraped back and not a touch of make-up up on her face. She looks younger, without the scarlet lipstick, severe blusher and the harsh black eyeliner she normally wears.

'You're up bright and early,' I say groggily, still feeling the aftermath of last night's drinking session.

'Yes, well,' she says pushing past me into the living room, 'I've something on my mind.'

She beckons me into the tiny kitchen area and turning on the kettle, she whispers, 'I'm worried about Bunny.'

I look at her blankly, not wanting to sell my new flatmate down the river. I've promised Bunny to keep my mouth shut and I fully intend on keeping my word.

A-J eyes me steadily. 'I know what's on your mind,' she says. 'But the truth is I've a fair idea that Bunny could be in trouble.'

'Was the beautician talking about her?'

A-J shakes her head. 'She didn't have to. I myself was talking to Bunny this morning. I could hear fear in her voice. I also caught a glimpse of her back and arms when she was changing and it wasn't a pretty sight. Nobody should have to live like that in this day and age.'

'But is there anything we can do about it?' I ask matter-of-factly. 'After all if there's *anything* I can do to help Bunny, I will. She's such an angel. I'm just at a loss to know what to do. Domestic abuse isn't something I've ever had to deal with before.'

A-J opens her bag, fishes out a disposable camera, and hands it to me.

'I want you to take some pictures.'

'Of Bunny? She's not going to let me do that.'

'Tell her I want some "before" and "after" pictures so that we can look back one day fondly on Bunny's disaster hair pictures . . . after we've turned her into a sex bomb of course.'

I understand now.

'You're a genius, Angela-Jean.'

'Don't mention it,' she says. 'Now, here is the plan. I'm going home to put on my face now but I'll ring you in about an hour to tell you what's going on, so start making yourself pretty.'

And she's gone before the kettle has a chance to boil.

Bunny opens her bedroom door.

'Was that A-J?'

'Yes it was,' I answer. 'She just popped in to go through some stuff with me about the new job. She'll be calling around again later. Remember the beautician will be in here in about fifteen minutes,' I say looking at my watch.

'Yeah, I know, I'd better jump in the shower before she arrives.'

'Mmm, listen, Bunny, I wonder would you do me a favour?'

'Sure,' she gives a big bright smile.

'I'd love some photos of you with your mad hair.'

'Oh okay. That sounds fun.'

God, that was easy, I think. So far so good.

'I've got a disposable camera in my room. I could take them now?'

'Now?' Bunny looks horrified. 'But shouldn't I have my shower first? And at least wait until the beautician comes and applies my fake tan? I look awful!'

'But they're just fun photos . . . just for me and A-J. So that when you're famous, and are swept off your feet by some hunky millionaire to live in the

Caribbean on a luxury yacht, we can always look back and remember the "real" Bunny we once knew.'

Bunny looks at me dubiously and I begin to feel I'm making a mess of things. Oh, why couldn't A-J have stuck around and taken the photos herself? She'd be much better at this than me.

'B . . . b . . . but the *bruises*,' Bunny says self-consciously rubbing her arms.

Oh no! I'm terrified she's going to cry again and this time it'll be all my fault.

'I'd better put on a jumper.'

'No *don't*. Hey, you wouldn't even notice them. And besides your vest top is so pretty, it would be a shame to hide it.'

I rush off to my room to get the camera before Bunny can even think about changing her mind. 'This'll take less than a minute,' I tell her sitting on the bed beside her.

Bunny relaxes and smiles and sticks out her tongue happily as I snap away. Then when I finish Bunny hops into the shower and I start getting ready to go out.

A-J phones just as the beautician arrives, to say she's on her way over. While Bunny is being smothered in fake tan, she and I will be going to lunch in a fancy restaurant to celebrate the launch of some festival. A-J isn't sure what it's about but says I'd better dress up anyway, just in case. Hmmm, sounds like fun.

16

We're sitting in a gorgeous little restaurant off Baggot Street, listening to some politician rambling on and on about a festival. It's being brought to Ireland for the first time to celebrate God only knows what 'cos I'm not listening to a word. Nor is anybody else by the looks of things. Some people are furiously texting under the table, others are just lashing into the free drink and some people are, believe it or not, talking to each other loudly, as if they were alone.

I keep looking out for famous people because Angela-Jean said there might be a couple of well-known people here. But so far, unless I'm *totally* blind, I don't see anyone here from TV or anything. I'm sure the politician is fairly well known in his own constituency but when it comes to his dress sense, unfortunately he's nothing to write home about.

After his speech everybody claps rapturously. Everybody is so glad the boring bit is over and they can now do what they came here for (i.e. enjoy a free lunch).

'Isn't it a wonder they wouldn't give the speech after the lunch?' I suggest, my stomach rumbling so much I'm convinced people outside in the street can hear it.

A-J gives a knowing smile. 'That's the whole *point*, sweetie. If they gave the speech after lunch, nobody would stick around for it. I'm sure they've learned that from experience.'

'Would you like some more wine?' She fills my empty wine glass to the brim, then reaches for a small dry brown roll and starts to nibble as we wait for our starters. I nearly keel over in shock. This is honestly the first time I've ever seen A-J eat carbohydrates.

'Are you going to write about this?' I ask out of curiosity.

'About this?' A-J looks surprised. 'No, no, not unless I'm really desperate. There's nobody here, is there?'

'But,' I say, frowning, 'there doesn't seem to be anybody *anywhere*, according to you.'

'It's true though, there isn't. Ah sure I'm not panicking yet. I only ever start panicking if at the end of the week I've still got nothing to write about.'

'Then what do you do?'

'Oh, I just start ringing band managers, model agents, publishers and PR agents for stories.'

'And suppose they don't have any?'

A-J just laughs. 'They *always* have stories, and if they don't, they make them up. They'll do anything to keep their little darlings in the news. Come to think of it, I keep getting these calls from a very annoying guy. His name's Larry and he keeps telling me about his band who are huge in Germany.'

'What did you say his name was?'

'Larry something. His band's called Heartbreak Hell or something silly.'

'You mean H Club Heaven?'

'Oh yeah, that's it.' A-J looks surprised. 'Do you know their music?'

'No, but I've been given the whole "big in Germany" rubbish. Larry is a complete chancer! He once invited me to dinner and bought me a cold Chinese instead.'

'Jesus. You do have terrible taste in men.'

'I know. I used to call him Mr Maybe. But after one date with him I knew he was Mr Not-if-he-was-the-last-man-alive.'

'Well, sounds like you had a lucky escape there! Anyway, if his band is that huge in Germany, why doesn't he hassle German magazine writers instead? That's what I want to know! Next time he rings I'll tell him to fuck off in the nicest possible way.'

Her phone goes off. She answers it and listens for a few minutes. 'Right, thanks for letting me know, Les.'

She turns to me. 'Oh, remind me to buy the *Evening Herald* later,' she says. ' 'Cos there's a picture of us in it apparently.'

I feel the blood drain from my face. 'In the paper?' I whisper. 'Our picture is in the paper?'

'Yes.' A-J, unperturbed, takes another sip of her wine. 'So remind me to buy it in case I forget.'

Forget? Is she serious? Oh my God, I want to rush

out and buy it now, this minute. I have never been in the paper before. There was a small picture of me once in *Gloss* magazine but I had a facemask on and two slices of cucumber on my eyes so nobody recognised me. But this is the first time I have ever been in the newspapers. God! I wonder will people recognise me walking down the street later on? Will I have to permanently wear my sunglasses to avoid being hassled? I wish we could leave now but A-J is telling the waiter she'd love an espresso and is being as blasé as anything about the whole thing.

I'd love to pop out to the newsagent, get a copy of the paper, bring it back here and sneak into the Ladies for a look. Of course, I couldn't look at it in public in case anybody recognised me and thought I was being vain. Could you imagine!

Eventually after waiting around as A-J practically air kisses the whole room (doesn't she ever get bored with all the pretence?) we pop into a nearby newsagent and A-J just grabs the *Evening Herald*, opens it up in front of everyone and shouts, 'Oh my God, I look like shit! *You* look nice though.'

I want to die, I really do. A couple of people look around at us probably thinking that we are (a) members of a girl band (a much *older* girl band) or (b) just a couple of obnoxious twits. I feel my face burn as I look at the big picture of us taken at the fashion show. I look like Miss Piggy. All I can see is my double chin. Good God, how many people are going to see that photo? I don't even like to think about it.

On our way back to A-J's flat, I feel pretty

depressed. I'm deflated actually. Why didn't anybody tell me I was so overweight? And how did the pounds pile on without me noticing? I mean I don't eat *that* much and never touch butter or beer. I usually just drink vodka and slimline tonic and nearly everything in my shopping basket is fat free. The woman that you see spending ages in the super-market aisles scrutinising the calorie content of every single food packet, is in fact me. I can also tell you the calorie content of every single chocolate bar on the market. Isn't that clever? If there was a national exam on calories, I would achieve first class honours! As soon as I get home I'm standing on those weighing scales, which have been gathering dust for the last few months.

I hate weighing myself but the scales don't lie. God, how I dislike dieting! Every now and again I go on a serious starvation diet, just like Angela-Jean. And I spend the day looking at my watch to see what time I can go to bed at because starvation days are very, very long and very, very boring. In the diet magazines they tell you to treat yourself to nice things to take your mind off your diet, but that doesn't really work. The minute I know I'm not supposed to eat food, that's all I can ever think about. And I buy inspirational slimming magazines with pictures of women who have gone from looking like whales to foxes. When I read how they have done it, it always gives me inspiration to do it too. But unfortunately those same magazines always have pages and pages of pictures of gorgeous-looking food, which is a fat lot of good! The other thing I do is drink nothing but Diet

Coke and eat fruit (not bananas though) and pots of broccoli and spinach (ugh!). And I take the DART train out to Dalkey and walk back to Booterstown. But it's so bloody hard that I always swear to myself I'm never going to let the weight creep back on. But it always does. Somehow it always bloody does.

'Do you think I'm fat?' I ask Angela-Jean.

'Well, you're not *enormous*,' she says, not taking her eyes off the road for a minute. 'But people always look bigger in the newspaper if that's what you're worried about. Don't dwell on it.'

'*You* don't ever look huge though.'

'That's 'cos I work hard at keeping myself slim. It's a full-time job, y'know? It's not fun but I've got used to the sound of my stomach rumbling,' she laughs.

I'm not sure I agree with all of this. I mean, surely starving can't be good for you. There's something pretty sick about listening to your stomach crying out in pain and going around feeling weak and not being able to think straight. Come on, surely to God there must be an easier way. Anyway I'd never want to be as thin as A-J. She looks like a clothes hanger, too asexual for my liking. No breasts, no hips, just straight up, straight down with a head on top, like a bus stop. I'm sure clothes designers would find her irresistible but most of them are gay so why bother trying to please them? Men are supposed to like a bit of meat in a woman. Everybody knows that, although ... although maybe I'm a bit *too* meaty, you know? I'd like proper curves and somehow I don't think a generous curve directly above the belt is exactly what most red-blooded males have in mind.

'Here we are,' A-J announces, parking the car on the street outside a trendy little mews (once somebody's garage obviously). 'There's no garden but there's a little balcony up there, so on the one or two summer evenings we happen to get in this country, we can sit up there watching the world go by while sipping a glass of wine.'

'Oh that's nice,' I agree, not liking to point out that the world doesn't actually go by here because it's a tiny lane with only a couple of parked cars to look at.

I wait for A-J to put the key in her lock and push open the door. Once inside I admire the small but impressive dining room/kitchen with everything so neat and minimalist that I'm actually afraid that my being there makes it untidy. A clever mix of vintage and spanking-new furniture gives the room an understated elegance. There's fresh tulips in a huge clear vase on the window-sill, lending the room that extra feminine effect. This is *obviously* the home of a woman with exquisite taste.

'This is a lovely place,' I say appreciatively. 'You're lucky.'

'Thanks.' A-J smiles with more than a hint of pride. 'I do love it, even though it's small. Do you want something to drink or eat? I've plenty of fresh fruit, if you like.'

Fresh fruit? Flowers? Gosh, I wish *I* could be this organised. I'm not the type of girl who buys flowers for myself although I almost wished I was. I mean there's nothing wrong with buying your own flowers, is there? And they brighten up a place. The lilies that Bunny bought for me still smell wonderful and put a smile on my face every time I come through the front door. But ours is a more homely lived-in, come as you please flat. Angela-Jean's place however smacks of chic independence. I'm in awe.

'I'll have just a water if you have it?' I say taking off my jacket and placing it carefully on the back of a delightful wooden chair.

'Still, sparkling or lemon flavoured?'

'Oh, still is fine,' I say, surprised with the formality of it all. 'I'm a tap water kind of girl myself, I'm not at all fussy.'

'Ice?' A-J offers as if she hasn't heard me.

'Oh no thanks, do you mind if I just use your bathroom?'

'Over there,' A-J nods towards the corner and I head in that direction.

When I open the door and step inside I momentarily forget why I am there in the first place. I feel like I've stumbled into Blue Eriu. Piles upon piles of lotions and potions, unopened boxes of expensive perfumes, foot creams, bath oils, body scrubs, Christmas box sets, soap sets, bumper boxes of talcum powder and the latest range of every type of make-up under the sun are stacked so high, I'd be terrified to touch any of them in case they collapsed in a heap on top of me and knocked me out. I am completely gob smacked. I feel like Alice in A-J's Wonderland. There's hardly room to move.

Suddenly I want to pick everything up and sample

everything, like a little kid who accidentally comes across Barbie's secret boudoir. This is girlie heaven. This is every beautician's fairytale. I want to stay here all day powdering my nose and sampling 50 shades of blusher. How does A-J ever leave her bathroom? And where the hell did she get all this stuff? I mean the contents of my own handbag are worth at least a couple of hundred euro, so the contents of this little bathroom must literally be worth thousands.

When I come out, A-J is sitting at the glass table sipping sparkling water with a slice of lime. Imagine actually slicing a piece of lime for your water – how cool! From now on I'm going to start doing things like that, instead of just rinsing the nearest glass and filling it with tap water as I usually do. I'm so inspired. As soon as I'm back home I'm going to arrange all my books in alphabetical order and put a purple plant in the window or something. And I'll have to get Bunny to remove some of the stuff from the living room. Since she moved in our place looks like an electrical shop at Christmas time!

'You've got so much nice stuff in your bathroom.' I pick up my glass and let the water quench my thirst. The wine I had at lunch has made my mouth quite dry.

'Stuff?' A-J asks while examining her nails carefully.

'All your products. They must cost you a fortune.'

'Oh them? I don't really use much of that stuff. And I certainly don't spend a fortune. In fact, I can't even remember the last time I spent money on beauty products. I usually get them all for free.'

'Free?'

Angela-Jean gives me a smile. 'I'm also a beauty writer,' she reminds me. 'Beauty writers don't pay for products.'

'Are you serious?'

God I'm so envious.

'Mind you,' A-J continues. 'You'd think with all the free gunk, that all the other beauty writers would be, well . . . beautiful. But most of them are hags, haha . . . it just shows that you can't buy good looks.'

Goodness, for a girl who can be quite kind, she can also be vitriolic about her competitors when she wants to be. I'm *so* glad I'm not on the receiving end of A-J's sharp tongue. God help any man who tries to win her heart.

'I don't feel bad about getting so much free stuff,' says A-J determinedly. 'After all, beauty writers are so badly paid, and you spend your time answering calls from pushy PR women, that anything free is actually very well earned.'

'So will I be writing beauty stuff too?' I ask, alarmed. 'I mean, I know really very little about beauty products.'

'So do most beauty journos,' laughs A-J. 'We're all bluffing. None of us knows what the hell we're talking about. But we never say no to the goody bags. You never know, maybe one day one of us will find a cream that truly removes cellulite, or a lotion that makes your skin look ten years younger, instead of the usual old rubbish they expect you to be grateful for.'

A-J finishes her water, and instead of just leaving

her glass in the sink to be looked after later, she pops it in the dishwasher. I'm so impressed I follow suit.

'Now,' she looks at me. 'We'd better go to the office and face the music.'

Suddenly I feel very nervous. How am I going to take my place in an office full of glamorous know-it-alls? Will I be exposed as a fake? I mean I know I did my time at *Gloss* but I was just a general dogsbody there. This is different however. I am going to be part of the team here in *Irish Femme*.

Half an hour later we pull up outside a dreary grey prefab building in Templeogue. I wonder why A-J has stopped her car here. I mean I can't see a shop about or anything.

'Welcome to *Irish Femme*,' Angela-Jean laughs.

I stare ahead in disbelief. This is it? It *can't* be! I mean where is the classy lobby with a uniformed porter and all the glitz and glamour I've been expecting? For God's sake even the *Gloss* offices, although slightly run down, were at least in town so you could spend lunchtime browsing around the shops.

'Are you shocked?' A-J enquires getting out of the car. 'Welcome to the glamorous world of fashion. Here we are!'

Dubiously I get out of the car and follow A-J into the prefab building. A bored, haggard-looking woman of about fifty is chewing gum at a battered old desk near the door.

'This is Fiona,' A-J announces. 'She'll be filling in for me for a few weeks, Mary.'

The woman called Mary mutters some kind of

disinterested greeting. I can tell she's very excited to meet me, not!

I then follow A-J into the *Irish Femme* open-plan office which is about as welcoming as an ice-cream parlour in the North Pole. I shiver, almost able to feel the sharp chill that seems to hang over the too-close-together rows of desks. A couple of girls look up in interest as A-J swans in, with myself in tow. They all look so young, and so completely dressed up, as if they are going to a dinner party or an awards ceremony or something. Am I missing something? A-J never mentioned a dress code or anything to that effect.

Suddenly I feel very stuffy in my beige, rather conservative trouser suit. Everybody else is drowned in accessories. Dangly earrings seem to be very much in vogue in *Irish Femme*. As do knee-high boots and funny-looking hair accessories. I almost feel naked and certainly feel boring.

'Angela-Jean,' one woman with obviously dyed-red hair calls out shrilly. 'How was the lunch?'

'It wasn't too bad,' says A-J taking off her jacket and hanging it on the back of a chair. 'No real scandal though. I'll need to get on the phone and start hounding people in the know for a bit of old gossip.'

'Get me an exclusive,' the red head says firmly. 'I don't want a full page rehashed from the tabloids. Hi, I'm Cecille, editor of *Irish Femme*.'

'Hello, I'm Fiona.' I shake her hand nervously, trying not to gag at the stink of hair spray.

'You've worked in *Gloss*?' she eyes me steadily.

'Er . . . yes.' Oh my God, what has A-J been telling

her? I hope this woman doesn't think I'm this really sophisticated journalist with a black book stuffed with hot contacts.

'Did you enjoy working there?'

'Very much so,' I lie, terrified that my facial expression will expose me as a fake.

Cecille purses her lips and waits for me to continue.

'But I learned a lot there,' I press on, 'and I can't wait to get back to writing features.'

Cecille raises a perfectly plucked eyebrow. I find myself shivering again. God, why doesn't anyone put on the heating?

'I've filled her in on some stuff,' A-J explains, having lost some of her usual arrogance in the presence of her scary-looking boss. 'Now I'll show her my desk and run her through the daily routine.'

'Fine,' Cecille says. 'Well, I'll leave you girls to it.' Her cold green eyes penetrate mine. 'You're in A-J's capable hands at the moment, but next week you'll be on your own, so I'll be expecting great stuff from you. *Irish Femme* is the best woman's magazine in today's very competitive market. Our standards are very high and we have a reputation to live up to. I wish you the very best of luck.'

A-J suddenly grasps my elbow. 'I'll show you to the Ladies where my locker is. You can use it in my absence.'

'Okay thanks,' I say feeling like a lost kid on her first day in school. 'And thank you too, Cecille. I know I'll really like working here.'

Cecille gives me a cynical 'we'll see' look. I hate her already.

Only when A-J has firmly shut the bathroom door behind her does she speak.

'Don't mind that old boot,' she almost spits. 'She needs a good ride to calm her down.'

'Jesus,' I whisper. 'What did you tell her, A-J? She thinks I'm some sort of fashion expert. Do you think she'll ring *Gloss* looking for a reference?

A-J flashes me an evil smile. 'Not a chance. Herself and Faith are arch-enemies. They were in journalism college together. They fell out over a man and Cecille never got over it. She still hasn't had a sniff of romance since.'

'Is Faith still going out with him?' I wonder aloud.

'Not at all. He dumped her and she then tried hooking up with Cecille again but was told to fuck off in no uncertain terms. Both of them got jobs in *Gloss* around the same time and their public catfights were fairly legendary. When Faith was made editor Cecille resigned and got a job here in *Irish Femme*. About a month later the editor went to Australia, Cecille stepped in and the rest as they say is history. Needless to say, we've all been living in fear since.'

'Are you afraid of her?'

'Well, I don't take much guff from her to be honest. I think she knows that I wouldn't take shit, although she does tend to wreck my head. Being the social diarist gives me a lot of freedom because I have to go to events and things. However, she does get to bully the poor trainees who are in for work experience or just graduated from journalism college. She takes great pleasure in treating them like dirt.'

'So why do they do it?' I ask, taking a peek in the full-length mirror, less than impressed at my reflection. I really must look into the Weight Watchers diet soon. I think that one works as long as you don't cheat.

'For the experience, darling,' A-J laughs. 'And most of them work for free too because they think it'll look good on their CV.'

'For free? No way?'

'Way, way,' A-J stresses. 'Now let's get back to my desk before Cecille has a chance to come looking for us. She times people's toilet breaks by the way.'

Back at A-J's tiny desk, I can feel all eyes upon us. They're all wondering who I am. The new girl. I feel like a schoolgirl. A-J makes a brief introduction but after five seconds I can't remember any of their names. They all end in 'ia'. There's Amelia, Julia and something else 'ia' which is completely unpronounceable.

They all look the same too. Highlighted straight hair and everyone is wearing something pink, even if it's just a hair clip. I'm really surprised actually. I thought these magazine 'chicks' would be really outgoing Vivienne Westwood types.

'Now,' A-J switches on her PC and checks her inbox. 'What do we have here? Let me see . . . the launch of a new restaurant, the launch of a new face cream, another launch of another new face cream, the launch of . . .' she gives a great big yawn, 'a boutique somewhere down the country, so no, no, no and no again.'

'No to them all?' I say in a small hopeful voice. 'Could we not even go to one of them?'

A-J gives me a pitying look. 'Believe me, Fi, these things are rarely fun. These events might sound like they're a great way to spend a night out, but it's still work at the end of the day. You see, there's no such things as a free drink. You can't enjoy the free booze without some bossy PR type practically knocking you out with a press release, and asking where your photographer is. Like, as if *Irish Femme* can afford to pay a photographer to trot along to all these silly things!'

'Then how do you get the society photos?' I ask out of curiosity. 'We didn't put society photos in the back of *Gloss* because Faith always complained that the same old faces kept popping up over and over again and she was sick of the sight of them.'

'The society photographers just email them into us,' A-J explains. 'They're booked by the PR people for certain events. So when Cecille receives them from the photographers, she then chooses the people she wants to put in. She loves doing that.'

'What else does Cecille do?'

'We're all still trying to figure that one out,' A-J whispers in my ear.

17

The three of us are standing uncertainly in a shoe shop. Angela-Jean is waving at various people as myself and Bunny stand awkwardly beside her. A skinny young model, bearing a remarkable resemblance to a baby giraffe, is going around with some dodgy-looking pink drinks on a silver tray.

'What's this?' A-J asks in a loud voice. The young girl nervously explains that it's a new type of drink on the market, a mixture of vodka, cranberry juice and something else. We all accept the drink gratefully. We seem to be the only people here except for some anxious PR women, the shop owner himself and a photographer who is doing his level best to ignore us.

'This is great, isn't it?' Bunny says, clearly impressed by the whole set up. 'Very glamorous, I must say. Are you sure we don't have to pay for the drinks?'

'Of course not,' A-J says rather dismissively. 'One never pays for drinks in this line of work.'

Bunny and myself exchange a glance while A-J looks at her watch with a distinct air of boredom. 'I hope this place fills up soon,' she sighs. 'It's embarrassing being here first. We should have waited for the place to fill up first.' But Bunny and I don't mind. It's a novelty being here even if we *are* only in a shoe shop.

'Can we try on the shoes?' Bunny wants to know. 'I'd love to buy some.'

'Well, I must admit they are pretty fabulous,' A-J says, aware that Bunny could quite easily snap up half the collection while barely putting a dent in her credit card. Bunny's eyes are shining as she sips her vodka concoction. She looks beautiful tonight. Her newly highlighted hair has been cut in layers framing her waif-like face. She looks like an angel, almost unrecognisable from the bedraggled mess that turned up on my doorstep not so long ago.

Suddenly the photographer, obviously bored with hanging around waiting for the real VIPs to show up, ambles over. He asks Bunny if she doesn't mind posing for a photo. Bunny blushes three shades of pink. 'Me?' she asks awkwardly.

The photographer then looks at Angela-Jean and asks her if she'd like to stand in the photo too. As cool as anything A-J places her drink on a shoe stand and agrees. She then slips an arm around Bunny's slim waist and grins as the photographer starts snapping madly. I have been left standing on my own, absolutely mortified. The photographer hasn't asked me to pose with them. I want to hide. Does he really think I'm that ugly? Does he think I'll break his bloody camera or what?

When the photographer stops snapping he then takes Bunny's name. He gives her a second look when she says her name as if she *might* be someone famous. He doesn't take A-J's name 'cos he seems to know her already. I've half a feeling he might want to take a photo of me on my own, because I can't *imagine* anybody being so rude, but he doesn't. He just moves towards the door where other people are starting to make their way into the shop. I want to die. I feel so ugly you just wouldn't believe it!

A-J starts chatting away as if she hasn't noticed the photographer snubbing me. But I can tell Bunny feels bad for me. 'He probably just takes people in pairs,' she squeezes my arm, trying to make me feel better. It only makes me feel worse though. I want to go home now.

I have finished my drink. Well, I *had* to look busy while Bunny and A-J were being snapped, didn't I? The vodka has already gone to my head. Suddenly I think the shoes are way nicer than when I first arrived. But as I don't have any money and will be paid buttons in my new 'glamorous' temping job at *Irish Femme*, there is no point trying anything on. How I wish I had just a fraction of Bunny's dosh. God, that's me just being petty, isn't it? I mean I'm glad Bunny has won the Lotto and everything but until now I just kind of didn't believe anybody actually won money. Until now it was just smiling people in the newspapers and on TV, not people that

I actually knew, not to mention people that I lived with.

'Another drink?' the smiling model wants to know. It doesn't take much to twist my arm.

'Yeah thanks.' A-J and Bunny help themselves too. So much for popping in for one then . . . it looks like we'll be here all night!

The shop is buzzing now, and although I'm still fairly smarting over the fact that I wasn't glamorous enough for that horribly ignorant photographer, at least the vodka seems to have hit the spot and I'm looking around the room with interest. I see Laura Woods from RTÉ as well as a couple of Ireland's most stunning models. They are so tall, slim and elegant that one part of me wants to run away and hide and another part of me wants to run over to them and hound them for their fashion tips.

Then I remember that I have to stay cool. I am a top fashion writer for a top magazine (yeah!) and I must remain chilled at all times.

'Oh thank you, I would LOVE another pink drink,' I beam enthusiastically. Bunny and A-J are drinking just as much as me so I don't feel too bad. I mean, I'm not the type of person who would go to the launch of a shoe shop just to get a free drink. God no. Although I have to admit when I was in UCD I used to turn up to any old talk just so I could get a free glass of wine afterwards. Sad? Moi? Oh maybe just a little bit. But I was young and broke then, and now I guess I'm older and . . . still pretty broke when I think about it. I'm not going to think about it though 'cos it's way too depressing. I'm just thinking of all the fun I'm going to have doing this job, even though my new boss Cecille is a bit of a monster. However, if A-J has been able to stick her for a couple of years, well then it'll be child's play for me to humour her for just a few weeks!

Suddenly we're joined by a woman of about thirty with long dark curly hair and a face full of thick orange foundation. She smiles revealing prominent teeth with a trace of purple lipstick smeared across them.

'Hi, Angela-Jean, you're so good to have come.'

'That's okay,' A-J returns the saccharine sweet smile. 'Let me introduce Fiona who'll be standing in for me at *Irish Femme* for the next few weeks.'

I shake the woman's hand as she looks me up and down suspiciously before offering me a press release and a CD.

'Thank you,' I beam wondering what the CD is. I do hope it's the latest one from U2.

Then she looks at Bunny curiously. 'And sorry, you're from?'

Bunny flushes scarlet as if she is an imposter who as just been caught gatecrashing the Oscars.

'This is Bunny Maguire,' A-J cuts in using a very firm tone of voice. 'Is she the only celebrity here so far? Are there any more arriving?'

It's now the PR woman's turn to look mortified. It's obvious she's racking her brains to remember who the hell Bunny Maguire is.

'I believe some of the *You're a Star* contestants might drop in. And Mandy Delby is here. You know, the model who is going out with that guy who plays for Liverpool. Or is it Chelsea?'

'I don't know,' says A-J as if she has just been told that the Pied Piper might be arriving along with the city's rat population. 'But I might have a word with her if nobody else turns up.'

Flustered, the PR woman then welcomes Bunny to the shop, and tells her to feel free to browse around.

'There's also a thirty per cent discount off tonight,' she adds hurriedly.

'Cool.' Bunny looks positively delighted. 'I might as well buy the whole shop then!'

'Oh yes, haha,' says the PR woman uncomfortably. 'Well, I'd better check on the rest of the guests. Enjoy your evening, girls.'

'Am I not supposed to be here?' Bunny asks anxiously as the PR woman scuttles off as if she has an angry terrier yapping at her high heels.

'Of course you are,' answers A-J defiantly. 'You're *my* guest. You're as entitled to be here as anybody else. I mean I'm hardly going to turn up to something like this on my own, am I? Anyway she probably thinks you're some kind of "IT" girl she hasn't heard of yet, or a visiting international celeb. I'll tell her you have a record deal or something. Or that you're a huge playwright in Japan. With a name like Bunny Maguire, you could be anyone, you know?'

'Do you think so?' Bunny's face flushes and I'm not sure whether that's because she is happy or because she is now on her fourth vodka.

Now somebody is making a speech. It must be the owner of the shop. We all face him as if we are listening but I know I'm not anyway. Instead my eyes are glued to a pair of knee-high mahogany-coloured leather boots. They are positioned right behind the man who is droning on about the history of the shop. Oh my God, I wish I had money with me. Why has my credit card been cancelled, and why do I have to get all my shoes re-heeled and re-soled every year instead of being able to splash out like Lady Muck here beside me?

Suddenly Mandy Delby is standing beside us grinning at nothing in particular.

'Are you enjoying the evening?' A-J asks her.

'Oh yes,' Mandy says vacantly.

'Do you like the shoes?'

'Well, I couldn't wear them because I can only wear special shoes because of my corns.'

'Right.'

'But you can say I like them in your column if you like. I don't mind.'

'Right. Thanks. So are you still going out with er . . .?'

'David. Yes, but it's early days yet. We're more "good friends" than anything else.'

'Good friends who have a good time together.'

'Er . . . er. . . yes. Oh, we'd better listen to the speech. If you need any more details it's best to call my agent. He always knows the right thing to say. Here's his card. I love your column by the way. I read it every month.'

'Week.'

'Week?'

'It's a weekly column.'

'Oh . . . oh . . .'

C'mon,' A-J announces the minute the speech wraps up. 'Let's get out of here.'

Bunny's face falls. 'But I haven't tried anything on yet. I can't possibly leave without buying something.'

A-J reluctantly agrees to hang around a while longer while Bunny tries on loads of different shoes and boots and staggers around the room. As we've learned before, Bunny isn't great at holding her drink and as she tries to walk up and down the shop in impossibly high heels, with everybody looking at her with interest, I keep my fingers crossed behind my back, hoping that she doesn't topple over.

After a few minutes, Bunny comes over to where we are standing with the exact same pair of boots that I have spent the evening lusting after. 'Do you like these?' she asks. 'Will you try them on? I just want to see how they look on somebody else before I purchase them. Just to be sure, you know?'

Oh God, why is she torturing me like this? What have I done to deserve this humiliation? I don't want to go walking around the shop in a pair of boots that I wouldn't be able to afford in a million years. Why can't she get A-J to try them on?

'Oh okay then,' I mutter as I bend down to take off my shoes. As I whip off my left shoe, I suddenly realise that there are three holes in the toes of my tights. Quickly I put my foot back in the shoe and hope to God nobody has noticed.

'Aren't you going to try on the boots?' Bunny enquires.

'No, if you don't mind, I don't really want to,' I say feeling like a bitch. 'I don't think I like them anyway.'

'I'll try them on,' offers A-J and slips off her heels.

She glides up and down the shop like a top model on the catwalk.

'I'll definitely buy them,' Bunny beams. 'And I'll get a second pair for you too, A-J.'

'No, you can't,' A-J insists. 'Honestly, I won't hear of it.'

'But you must accept,' Bunny insists as my heart sinks below sea level. If I had tried them on, would Bunny have bought them for me? Why oh why did I come out tonight with holes in my tights like an old bag lady? I've got to get a grip and remind myself that I'm now one of the jet set ... hmmm. I must be prepared for all eventualities.

Bunny and A-J are still arguing over the boots when Bunny storms up to the counter with her credit card. She has about six pairs of boots and shoes lined up. The total comes to just over a thousand euro (including the discount). She doesn't bat an eyelid though and casually signs the credit card receipt.

At this stage, the PR woman with the lipstick on her teeth is practically falling over herself with bursting curiosity trying to figure out who the hell this Bunny Maguire woman is.

'Your friend Bunny is fabulous, isn't she?' she

gushes to a fairly pissed-off-looking Angela-Jean who has been trying her best to leave for the last half an hour. 'If you've been to one of these things, you've been to them all,' she's been whining to anybody who will listen.

'Bunny is always the life and soul of every party,' A-J confides in Ms PR as my ears prick up in astonishment.

What's all this about then? A-J has *never* gone out with Bunny before. Nevertheless A-J continues to rave about my new flatmate. 'Oh yes,' she enthuses. 'A party is never a true party until Bunny shows up. Unfortunately though, Bunny is too busy to go out. She's only just back from filming in LA. But she loves the way she can just walk around Dublin without being hassled.'

When we eventually leave the shop, Ms PR, all fired up by the bullshit A-J has been feeding her, practically accosts Bunny with her card, 'If you need anything, *anything* at all, please don't hesitate to call,' she enthuses as a startled Bunny stares at her blankly. 'By the way have you received your goody bags yet, girls? Hang on there a minute.' She rushes off to the counter and comes back eagerly with three bags. I am so delighted. This reminds me of when I used to go to kiddies parties and you always got a 'going home' present which softened the blow of your mother turning up just when you were really starting to have fun.

'What's in this?' Bunny asks loudly, as A-J shoots her a thunderous look.

'Oh, you are just too funny; it's true what A-J was saying about you. You really are the life and soul of the party. Do you do comedies?'

'Excuse me?'

'Comedies?'

'Oh yes, I like them a lot,' says Bunny. 'Have you seen the second *Bridget Jones* film?'

'Oh my God, are you in it?' the PR gasps.

Bunny looks completely baffled.

A-J cuts in immediately. 'Well, we'd better be off now – thanks again!'

Ms PR gives a false little laugh and waves us good-bye. 'I look forward to seeing you ALL again very soon, especially you, Bunny. I'll get the new *Bridget Jones* on video and look out for you. Best of luck in New Zealand, Angela-Jean. Don't come back with too much of a tan or you'll make us all quite jealous.'

'God, she was a bit weird, wasn't she?' Bunny says as soon as we are out of sight. Then she starts to rummage in her goody bag like a child with a Christmas stocking. Eagerly she pulls out a deep-burgundy nail polish, followed by a large bottle of nail polish remover, a velvet-covered nail file and a small box of sweets. 'Wow,' she exclaims. 'This is cool, so really nice of them. I'm definitely going to go back to that shop again. Hey!' she turns towards me. 'Did you check out your CD?'

'Yeah,' I say, 'it's a CD with photos of shoes on it.'

'Oh.' Bunny looks disappointed, but not obviously as disappointed as I was when I discovered about my 'free' gift truth. Bunny, I must admit, is hilarious though. I mean she keeps going on about how nice everyone in the shop was, and how thrilled she is with her goody bag. What's wrong with her? Jesus, she's just blown the same amount of money on footwear in five minutes, as most people would spend in a year, and she gets excited about a nail polish 'cos it's free! I don't get these people. Oh my God, I'm only one day in this job and I'm already getting blasé about the whole scene. Hell, what on earth am I going to be like in a month's time?

'I don't really want to go home just yet,' Bunny suddenly announces. We're walking towards Grafton Street, and Bunny is laden down with all her shopping bags.

'Well, I'm definitely going home,' A-J insists. 'I'm going to New Zealand in a few days' time and I haven't a thing organised. You go on somewhere for a drink though, but be careful, Fiona, we need to be in the office at 9.00 tomorrow morning. If you're not on time, Cecille will eat you for breakfast.'

'Could you do me a huge favour and take my bags A-J?' Bunny asks. 'You could give them to Fiona in the morning?'

'Sure,' A-J smiles, 'and listen, thanks a million again for those boots, they're to die for.'

'No worries.' Bunny air kisses A-J farewell. Yikes, she's learning fast!

'Right, where will we go?'

'Where do you fancy going? I'm easy, but you heard A-J, my head will be served for breakfast tomorrow if that weapon doesn't see my face bright and early in the morning.'

'Tell her you were out looking for scoops,' Bunny suggests innocently and I can't help laughing at the idea.

We go to Cocoon in the Hibernian Mall. The place is full of beautiful thin people and immediately I feel like Mrs Blobby. A few heads turn as Bunny makes her entrance. So it's not just the PR woman who finds her fascinating! Even I have to admit there's something pretty irresistible about Bunny. She doesn't have a clue about anything, yet she somehow manages to sail through every situation. I guess, to be somewhat crude, she's the type of girl who would fall into a pile of shite and emerge smelling of roses.

In Cocoon, Bunny wants a look at the cocktail list. I'm aware that I can only stay for one. Yes, one. Just the one. I go for a Sex on the Beach and Bunny opts for a Bloody Mary.

We sit near the door watching the people come and go. It's like being on a film set. Bunny is in her element. She says that in the village where she's from there are no trendy bars, just old men's pubs with no music and plenty of grumpy old guys who don't speak. She says there's only one bar where young people go but that everybody there has gone out with everyone and if anybody new showed up, it was big big news.

'Seriously though,' she confides in me, 'even if *you* were to come down for a night you'd be treated like a celebrity. It's pathetic.'

'But surely nights out down the country are great craic though.'

Bunny takes another sip of her drink and makes a face. 'Great craic if you're only there for a night or two but God, if you're stuck there for any length of time, it'd just do your head in.'

'But don't you ever go to a bigger town? I mean, where's the next biggest town to you?'

'Dundalk. That's fun 'cos there are loads of pubs there, but you have to know which pubs to go into. Like Ridley's is fun and there's a nightclub upstairs too. The talent can be good there occasionally if you're lucky, and then there's McManus's – that's really popular with the DIT students, and there's a few more pubs around but I dunno, I suppose deep down I was always determined to get to Dublin and live here properly.'

'And is it all you thought it'd be?' I ask. 'I mean Dublin may seem big but if you go out every night it becomes a village. You see the same faces week in, week out, and it gets tedious after a while. I'm always thinking of moving off to London.'

'We all want to move on, don't we?' Bunny asks dreamily. 'I bet if you were in London, you'd probably want to live in New York.'

On that rather pensive note, I leave Bunny to go downstairs to the Ladies to powder my nose. It's late now so we'd better not stay out for much longer. We can head out properly later during the week, maybe on Friday. Maybe try Renards or somewhere and see if we can spot Colin Farrell.

I look in the mirror and give my hair a quick brush. I notice that I'm not looking too hot. Actually that's an understatement. I look woeful. No wonder that photographer ignored me! Then again, maybe the vodka is making me paranoid. Perhaps I've just had one too many.

When I get back to the bar, Bunny has ordered another two cocktails. My heart sinks. What is she playing at? It's all right for Madame here to get drunk but she doesn't have to get up in the morning, does she? Every night is Friday night for Bunny.

'I can't drink that,' I tell Bunny in no uncertain terms.

Her face falls visibly but her poor-little-lost-girl look isn't going to work on me this time. It's late. My bed is calling.

'But I'm so in love,' she says, placing a hand dramatically on her heart. 'I'm not joking, I have just seen the man of my dreams.'

'Right, I believe you,' I say, 'but he'll have to stay in your dreams 'cos I've a long day tomorrow and don't fancy getting fired before I even start. So c'mon, drink up.'

Bunny looks at me with a sorrowful look in her eye. 'You think I'm joking, don't you? Well, I am not. When I was up at the bar ordering the cocktails, I asked the barman to be sure to give me two of those umbrella yokes to put in the glasses. Then I noticed this guy standing beside me. This total vision.'

'I'm sure.'

'Seriously. He was like my dream man, tall dark

and handsome. You know when people talk about love at first sight?'

'I nod wearily.

'Well this is the first time I've just looked at somebody and thought, "Oh my God, I think this is it!"'

'Did you talk to him?' I ask, picking up my glass and sipping slowly.

'Kind of. He asked me what I was celebrating and I didn't like to say we were at a shoe shop thingy so I said I was celebrating my birthday. I couldn't stop staring at him 'cos he was so good-looking like . . .'

'You *must* point him out so. A handsome man is so rare in Dublin these days that unless I see it with my own two eyes, I won't actually believe it. Where is he?'

I'm almost sure that if I see him I *won't* find him that good-looking. Not being mean or anything but privately I reckon Bunny thinks most Dublin men are good-looking. She's just not used to city boys, but she'll learn fast. They're all too spoiled. You see, most Dublin women don't think their sons are good enough for anybody and they, the little devils, just happen to agree.

Bunny looks around but can't seem to see him. 'He must be sitting just around the corner,' she says. 'You can't miss him, he looks like a classier version of Colin Farrell.'

Good Lord! You can't bring Bunny anywhere!

'Do you know what he did?' she continues. 'He asked me what age I was and then he paid for the drinks and said "Happy Birthday".'

'Really?' Now I am pretty impressed. It's not often an Irish man makes that much of an effort. Usually their idea of chatting you up is asking for a cigarette.

'Of course, I didn't want him to pay but I was flattered. I couldn't exactly tell him to keep his hand in his pocket because I won the lottery now, could I?'

'No,' I agree. 'It's best not to tell too many people about your winnings. The less they know the better. Anyway count yourself lucky. I can't even remember the last time anybody even bought me a coke never mind a couple of cocktails. I must get a look at him myself on our way out.'

'Are we really going?' Bunny looks crestfallen.

'Yes, we are. I've explained why. But we can go out properly at the weekend.'

'But what if I never see that guy again? I have to at least find out his name!'

'If it's meant to be, it will be,' I add using that tired cliché, and then adding yet another one. 'What's for you won't pass you.'

I stand up and put on my coat and Bunny does the same.

'Now, be sure to point him out on our way out,' I tell her. 'I want a good look at this extraordinary man.'

'Okay,' Bunny wraps her scarf around her. 'If you don't think he's good-looking too, I'll eat this scarf.'

On our way out, I anxiously scan the room for this 'dream' man whoever he is. It's not until I reach the door that he suddenly turns around and immediately our eyes lock. Too shocked to speak, or even acknowledge him, I keep walking and only when I'm outside do I take a deep breath and exhale slowly.

'Was he the guy in the white shirt?'

'Yes.' Bunny has a faraway, dreamy look in her eyes. 'Isn't he divine?'

'He is very good-looking,' I say sharply, 'but looks aren't everything and it's best you forget about him.'

Bunny's face clouds with confusion. 'Why?'

'It's for your own good,' I warn her.

'Are you telling me you know him? Do you know his name?'

'His name is Connor,' I tell her stiffly, putting on my gloves. 'And he's about to become a dad.'

18

I'm exhausted. I'm wide-awake. And unfortunately I have to get up in two hours' time. My little bedside clock is ticking loudly, and the light from the full moon outside is forcing itself through the gap in my curtains. I wish I could sleep and I wish I could forget about Connor but I can't. What is wrong with me? Why did I have to see him tonight? And why did he have to hit on Bunny of all people? And why oh why is he so bloody good-looking?

How many times do I need to be warned off handsome men? They're players. They don't have to work hard to get women. They don't have to be funny or charming or anything really. They just have to basically stand there and poor fools like Bunny just melt. Thank God, I'm strong though. I mean, I saw Connor looking at me in Cocoon like I was the only woman in the room, despite the fact that he had been chatting my flatmate up minutes earlier. And although I have to admit it pained me to see him, I'm glad I was able to walk out the door. Men shouldn't be allowed to have such beautiful faces. They only use their looks to hurt women. Connor should have a health warning stamped to his forehead. And where was Ellie, the mother of his child? The fact that she used to be my best friend obviously doesn't put him off. He must have a really twisted sense of humour. Well I wish he'd bloody well disappear. Why can't I even go out for a quiet drink in town without bumping into him? And now to top things off, I can't sleep, thinking about him!

I seem to have barely closed my eyes again when my alarm goes off. I groan, roll over and knock it to the ground causing the batteries to fall out. Right, I'll give myself five minutes to get up . . . or ten minutes . . . God, I'm so bloody tired.

Eventually I drag my reluctant body into the shower. Strangely enough I'm dreaming of A-J's bathroom. After a few weeks working in *Irish Femme* I'll have a bathroom just like hers full of delicious products to pamper and preen myself with. It's enough to put a smile back on my face.

It takes me over half an hour to drive to Temple-ogue. I'm early, believe it or not, but A-J is already at her desk, checking her emails with a large cup of steaming black coffee in front of her.

'Morning, Sunshine,' she calls to me cheerfully. 'Did you stay out for long last night?'

'We had just one drink after you left,' I tell her. 'So it wasn't that bad. I was a good girl, home by mid-night.'

'See anyone exciting?'

'Nobody exciting. But I did see Connor unfortunately. Kind of put a dampener on the evening.'

'Connor? As in the guy who's engaged to your friend Ellie?'

Suddenly I feel kind of ill. 'Engaged?' I ask in a strained voice. I have to sit down.

'I didn't know they were getting married. Where did you hear that?'

A-J shrugs. 'Can't remember now, I think somebody said it to me last night at the shoe shop. Well I suppose, it's natural though, isn't it? I mean if Ellie's pregnant, and they're living together . . . anyway, who cares? Listen, why don't you start making yourself useful. Actually get yourself a coffee first and then you can start opening my post. I've got a shitload of stuff in today. It's always kind of mad a month or two before Christmas. The beauty companies start sending you all these parcels of crap.'

As I boil the kettle in the corner of the office, A-J points out that there is a weekly charge of one euro, which covers unlimited coffee, tea, sugar and milk.

'See the white plastic container there? You're to put your euro in that and then tick off your name from the list. Cecille types up a new list every Monday to make sure everyone has paid. It's not worth a curse pointing out that Cecille is the only person in the office who takes milk in her coffee. Those are the rules.'

I make myself a black coffee and then fish in my purse for a euro. I see my name has already been added to the end of the printed list so I tick it off with a red pen. As I do so, I can't help thinking how unglamorous *Irish Femme* is. I mean, in what other job would the boss have so much time to be making up all these silly rules?

I sit down again beside A-J and start tackling her enormous pile of post. Like a kid on Christmas Day I tear open the parcels first, although admittedly I don't go as far as shaking them or anything. The first parcel contains an orange-scented candle. It is accompanied by a press release about some shop that sells new age stuff and an invitation to come in for a browse.

'Will you be browsing?' I ask A-J.

'Hardly. I'm going to New Zealand, remember? But *you* can browse if you like. Keep the candle anyway. It'll look nice in your flat. Or give it to Bunny as a present. By the way, how was Bunny's head this morning? She'd quite a bit to drink, hadn't she?'

'I don't know, I never see her in the mornings. Oh, the joy of being a Lotto winner! Sure, why would she be bothered getting up for anything? God, sometimes I'm so jealous. Especially when I have to get up in the cold and the dark and her Ladyship and Timmy are still in the land of nod.'

'That'll be me in New Zealand,' A-J says happily. 'Getting up with the sun, with none of that alarm clock hell. I think there's something very unnatural and cruel about being jolted out of your sleep at the crack of dawn five mornings a week, don't you?'

'Agreed. Hey, you've got an invitation to the launch of Westlife's new album.'

'I do? Cool, they're always fun. When is it?'

I glance at the invitation. 'Not for another few weeks.'

'Sugar, that means I can't go. I won't be here. Oh well . . . you can go in my place. Bring Bunny, I bet she'd enjoy it. But be sure to warn her against hounding the guys for autographs though. That'd be really embarrassing.'

'Yeah, she certainly has a thing for hot guys. She nearly fainted when she saw Connor in the bar last night. Now I know he's completely beautiful but still, her reaction was way over the top.'

'He could be a male model or something though, couldn't he?' A-J says, busy deleting press releases from her inbox.

'Yeah, but he's too clever for that. I couldn't imagine him parading up and down a catwalk wearing silk boxers and a red rose in his teeth. He's really deep. There's so much going on in that head of his. I just wish I could get inside it.'

'I think you've got the hots for him.' A-J gives me a wicked smile.

'No, I don't.'

'You can't fool me.'

'I don't fancy him at all,' I say, feeling myself blushing. 'And especially not now that he's a family man and all that. All I'm saying is that it's unusual for a guy to be so good-looking and intelligent. It's just an observation.'

'He's almost perfect then, except that he's taken.'

'Quite.'

'Morning, ladies.' Cecille interrupts us in a loud

booming voice. 'How was the shoe-shop opening? Any stories out of it?'

'Um, Lainey H is pregnant again.'

'Good, good, I haven't read that anywhere yet, have I?'

'No, I'm keeping my fingers crossed nobody else will run it before me,' A-J tells her. 'She hasn't announced it to the press, I just happened to hear it through the grapevine but I'll confirm the news with Lainey herself just before we go to print. Don't want her to think I'm running an exclusive though, in case the silly twit goes and tells one of the Sunday papers. You know what those silly rich men's wives are like.'

'Mmm. What else? Any marriage break-ups, unplanned pregnancies, new salacious stories, models going out with footballers, that kind of thing?'

'Um, not at the moment, I'm working on a few leads though,' A-J promises and I almost feel her blood pressure rising myself. I mean, what if *nothing* happens, suppose *nobody* splits up with anybody this week or is caught carrying somebody else's love child? What do you do then? After all, you just can't go to print with a blank page where the official gossip section is supposed to be, can you?

Cecille's mobile phone rings and she goes out to answer it. A-J makes a face behind her back. 'Where does she think we are, Beverly flipping Hills? I wish people would realise that not much goes on in this town on a weekly basis, you know? Dublin really isn't that exciting. I am sick of writing about silly empty-headed people and their silly empty lives.'

'There's a lot of pressure involved writing this column, isn't there?' I say doubtfully. After all, if A-J finds it difficult getting stories, then what chance do I possibly have? I'll be like a fish flapping on the ground. I wonder if it's too late to pull out.

We're interrupted by one of the 'work experience' students handing us the daily newspapers. I have now learned that the 'work experience' kids come in to find out about the world of fashion writing but invariably end up spending most of the week making tea, posting letters, answering the phone and delivering newspapers. I reckon it's enough to ensure that they never set foot in a publishing office again.

I continue sifting through A-J's mail. You wouldn't believe the crap she gets sent. There's two tickets to see some obscure one-man show in Donegal on Wednesday night, the launch of a new range of luxury tights in a city centre hotel on Thursday (refreshments included), a sunglasses case with a business card enclosed (but no sunglasses unfortunately), a slice of stale wedding cake (I kid you not!) to promote a big wedding fair the following week, and a clothes hanger to promote a new boutique.

'Is this the norm?' I ask A-J as I begin to shred press release after press release thinking what an unbelievable waste of trees this all is.

'More or less,' she shrugs. 'Sometimes it's busier than other times. Like in the summer, it's pretty quiet 'cos everybody's away and you end up racking your brains trying to turn otherwise mediocre news into something hot. October and November are usually pretty mad months as all the big retail companies fight for newspaper coverage before the big Christmas rush.'

'Do you ever get like really nice presents though?'

'Mmm.' A-J screws up her face trying to remember. 'I once got a free mobile phone, and I've also got some very good creams and make-up as well as a couple of free massages in luxury salons. And I also have a fabulous sterling silver clock that I got at some launch, but most of it is Christmas cracker stuff, and to be honest it just takes up a lot of space in my place.'

'Still, it's better than nothing. All I ever got in *Gloss* was some cheap glittery eye shadow that nobody wanted, a couple of novels with gaudy bright pink covers that nobody wanted to read, and a CD from a folk group I'd never heard of before or since. Faith, on the other hand, used to practically need a suitcase to drag everything home every evening. She could have set up a gift shop with all her freebies.'

A-J laughs. 'Do you know what I think would be really glamorous?'

'What?'

'To have a really well-paid job where you could go into any salon you liked for a facial, or buy any creams you wanted in Brown Thomas, or go into Hughes and Hughes and buy the book of your choice instead of being given a free book that will bore you to tears, or cheap crappy make-up that'll probably make your skin break out in a rash . . . so . . . so yes of course, as you know *Irish Femme* is the crème de la crème of the magazine world, and therefore it's in everybody's interest that we write the kind of articles that our customers want to read.'

Hang on, why is A-J suddenly speaking like a wound-up walkie-talkie doll? Aha. Now I understand. Cecille is approaching the desk so I start nodding vigorously as if I'm a nervous student having a maths grind. I also pretend to take notes but I'm really only scribbling my name over and over again. It's pretty hard to relax with that old cow breathing down our necks.

At 11.00, it's time for our ten-minute break. In the stuffy little canteen A-J tells me that Cecille is off to the press screening of the new Brad Pitt movie after lunch. I ask her why she isn't going to the premiere herself. 'Oh that's because Cecille does the movie reviews,' A-J explains.

'Well, at least she does something, I'm so glad to discover that,' I whisper. 'For a while there I was convinced Cecille's only function in life was bossing other people around.'

'She doesn't really write reviews,' A-J confides in a low tone. 'She downloads them from the net and then puts them into her own words. Not that you heard it from me or anything . . .'

'No way, that's outrageous!'

'And so the *main* thing is that our advertisers are happy,' A-J then says in a loud, exaggerated voice. 'After all *they* are the people who pay our wages. Our customers are our priority.'

I don't even have to turn around to confirm that Cecille is hovering behind my back.

We're back to our desks before we know it and A-J is busy cutting out snippets from newspapers that she thinks might be useful leads for her gossip column. I, on the other hand, am going through back issues of *Irish Femme* to familiarise myself with the kind of features they usually write about. To be honest, it's much the same thing every week.

'How to lose weight and feel great' 'Eat all you like and STILL lose those pounds' 'The bikini diet' 'How to be the perfect hostess' 'You're never too old to fall in love' 'Which night course is the right one for you?' 'How to tell if he's having an affair'.

God, to be brutally honest, it's all a bit depressing, isn't it? And why do they have boring diets on one page and recipes for chocolate treacle cake on the next? And if all men are having affairs, then why do we do little self-tests to see if HE might be the one for US? If I had editorial control I'd do it differently. I'd commission articles like:

'How to hurt when he does the dirt', 'How to get HIM to lose weight', 'How to manage your own finances', 'Your guide to a great night out with the girls', 'How to be a selfish singleton!'

Then again, those kind of articles might cause a major sales slump and then the advertisers whom we so obviously worship, wouldn't be too happy. But why do we do it to ourselves? Why do we want to lose weight, look great, be intelligent and funny at all times (without obviously being intellectually superior or poking fun at our partners)? Why do we go to the gym immediately after child-birth in order to get back our pre-pregnancy figures? Why do we record TV cooking shows so that one day we will actually try and make that scrumptious meal for somebody whose idea of doing the cooking is dialling the local take away? And why do we have to make sure that everything is always so bloody perfect when all we want to do is have a 'no make-up, tracksuit day' and watch *Desperate Housewives*?

Hang on now, sorry about that . . . rant over. I promise. I don't know why I always get so carried away. After all, it's not like *I* ever cook or try and be superwoman for anyone!

'So who are the celebrities being interviewed this week?' I ask, hoping that maybe I'll be given the happy task of interviewing the likes of Brad Pitt or Jude Law.

A-J gives me a somewhat pitying look. 'We don't interview international celebs in here,' she explains. 'Those interviews are bought in from an international agency. Sorry. Sometimes the deputy editor gets to interview the stars who are in town but that's about it.'

'So who do *you* get to interview then?' I ask, feeling a bit downhearted. I had envisaged long lively chats on the phone with Victoria Beckham, Leonardo Di Caprio, J-Lo, Orlando Bloom etc.

'Oh you know . . . the local celebs,' A-J says with a surprisingly straight face. 'The cast of *Fair City*, RTÉ newscasters, radio djs, up and coming models and boy bands . . .'

'So nothing to get too excited about then?'

'No.'

God, what a let down! I mean, I could get talking to those kind of people at the fruit 'n' veg counter in my local supermarket, you know? Suddenly I can't wait for lunch. My stomach is grumbling and A-J is in a sour mood after some PR person rang to ask why her client, a celebrity make-up artist, hadn't received any coverage in *Irish Femme* so far. Apparently nobody turned up to the launch of her make-up demonstration in the back of somebody's shop. Now her PR person (who just happens to be her sister as well) is on the phone letting off steam. After A-J ends the conversation rather abruptly, she phones Mary in reception to inform her that under no circumstances is that woman to be put through again.

'You see,' A-J turns to me, her dark eyes flashing, 'it's people like that who make my working day hell. Here I am trying to write features, answer emails, and generally get things done, and then some up-her-own-arse idiot rings disturbing me and actually has the chutzpah to think that we owe her something. Well I'll make damn sure she doesn't get any coverage in *Irish Femme* ever again after today's little outburst.'

I stay quiet. Jesus, I don't think I've ever met anyone who's liable to fly off the handle quite as fast as A-J. Maybe it's the lack of food. When I don't eat I often find I'm a little more intolerant, tearful and irritable. A-J picks up the last unopened newspaper and flicks through it as I answer an incoming call from a charity fundraiser looking for a plug in the magazine.

I take down the website address and tell her I'll see what I can do. Somebody else rings about a competition they want to run to promote an Australian wine. They promise the winner a trip of a lifetime to Northern Australia. I take down their details too as I'm sure this is an offer *Irish Femme* won't be able to refuse. Then somebody else rings wondering if they're through to the Well Woman Clinic and a young man rings looking for work experience. As I end by telling him to send in his CV, A-J gives a little cry.

'What?' I ask, panicking slightly. 'Was that not the right thing to say?'

But A-J isn't listening. She's staring at a large photo of . . . oh my God, it's herself and Bunny at the footwear launch! Bunny looks absolutely stunning, like a film star. In fact both girls look like models – no wonder I was asked to step out of the photo!

'What does it say?' I ask, craning my neck for a better look.

'*IT girls Angela-Jean Murray and Bunny Maguire also enjoyed the evening*,' reads the caption underneath. 'God that's hilarious. I wonder how Bunny will feel about being called an IT girl, haha.'

'I'm sure she'll be stunned,' I say truthfully. 'After all, last night was only her first night out in Dublin, apart from the time we ended up in hospital.'

'She could be a star . . .' A-J stares at the photo with interest.

'What do you mean?'

'Well . . .' A-J says slowly. 'She looks like a star, she's beautiful, single, quirky and nobody knows who

she is apart from the fact that she has money to burn
. . . perfect.'

'But you can't be a star for no reason,' I interrupt.
'I mean you have to actually do something, like sing
or dance or . . . I dunno, read the news . . . you can't
be a star for just doing nothing at all.'

'In this town?' A-J raises a perfectly arched brow
and gives a knowing sort of smile. 'Do you want to
bet?'

19

'It doesn't look like me though.' Bunny stares at the photo in amazement. 'I look completely different. It's unbelievable. I can't thank you and A-J enough.'

'Hey, all it took was a couple of trips to the hairdresser and one or two beauty treatments. Money can buy almost everything.'

'I'm worried though,' Bunny says with a frown.

''Bout what?'

'My ex, Shaney. If he sees this, he's not going to be too happy.'

'Remember he *is* your ex though. So he has no hold over you whatsoever,' I tell her. 'Now, show me your CV. Have you finished writing it up yet?'

Bunny hands me a sheet of paper with all her details on it. It's a standard CV stating her date of birth, school, grades, and work experience which includes working in a funfair, a stint in Dunnes Stores' grocery department, a part-time job in a local petrol station, temping in an accountant's office and a bit of babysitting. Nothing that'll have any employer banging down the door, I'm afraid.

'We really need to spice this up a bit,' I tell Bunny.

I still can't understand why she is so hell bent on getting a job anyway. Surely she should go mad for a bit, live it up, do a bit of travelling and stuff. But Bunny herself thinks it's a big enough deal coming to Dublin, without heading off to France or somewhere where she doesn't speak the language. And she says she can't stick another day watching the likes of *Neighbours*, *Police Rescue* and *Judge Judy* while pigging out on rubbish.

I notice Bunny looking at me anxiously.

'You mean I should lie?'

'Well not lie *exactly*,' I say cautiously. 'But you have to sound like you've more experience than this. I mean, what kind of job are you looking for anyway? What floats your boat? You don't want to be stuck in an office all day, do you?'

'Not really,' Bunny shakes her head. 'I'd like to work maybe part-time and then I'd have time to learn to play the guitar.'

'Play the guitar?' I ask. Goodness, Bunny certainly has a knack of surprising you. Just when you think you're beginning to know her, she goes and contradicts herself.

'I've always wanted to sing and play the guitar,' she says. 'But I could never afford lessons and my mother ... when she was alive ... suffered from migraines so I wasn't ever allowed to make any noise. After she died, I bought my first guitar but my ex smashed it to pieces one night after a particularly horrible argument.'

'What a bastard!'

'You're telling me. I still can't believe I managed to get away from him. I'm half afraid I'll bump into him any time I leave the flat.'

'Don't worry about that thug,' I say. 'He can't touch you now.

'I rang Dave earlier,' Bunny then announces, out of the blue.

She's sitting up on the sofa painting her toenails with the free nail polish from the launch last night. 'Dave, as in my older brother.'

Dave? Brother? Bunny has a brother? Oh yes I forgot. For some strange reason I keep thinking Bunny is an only child. She rarely makes reference to any of her family. God, it just goes to show how little I actually know about my flatmate, doesn't it?

'Right.' I answer hesitantly. 'Great . . . did he have any news from home?'

I nearly bite my tongue. What kind of an ass am I? Bunny's parents are dead. Jesus. What good news could he possibly have? But to my surprise Bunny doesn't look too upset.

'Nothing major,' she answers chirpily. 'My brother is going around to the flat I used to share with Shaney to pick up my belongings.'

'Oh God, will he be okay? I mean will your ex cooperate with him?'

'Oh yes, there'll be no problem. My brother's bringing a pal along.'

'Oh that's good then. It's a pity they didn't try and get your stuff earlier though. From what I've heard about Shaney so far, I'd say he would have no qualms about pawning off half your belongings.'

'My things will be fine. My ex doesn't really want to cross my brother and his pal.'

'Oh.'

'They would have called earlier but they weren't around.'

'Were they away?'

'Yeah.'

'On holiday?'

'No. In prison. Now back to my CV, are you going to help me with this or what?'

'Hey, look at this,' A-J shrieks with laughter. 'That dreadful woman who does the PR for that shoe shop is looking for Bunny's address. She wants to invite her to the private showing of a luxury new lingerie collection in the Westbury Hotel next week.'

'But why?' I ask in puzzlement. 'Why would she want to invite Bunny? She doesn't even know her.'

'I told you before. *Anyone* can be somebody in this town. She obviously thinks Bunny is some rich kid with a trust fund. Well, come on, you can hardly blame her. Bunny was going fairly mad with her credit card the other night. And the fact that she appeared in yesterday's newspaper described as an "IT" girl can't have done her reputation much harm either.'

'But they don't *really* think she's an IT girl, do they?'

'Of *course* they do,' A-J is adamant. 'What's an IT girl anyway? Who decides? Bunny can be Dublin's IT girl if she wants to be. What's stopping her? We can help her achieve her dream.'

'I'm not sure it *is* her dream though,' I say quietly, thinking of Bunny's tragic history, the sudden death of her parents, the abusive ex-boyfriend, the brother who's just done time . . .

'Nonsense, Bunny is the perfect IT girl. I'm going to run my column this week with controversial headlines. *"Bunny denies she's dating any of the boys from* Zoo*"*, or how about *"Bunny slams rumours of diva behaviour at recent fashion show"*, or *"Bunny hotly denies affair with dishy millionaire"*'.

'But why should Bunny deny anything?' I say, completely taken aback. 'She hasn't even *done* anything. And anyway nobody knows who she is.'

'Not yet,' A-J says smugly. 'Not yet. But they will.'

With that, another PR company phones and A-J starts chatting away amicably. 'Tonight? Yes, lovely. Of course we'll be there. Who stars in it? Fantastic. I love Ewan McGregor. And I'll be bringing my stand-in if you don't mind, Fiona Lemon. She'll be writing my column when I'm away and I'd also like to bring Bunny Maguire . . . Bunny Maguire, yes, she's in town at the moment. She's probably tired after her flight from Barbados – her folks have a lovely house out there. They're neighbours of the Kidds, you know, Jemma and Judy. Sorry, I mean Jodie and Jemma. And God do they know how to throw a party! But I don't think Bunny has any engagements tonight. Great, well, we'll see you later then.'

'We're going to the movies.' A-J puts down the

phone and smiles at me gleefully. 'You, me and the "IT" girl.'

'But you never explained who Bunny was,' I say. 'You're such a chancer! And what was all that about a family holiday home in Barbados?'

'*That*, I said on purpose. There's nothing like a bit of international glamour to make the Dublin social set go wild for you,' A-J explains firmly. 'Let them rack their brains trying to figure out who Bunny is.'

I barely eat for the rest of the day. I have a fear of some photographer asking me to step aside at the film premiere tonight as I look on in quiet mortification yet again. If I starve, I might be down a pound or two later. All I've had today is two Weetabix, some slimline milk, and one half of a Twix, which isn't too bad, is it? The way I look at it is, if A-J can get by without eating, so can bloody well I.

Just before lunch, I find myself yet again shredding press release after press release as a shivering A-J types up her copy wearing fingerless gloves (it's so bloody cold in this draughty office!). Across the desk, barely hidden by a thin partition, Sue, the haggard-looking ad exec, who has been with *Irish Femme* for longer than anyone can remember, is frantically ringing companies who have not yet got back with copy approval on their ads. Purple in the face, she explains to yet another anonymous secretary that yes, the matter *is* very urgent.

Cecille, meanwhile, is pacing up and down the room, her face like thunder, shouting into her mobile phone about deadlines. Tomorrow, lunchtime, is when the magazine goes to print and I suddenly realise that this is by far the least fun part of the week.

Then, out of the blue, Angela-Jean, who has wisely kept her head down all morning, is called in to Cecille's tiny office, which is only separated from the main open-plan one by a single pane of glass and a partition wall.

'God, help me, what have I done now?' she mutters through clenched teeth and makes her way towards Cecille. I hear Cecille telling her to sit down and I feel nauseous. Is she going to berate her for employing me? Am I not good enough? Am I going to be told to clear my stuff at the close of day? I feel weak, and not just because I haven't eaten.

A-J and Cecille seem to be talking for ages in low voices. I know they're talking about somebody. If it's me, I just wish they'd hurry up and fire me so I can get out of here. This is worse than being back in school. Am I going to get detention or simply have my report card marked? I can't concentrate. I'm trying to proof some copy that A-J has printed out for me but the words are all blurring together. What will I do if they tell me to go? Could they possibly have somebody else lined up?

Suddenly A-J emerges from Cecille's office. Her eyes are dull and heavy lidded. She walks towards me and says in a sombre voice, 'Fiona, can I have a word with you in the canteen?'

I follow A-J into the tiny empty canteen. She shuts the door for extra privacy.

'Cecille doesn't want me here, does she?' I ask.

Judging from the sober look on A-J's face, this is indeed the case.

'Doesn't want you? Where did you get that daft idea?' she says dismissively. 'Don't be ridiculous. Now, do you want some coffee?'

'But we've had our break. I . . .'

'Cecille says we can have a coffee so we can discuss this in private.'

'Discuss what?' Jesus, what the hell is going on? I wish A-J would stop being so bloody mysterious.

'Well, we're having a mini crisis. Cecille is fuming because Lolly, our resident stylist, has quit.'

'Oh.'

'And there's more. It gets worse. She's moved over to *Gloss* to work for Faith.'

'Right, that's not good is it? But it's hardly a life-or-death situation all the same.'

'Lolly told Cecille she'll never set foot in this office again after a blazing row and Cecille told her she'd sue her for breach of contract for not giving enough notice.'

My eyes widen in surprise. That must have been some catfight!

'But then Lolly,' A-J continues, 'says she'll sue Cecille for bullying and harassment in the workplace.'

'You're kidding!'

'I'm NOT,' says A-J excitedly as the kettle starts to boil over.

'But why did she confide in you and why are *you* confiding in *me*?' I ask in amazement.

'The thing is,' says A-J, as she grabs two mugs and

carefully drops a spoon of cheap instant coffee in each, 'she has nobody to do the styling for this week. Lolly was supposed to bring the clothes to the photographer's studio this afternoon and then bring them back to the shops tomorrow like she always does.'

'And can they not just leave out the fashion pages for this week?'

'No, that's out of the question. Cecille promised one of the big chain stores, which also happens to be one of our main advertisers, that she'd fill half our fashion pages with their clothes. It's a case of "you scratch our backs, and we'll scratch yours". So we now don't have any clothes for the pages. I mean we *could* get the fashion company to courier out some clothes but if we just feature their clothes, the readers might smell a rat. We have to mix and match, you know?'

I dunno. It all sounds a bit silly and far-fetched to me. Why can't they just get someone to scoot around town today for a couple of hours, picking up bits and bobs in the various shops. Problem solved. I offer my humble opinion to Angela-Jean.

'Easier said than done. You can't easily get a stylist at such short notice, especially since Cecille has fallen out with most stylists in this town anyway. None of the good ones will work for the peanuts she's prepared to pay. I mean, who, in this day and age, can afford to swan around town all day carrying bag loads of clothes, and not care that they're basically scraping a living. People like that don't exist. At least . . .'

A-J and I look at each other and then the penny

drops. I know what she's thinking. She's wondering whether Bunny will do it. This is what this whole thing is about, isn't it? She's reading my mind.

'You don't suppose . . .' A-J begins hesitantly, putting down her mug of coffee and frowning as if the idea has just suddenly occurred to her. But I didn't come down in yesterday's shower and the idea of Bunny becoming a fashion stylist for one of Ireland's leading women's magazines is simply ludicrous.

'No. I know what you're thinking, A-J, but it's out of the question. You need experience to do that job.'

'Listen, it's not that difficult,' A-J persists with a determined look in her eye. I know that look. It means she has no intention of backing down. 'I will write out a letter for you with *Irish Femme* headed notepaper and my contact number here in case you run into any trouble. You don't have to troop all around Dublin or anything like that. Three or four shops should do it. We'll give you the taxi fare out of the petty cash box.'

'Me?' I ask, astonished. 'You want *me* to be the stylist?'

'Who did you think I meant? Bloody Santa?'

'No,' I laugh. 'Sorry I don't know how I got the wrong end of the stick but for a minute there I was thinking of Bunny, but . . .'

'Bunny!'

Oh my God, I can almost see the light bulb going off on top of A-J's head. I groan inwardly, wondering how deep a hole I have dug now for poor Bunny to dive headfirst into.

I say nothing, hoping that A-J will decide herself that it's not a great idea, without me having to spell it out.

'You're so right. Bunny *is* looking for a job, isn't she?' A-J continues.

'Yeah, but she hasn't got a clue about fashion. I'm not just saying that. Bunny herself would happily admit it. Sure, you were hired to dress her, remember?'

'You don't *have* to know anything about fashion though,' A-J says fishing out her mobile phone. 'Most stylists in this country don't have a clue either. Have you seen the state of some of them? Sure most of them don't even own a hair-brush!'

I laugh, despite myself. Doesn't A-J have any respect for anybody?

'Now,' she says in a matter-of-fact voice. 'What's the number of your place? I hope to God Bunny is at home.'

I watch with a mixed feeling of amusement and disbelief as A-J somehow persuades Bunny to become the new stylist of *Irish Femme*. I would actually love to see Bunny's face right now. Sure it was only this morning she was saying how much she'd love to work in a really posh department store but wasn't sure she had enough experience. She said she was afraid they might look down on her. What a difference a day makes!

'Don't you worry about that, Bunny. If anybody dares dismiss you, I'll personally come in and break their legs,' A-J reassures my flatmate in her usual charming manner. 'Anyway you'll be doing *them* a favour by giving them free advertising. You can't buy that kind of publicity you know. Yeah . . . absolutely . . . no of course they won't suspect you're not the real thing, most stylists look like they've been dragged through a hedge and back again. You'll look like a supermodel in comparison.

'Just wear something you bought the other day when we went on our shopping spree. Yeah, you'll look fab. Vintage stuff is all the rage this season so you can basically wear any old thing. Pull something out of the bin and wear it with wellies. They're in season too believe it or not!'

I try not to laugh at A-J's helpful styling tips.

'Now, this is your brief,' she tells Bunny. 'Have you got a pen handy? Right now, you need to get about ten tops for under fifty euros. Get them from three shops so you won't look like you're lazy and just stopped off at one place. And try to stay away from those awful browns and greens that are supposed to be "in" at the moment, do hear me? And no ponchos, God forgive me, but whoever thinks a knitted blanket with a hole through the top for one's head is stylish, deserves to be shot. Have you got all that? I'll write a headed letter for you right away and leave it in reception. No, I won't be here this afternoon. Just pick it up and get the taxi to wait for you. And remember to keep all your receipts. Good luck, my darling.'

'Poor, poor Bunny,' I say shaking my head as I stand up to rinse my coffee mug. 'She doesn't know what she's getting herself into, does she?'

'That's the only way to learn,' says A-J pragmatically. 'If you're thrown in at the deep end you have to swim up to the top for air. Bunny will be fine. I think you underestimate her, Fiona.'

'What do you mean?'

'Just that . . . sometimes I think you underestimate the girl.'

21

'My feet are covered in blisters,' moans an exhausted-looking Bunny. I find her on the sofa, her swollen feet soaking in a basin of soapy warm water and the *Irish Independent* covering her face like a mini tent.

'How was it?' I ask sympathetically.

'Awful,' she says, looking as if she's about to burst into tears. 'Simply horrible. Most of the shop assistants weren't a bit helpful even when I showed them the headed letter signed by Angela-Jean. It was as if they didn't trust me. I mean, did they think I would run away with their stuff, never to be seen again? Do I look like a thief?'

'Of course not. It's just that they didn't know you,' I say trying to cheer her up. 'Once they get to know your face, it won't be so bad. Promise.'

'I always thought being a stylist would be such a glamorous job though.'

'So does everybody.'

'Interesting. It just goes to show that you shouldn't go around thinking everyone's life is much more glamorous than your own.'

'Did you get great stuff though?' I ask sticking my head into the fridge hoping to find something that isn't too fattening. Now that I'm expected to go to launches and stuff as part of my job, I'm anxious not to be eating too much. I know I should really join the gym but the idea of running on the spot along with a load of other sweaty individuals isn't exactly appealing. And I would rather chew off my own arm than lie down on the ground doing sit ups on a thin mat surrounded by thick-looking bodybuilders.

Bunny sighs. 'It's no easy task trying to find trendy tops in this city for less than fifty euros but I did my best. The problem with going around the shops all afternoon though was forcing myself to keep my own credit card in my bag.'

'Did A-J mention that you've been invited to the launch of some fancy lingerie at The Westbury Hotel next week?'

'Um . . . yeah. She mentioned it when I rang her this afternoon about some sales assistant giving me a load of grief. I don't want to go to something like that on my own though. Will you come with me?'

'I'll try my best. Hopefully Cecille will let me out of the office.'

'We won't have to try stuff on though will we?'

'Are you joking?' I laugh. God, the idea of it! 'No, we'll watch the models parade up and down and all we'll have to do is drink champagne and enjoy the show.'

'Oh I see, that's okay then. Aren't the models mortified doing that though? God, I think I'd rather die than have to parade up and down in my smalls while ladies who lunch guzzle champagne.'

'I dunno if they are or not. I suppose I've never really thought about it. But it's their job. They're probably used to it.'

'I wouldn't say you *ever* get used to doing that,' Bunny says with a shudder.

'So tell us about the tops. Did you pick up some nice ones? No ponchos?'

'No, I didn't dare disobey A-J's orders. It'll be different when A-J goes off to New Zealand next week though. I'll be able to have more control over what I put in the fashion pages.'

'You mean you're going to continue?' I ask in amazement. 'I thought you said it was awful?'

'Well, yeah, it was,' she says taking her feet out of the basin and wiping them dry with a big fluffy towel. 'But that's just because it was my first day. I'll get used to it. And as I said, it'll be different when A-J heads off to New Zealand and I'm my own boss.'

'You'll still have to answer to Cecille though,' I warn.

'I can handle her,' Bunny looks at me levelly. 'She's the *least* of my worries.'

Someone knocks loudly on the door, making me jump.

'Are you expecting anyone?' I ask Bunny.

'No, are you?'

'Well no,' I say looking outside. I see Dervala's car outside and breathe a sigh of relief. Thank God. I hate having to say no to people looking for sponsorship or people trying to sell me household appliances I definitely don't want.

Dervala bursts into the room, full of life and energy.

'Wow,' she stops in her tracks when she sees Bunny.

'Is that you?' she shrieks. 'For a moment there I thought Fiona had got herself a new flatmate. You look stunning. Actually I saw your pic in the paper. IT girl? I say now, isn't that very grand! You'll soon be the Tara Palmer-Tompkinson of Ireland. So what are you two girls up to? Fancy coming out tonight?'

'What's the occasion?' Bunny wants to know.

'Oh, Dervala never needs an excuse. Let me see, it's pay day, Derv, right?'

'Yeah, well I can't think of a better excuse to go mad, can you?'

'Well I definitely can't go out,' I say firmly. 'We go to print tomorrow so the pressure will be on big time.'

'We go to print tomorrow ... oh la la,' says Dervala, obviously taking the piss. She takes a mock bow as I just shake my head. I'm standing my ground. I'm not budging. There is absolutely no way I am going out tonight.

'I wouldn't mind going out,' Bunny pipes up suddenly, much to my amazement.

'You? But I thought you were exhausted!' I can't help exclaiming.

'Well I was, but I'm not any more. My feet don't feel sore now. Anyway, what else would I be doing? Sitting in watching television with you?'

I am momentarily stunned. I mean I'm sure Bunny isn't deliberately trying to insult me but I have to admit I'm not terribly thrilled by her throw-away remark.

'The girl has a right to go out if she wants,' says Dervala, being her usual loyal self. Dervala's the type of woman who runs with the hare and chases with the hounds. She wouldn't understand true friendship if it jumped up and bit her in the butt. 'Come on, Buns, get ready and we'll paint the town red hot.'

'Okay so.' Bunny stands up. 'But where will we go?'

'Why don't you ring your pal A-J to see what's on?' Dervala suggests.

Horrified, I tell them I don't think it's a good idea to ring A-J. Tomorrow the magazine goes to print, she's been working flat out and has to organise everything tonight before jetting to the other side of the world.

'I'm sure she wouldn't mind,' says Dervala brazenly. 'Have you her number, Bunny? Just give her a quick ring there. If she says no, she says no. What of it? A dumb priest never got a parish, right?'

Bunny, egged on by Dervala, picks up her fancy new mobile phone, which is so unbelievably tiny I'm surprised she can even punch in the digits properly. The next thing I hear her talking animatedly into the phone.

'Hiya, A-J. Listen it's Bunny here. I'm so sorry to ring you when you're under such pressure with packing and all ... oh really you've everything packed? Well, that's great.' She gives Dervala a big thumbs up, completely ignoring me. 'But anyway the reason I'm ringing is 'cos we're at a bit of a loss here. We want to go out but aren't sure where to go. Anyway, we were wondering if you could ... oh brilliant. Are you sure you don't mind? All right, we'll call over later and pick up the invitations. Yeah, I promise, if I see any of the stars misbehaving, I'll be sure to tip Fiona off. Haha. No, no, she's not going out tonight. Deadlines and all that, you know yourself. See you later then!

'Sorted,' she snaps her mobile closed with a grin. 'A-J say she's got tickets for a bunch of various gigs. There's the launch of a CD, the launch of book and a party sponsored by one of the big drinks companies which goes on to the small hours.'

'Way to go, girl!' Dervala high fives her. Then she turns to me. 'When you start this gig, we'll be able to go to these kind of events all the time. I can't wait. God love our poor livers though – I don't know how they'll cope!'

I say nothing. I still can't believe they've arranged to go out without me. I mean, I know they didn't go behind my back or anything 'cos I was standing here the whole time but I can't help feeling like Cinderella, who's not going to the ball. And the most annoying thing is that Bunny and Dervala wouldn't even know each other if it wasn't for me. And they wouldn't know A-J if it wasn't for me. So technically they wouldn't get these invitations if it wasn't for me. Yet they are going out and I'll be left sitting in alone watching soaps on the box, all because of this bloody temp job that I've signed myself up for.

And then I'm struck by a sudden thought. And it's not a particularly pleasant thought. You see, I've just realised that although I am only filling in for A-J while she's away, Bunny isn't filling in for anyone. That means that when A-J returns, I'll be turfed out on my ear while Bunny will get to keep her styling job. Not that I'm resentful or anything . . . I'm happy for Bunny and all but . . . but hell she doesn't even need the money!

Do you think I'm being just a bit neurotic here? After all shouldn't I be happy that Dervala and my new flatmate seem to have clicked? Wouldn't it be worse if they didn't get on? I shouldn't worry about something so petty. I mean, they have invited me along. I'd be welcome to join them if I wanted. And besides, there'll be plenty more fun nights out, I think to myself, trying to ignore the shrieks of laughter coming from Bunny's bedroom over the music.

I can smell the wafts of perfume coming from the room, but it's the laughter that's getting to me. They say half the fun of a girl's night is getting ready but this is taking the biscuit. I want them to leave the flat so I can wallow in peace. I switch on the TV but nothing's on. I flick from channel to channel but have no luck. There's just so many programmes about searching for the dream home at the moment. It's

depressing for the rest of us to watch. The way I'm
going I'd be lucky to ever own a shed of my own.

Oh, to marry a rich man. A rich, good-looking
man, who's funny and kind, honest and intelligent,
tall with blue eyes, someone like ... a vision of
Connor's perfectly sculpted face suddenly flashes
before my eyes. Now where did that come from? I
should absolutely not be thinking about that
scoundrel. Connor, no matter how gorgeous he is, will
never be mine. He's Ellie's and the father of ... God,
I don't even feel comfortable thinking about him. I
wish to God I'd never met him.

'Hey, do my thighs look big in this?'

Dervala stands between me and the TV, poured
into one of Bunny's designer minis. She looks like
she's struggling to keep her tummy in and it's not
working. Some girls, very few mind you, can get away
with wearing pieces of string for skirts. Dervala isn't
one of them.

'Your legs aren't big, no. But won't you be cold?' I
ask diplomatically. 'The forecast isn't great for
tonight.' What can I say? Honesty is not always the
best policy when you're telling friends what they
really look like. I'm not her mother. I don't have the
power to yell, 'You're not going out like that, missus.
You look like a whore! What kind of message are you
trying to give off, eh? Eh? You're not going out of my
home dressed like that!'

Dervala just shrugs. 'We'll be getting taxis to the
venues. It's only Thursday so we shouldn't have any
trouble getting them. I don't want to be carrying a big

coat around with me. I couldn't be arsed, you know?'

'Well it's whatever you feel comfortable with, Dervala. I know I probably wouldn't . . .'

'What do you think?' Bunny suddenly emerges from the bedroom and I am stunned into silence. For somebody who looked like a complete wreck a couple of hours ago, she has suddenly managed to transform herself to a stunning creature. Her grey eyes look huge under her thick dark lashes and her highlighted hair falls loosely over her slender shoulders. She too is wearing a micro-mini but effortlessly pulls it off because she is so thin. Her legs look well with her immaculately applied fake tan. No streaks. Beach legs. Bunny belongs in St Tropez. Not in my Dublin flat. She looks like a piece of chic art while Dervala looks more like a cheap tart. Immediately I vow to stop eating for good.

'You look amazing,' I say truthfully. 'You're a knock out!'

Bunny runs towards me and gives me a big hug. 'You're always so, so nice to me,' she says, sounding vulnerable and grateful. I almost feel guilty for resenting the girls a fun night out. I mean, what kind of a monster am I anyway?

'I've been chilling a bottle of champagne in the fridge,' Bunny says excitedly. 'We're going to drink some before we go out to put us in the mood. Will you join us for a glass?'

'Oh why not? I might as well,' I say. 'Thanks.'

Seconds later we're all sitting around drinking Bunny's champagne. I sip it slowly, while Bunny and

Dervala drink with slightly more speed.

'So where are you going to go first?' I ask them.

'Well, we're thinking of going out to Swords first,' says Dervala.

'Swords? Sure that's miles away.'

'Yeah but there's a launch of a new boy band's single in a pub out there tonight and Dervala says we might get the phone numbers of a few hunks,' Bunny giggles.

I'm not sure if I like the sound of that. Bunny might think this is all a bit of innocent fun but I bet she's never been on a session with anyone like Dervala before, apart from our disastrous first night out. If you looked up 'man eater' in the dictionary, you'd probably stumble across Dervala's name. But what can I do? Bunny's a grown woman and I can't go around being her chaperone. I'll let her have her night out and that will probably be the end of it. Most people who experience a night out with Dervala never go back for seconds.

Right then, the champagne is nearly gone and the taxi has arrived to pick them up. They blow me kisses, offer me one more chance to change my mind and then leave. The flat is eerily empty. I'm so bored. I need company. God, I really wish Ellie was still my friend. I'd love to call her up for a chat or something but I can't. I can't think about herself and Connor. I should be happy for them but I'm not. I've tried and failed. I don't know what's wrong with me. I had a dream about Connor last night and we were in a boat in the middle of the sea and we were laughing. It's all a bit vague now, but when I woke up I felt warm and happy until I realised that none of it was true, and I was so so shocked that in my dream I imagined that I was in love with somebody who didn't belong to me and never would.

I try ringing Mum but Dad answers the phone and tells me she's playing in a bridge competition. He doesn't seem to want to talk so I hang up and dial my sister instead. Gemma's always on for a bit of a natter.

'Listen, I'm on a date at the moment,' she says in a low muffled voice. 'I'll give you a ring tomorrow and tell you how it went.'

Oh great, I think, sinking into a kind of mild depression. I really feel like Billy-No-Mates now. Everybody is too busy for a chat, too busy getting on with their lives and now that my fair-weather friend Dervala has paired off with my new flatmate, they don't really need me either. Bloody brilliant!

I decide to go to bed with a book. At least I'll get a good night's sleep and I'll be feeling refreshed in the morning. I curl up with the latest from Marita Conlon-McKenna. After half an hour I'm still reading so I force myself to put it down, switch off the light and drift into a deep, deep sleep.

Within hours I wake with a jolt. Peter Andre's 'brother' is standing at the foot of my bed.

22

'What the hell is going on?' I scream, as I suddenly realise that (a) I'm not having a nightmare and (b) he is who I think he is.

'What's the story?'

'Story? What's the story?' I feel like exploding. 'What are you doing in my room?'

'Listen, there's no need to be so aggressive, your friend is shagging my brother and what am I supposed to do? Join in?'

'Bunny is with your brother?' I say, feeling sick to the stomach.

'Who's Bunny?'

I get out of bed, pull on my dressing gown, push your man out the door and into the living room. The living room lights are off but as the curtains are open and the street lights outside are bright, I can make out a big hairy butt in the middle of the floor, giving it loads. Underneath that butt, somebody is making a lot of groaning noises. I recognise the voice. It's

Dervala. And ohmigod, she is having sex. And ohmigod I am watching. And so is your man's brother. This is like stumbling on to a porn set. Only I know the people involved. This is obscene.

'You have two minutes to get out of here or I will call the guards,' I manage to say in a stone-cold voice although my heart beat is getting faster and faster. The hairy butt suddenly stops moving up and down, and Dervala says 'Ah Jesus, Fiona, what's your problem? Here would the two of you ever give us a bit of privacy, you pervs.'

She cackles like an old witch. She's obviously off her head on something stronger than champagne.

'I mean it, I'm phoning them now,' I threaten. 'I'm not putting up with this. Where's Bunny? Is she in her room?'

'Who's Bunny?'

I storm into her room. Her bed is empty. It's still made. Good God, where the hell is she? What's going on?

I come back into the living room where Dervala and her 'date' are pulling on their clothes. The 'brother' is standing at the door having a cigarette. They are all completely out of it and it's pretty scary, but not as scary as Bunny's disappearance.

'Where is Bunny?' I ask once again when the 'lads' have finally cleared off.

'She met someone,' Dervala says sulkily trying to pull on a second shoe.

'Who?'

'I dunno, some rugby player.'

'And she went home with him?'

'I guess,' Dervala shrugs.

'And who let you in here?'

'Bunny gave me the keys. I told her I couldn't go back to my place 'cos obviously I live with my folks'.

'So it's okay to wake me up and have sex on my living-room floor but it's not okay for you to do it in your own home?'

'Jesus, what's wrong with you?' Dervala says angrily. 'I used to think you were my friend but now I just think you're a bit of a nut, do you know that?'

I take a deep breath and exhale slowly. Dervala is obviously very tired and emotional so there is no point in fighting with her. Nobody ever wins an argument with a drunk anyway. And much and all as she has annoyed me this evening, I can't possibly just throw her out on the street either. I offer to ring her a taxi.

'S'ok,' she mutters. 'I'll walk.'

'You bloody well won't,' I say picking up my phone and dialling a local taxi firm. 'But you'd better tell me what happened to Bunny though.'

'She got lucky,' Dervala shrugs. 'It does happen to some of us sometimes you know,' she says scathingly.

I'd like to ask her what 'luck' was involved in inviting some sleazy guy back for a meaningless shag, but I don't. I just can't wait for the taxi to arrive.

Within minutes she's gone. I say good-bye but she doesn't reply.

Another one bites the dust, I think as I crawl back to bed again. What is it with me and friends? First

Ellie and now Dervala. What next? Will Bunny move out if she ever comes back in the first place? Do I start trawling the net looking for mates? Even A-J is leaving the country tomorrow and I won't see her for at least six weeks. I check the bedside clock. It's 5.30 a.m. I have to be up in two hours' time and I couldn't possibly be more shattered. So much for a peaceful night's sleep!

23

It's 11.00 a.m. and the magazine has just gone to print. The relief is enormous. I can't even begin to describe the pressurised atmosphere that hung in the office for the first two hours this morning. Maybe it's just because I had a broken night's sleep but I just can't believe that a magazine that has been up and running for so many years is so disorganised. Everything that could possibly go wrong, did. Someone rang at the last minute to pull an ad, an agent of somebody vaguely famous rang to say we couldn't go ahead with the piece on her happy marriage as her husband had just left her, Cecille's computer crashed so she had to use A-J's. Some footwear company was supposed to courier over shoes to photograph for an ad but they never arrived.

Anyway amazingly enough, everything got sorted between clumps of hair extensions being torn out, people called on for last-minute favours and a few bribes and threats thrown in for good measure. Then this afternoon, just after lunch (A-J and I went out to The Square in Tallaght for a treat!), Bunny rings to tell me she's okay adding that she's a bit worried about Dervala. I tell her that Dervala is fine although she may have picked up something nasty last night. Bunny sounds relieved and then asks what can she do about her key? She says she has no way of getting in because she has given Dervala her key. I say that it's too bad but there is nothing I can do about it until this evening. That'll teach Bunny not to hand out her house key, I think.

'If I call to your office, will you give it to me?' she pleads. 'I've got to get home and change. I'm still wearing my mini from last night but the fake tan on my legs is rubbing off and I look a complete mess.'

Jesus, I suddenly have this vision of Bunny rolling up to the offices of *Irish Femme*, wearing last night's make-up and looking like a whore gone wrong. I try not to have a minor panic attack.

'But you can't come into the office!' I shriek causing people in the café to turn around and stare openly. 'Cecille has us all at a very important meeting this afternoon and nobody is allowed to leave the office under any circumstances to give out keys or anything else.'

A-J gives me her infamous 'raised eyebrow' look. She's obviously intrigued. Bunny promises that she won't disturb me at all and has no intention of calling in person but she asks if Johnnie can get them from reception while she waits in the car.

'Who's Johnnie?'

'Er . . . um a friend,' she says sheepishly.

'Right.'

'We're going to a function tonight so I desperately need to change. It's a matter of life or death.'

'Okay.'

A function? I'm bursting to find out what kind of function but don't like to quiz her over the phone.

'Was that "The Boiler"?'

'Yep,' I laugh. A-J has christened Dervala and Bunny 'Dummy' and 'The Boiler' after I told her about last night's antics. But whatever about Bunny disappearing off with some stranger in a club, it was the Peter Andre look-a-like and his moronic brother that had her clutching her sides to prevent stitches.

'One day you'll see the funny side to it too,' she kept saying in between the loud snorts.

Funny. Up until now I've always wondered if A-J had a sense of humour. Apparently she has, albeit a fairly dodgy one.

'So what did she want?' A-J tries stabbing a celery stick with her plastic fork.

'She needs her keys. She's got herself a date tonight, would you believe?'

'With who?'

'Dunno, some guy called Johnnie. He's probably a fruitcake like herself.'

'Ah, Bunny's nice. She's just a big kid really. All that money and no sense. Bless her.'

'Yeah, I suppose. She's had such a tragic life. Hopefully things will only get better for her now. I hope for her sake though, that she doesn't start hanging out with losers and getting herself into all kinds of trouble.'

'Remember you're her flatmate, and not her surrogate mother though,' A-J says in a warning tone of voice. 'Come on, missus, we'd better get back to the office for my "going-away" party.'

There's about ten of us sitting around the canteen table pretending to have fun. On the table is a big pepperoni pizza (not much good to me!), a sponge cake with cream and two warmish bottles of white wine. Cecille then starts pouring the wine into ten plastic glasses as A-J looks on glumly. She said she already asked Cecille not to make a fuss but her plea only fell on deaf ears.

In the car earlier she said Cecille has some deal with the local supermarket on pepperoni pizzas, cakes and cheap wine 'cos apparently somebody leaves *Irish Femme* every couple of months.

'Do they all get the same pizza and cake?' I asked, surprised by such blatant predictability.

'Are you joking? Some people get nothing but a curt "clear your desk".'

'No way!'

'Oh yes way, one girl said she was leaving to go to a rival magazine. She was told to get out immediately because Cecille didn't want her taking any contact sheets with her.'

'So you must really be in the good books if she's throwing a party for you and you're not even leaving?'

'Yeah, I suppose I am,' A-J said and I got the

distinct feeling she didn't really want to talk about it any more.

So anyway here we all are in the dreary canteen with its list of infantile rules on the wall telling everybody to wash up after themselves and so forth. Cecille raises her plastic cup first and we all follow suit, even old Mike who has been working with *Irish Femme* since day one, although nobody quite seems to know what he does, least of all himself.

'I would like to raise a toast to A-J,' she starts enthusiastically.

'Hear hear.'

Fake smiles are beamed across the room. A-J pretends to come over all shy suddenly but because we all know her, nobody is taken in.

'I'm sure we'll all miss A-J on her travels but we wish her all the . . . Holy Fuck!'

Everybody looks astounded as Cecille rushes to the window. What's going on? Is somebody breaking into Cecille's car? Surely nobody would want that old banger! Everybody else is now looking out the window. I crane my neck for a better view. And now I know why everybody is so interested. There is a complete hunk getting out of a spanking new Beamer. He's tall and athletic looking with broad shoulders and hair a bit like David Beckham before he shaved it all off, and none of Beckham's horrible tattoos.

'Is somebody supposed to be doing an interview with him?' Cecille asks excitedly. 'Who organised it? Should we get another bottle of wine?'

But nobody knows why he's here.

'Who is he anyway?' I ask Cecille.

'Do you really not know who he is?' asks A-J with a smug smile. 'That's Johnnie Waldren, Ireland's hottest rugby player. And I have a fair idea why he's here. Look at his companion. Recognise her?'

With that, I peer outside trying to get a glimpse of the person sitting in the passenger seat. And yes, there she is, with her long unbrushed highlighted hair and huge designer sunglasses.

'Way to go, Bunny,' A-J says admiringly.

24

'That was *your* flatmate sitting in his car!' Cecille exclaims. 'I don't believe it!'

'That's Bunny Maguire,' A-J says teasingly.

'Our Bunny? You mean that young one who was styling for us earlier on this week?'

Sharon, the deputy editor who hardly ever says a word, suddenly perks up. 'Oh do you think herself and Johnnie would do an "at home" type of spread?'

'I wouldn't say she'd do anything like that,' I say. 'You see Bunny's quite private. She doesn't approve of people who want to show the world and his dog their homes.'

'Well, maybe she could do "My beauty regime"?'

'Yes indeed,' A-J cuts in. 'Now *that* would be more Bunny's scene. She's a real lady, not one of those hairy smellies who love to show off on pages and pages of magazines. Plus she probably wouldn't talk about her relationship because she's very private like that. *Very* discreet altogether.'

She catches my eye. I look at her worriedly. I feel about ten years old.

'Anyway why are we talking about Bunny?' Angela-Jean continues, ignoring my puzzled face. 'What about my flipping toast?'

Fake laughter follows. And somehow, unbelievably, we manage to finish drinking our vinegar-tasting plonk.

A-J texts me a 'Good luck' message from the airport. It'll take her a full day to get to New Zealand. I really envy her. In a way I'm glad she's going because now I'm on my own and can put my own stamp on the social diary. But I'm petrified of messing up too. At least with A-J sitting beside me I wasn't so terrified of Cecille. I tuck my feet underneath me on the sofa. I'm really looking forward to relaxing this evening. I've got an armload of invitations for next week so I know this weekend is kind of my last chance to slob around the place with no make-up. My only worry is that Bunny will walk in with the hunk and then I'll really be mortified.

How does she do it? I wonder as I flick through *Irish Tatler* and look at all the new fashion photos. As soon as I get my next pay-check I'm going to splash out on a new outfit. A size 12 outfit. There is no way I'm buying something so I can 'grow into it'. I've been quite good recently, sticking to fruit and vegetables. But it's all a bit boring. Sometimes I read magazines, where famous thin women say they love nothing more than eating fruit 'n' veg and their only 'vice' is the odd glass of wine with dinner. I know that kind of lifestyle is all very commendable but Jesus, it's a bit boring, isn't it? I mean I don't think you need to get trollied like Dervala did last night, but you do have to kind of let your hair down now and again, don't you?

I've been walking a bit too, proper brisk walking. There's no point strolling around pretending to exercise. But I don't boot around the place swinging my arms either like I'm going to war. Women who do that always look a bit mad. So yeah, I'm walking fairly briskly, which is supposed to be brilliant for keeping trim. The only thing is that it's very boring walking around when you're not heading for any particular destination. I'd love a Yorkie now. Or a Kitkat. Or a Moro – I haven't had one of those in ages. Wasn't it so much simpler being a kid? When you ate a bar of chocolate you didn't think twice about the calories. No you just opened your gob and scoffed it in case one of your siblings robbed any of it. Oh yes, those were the days!

I continue flicking through *Irish Tatler*, pausing to scrutinise some of the beautiful people who usually pop up on the back pages. You see, I'll have to write about people like that over the next few weeks so it's very important to familiarise myself with all the names and faces. That's right.

I wonder how Bunny is getting on with her date. She mustn't have been half as drunk as Dervala last night if she had the energy to go to a function with Irish rugby's answer to Brad Pitt. Well she certainly did better than Dervala did with the toe rag she dragged in here. The more I think about last night's little 'indecent incident' the more my blood pressure rises. No matter what A-J thinks, I will never ever find that funny.

I get into bed and switch on the telly. I may as well catch the end of the *Late Late Show* since I haven't seen it in a while. But as soon as I pick up the remote, I hear a loud banging on the door. I wonder who the hell that is. Don't tell me Bunny has gone and handed away her keys two nights in a row. Anyway why would she be back this early? I glance at my watch but it's not 11.00. I look out the window to see if I recognise my mother's car but there's no sign of it. And then I hear a voice; a thick aggressive voice, shouting through the letterbox.

'Bunny? Bunny, are you in there? It's Shaney. Did ya think I wouldn't come looking for my money?'

'How does he know where I live?' Bunny asks, stricken.

'I have no idea.'

'Maybe he saw my picture in the paper?'

'Yeah, maybe.'

'What'll I do?'

'I don't know. What do you think you should do? How does he know you won the lottery? And anyway, why does he think he deserves any of it? What a fucking prick!'

'Yeah,' Bunny lowers her eyes and stares at her hands.

'You bought the ticket, didn't you?'

'Yeah.'

And then I begin to wonder if Bunny is telling me the truth.

'Well . . .' I say slowly, picking up Timmy, who has just strolled in from the kitchen, and putting him on my knee. 'If you're telling the truth, you've nothing to worry about, do you? If he starts hassling you I've no problem calling the guards.'

'Oh God, don't do that!' Bunny says, shocked.

'But he can't come around here disturbing me. This is *my* flat as well you know.'

'I know but I don't want to involve the guards. I'll move out if that's what you want.'

'Now, listen, we'll have none of that talk,' I say gently. 'I just don't understand why he thinks he can come around here and bother you like this.'

' 'Cos, he's a freak,' says Bunny, chipping off bits of last night's nail varnish. 'I bought the ticket with my *own* money.'

'I know you did.'

'Normally we would do the same numbers every week and get eight euros worth.'

'Really?'

Aha! Now, we seem to be getting somewhere.

'Yeah but on that particular Wednesday, I forgot to get the money off him. So I only bought four euros worth 'cos I only had a fiver on me.'

'But he doesn't know that, does he?'

'No.'

'You've got to tell him.'

'I don't want to speak to him at all,' Bunny shakes her head firmly. 'Not after what he did to me.'

'Can your brother not talk to him?'

'My brother wouldn't talk to him, he'd kill him.'

'He'll be back though, you know that, don't you?' I look her straight in the eye.

'I know. I'll think about what I'm going to do later.

I'm too tired to think properly right now.'

'Well, God, you've certainly been on the batter for the last two nights. I believe you're seeing Johnnie Waldren.'

'How do you know?' Bunny's eyes nearly pop out of her head.

'Ah sure the whole office in *Irish Femme* saw you sitting in his car,' I tell her trying not to laugh at the expression on her face. 'Don't worry, the paparazzi aren't on to it yet. But it's not every day a hunk calls into our humble offices in person.'

'He is a bit of a hunk, isn't he?' she says coyly. 'But I don't want too many people to know at this early stage.'

'So you're going to see him again?'

'Of course! It's not every day you meet a lovely guy as well. He's really intelligent too, not like some of those rugby players you'd meet who've obviously had one too many kicks in the head.'

'But were there no press at the function last night? Once it gets out that you're dating a rugby hero, people might want to know about it.'

'Are you serious? Why would they want to know anything?'

'Well, we don't have that many celebrities in Ireland so anybody of any interest becomes a major interest. I mean some rugby players are always in the papers and they're damn ugly. Your fella looks like a superstar. And anyway everyone wants to know about you now. A-J has been telling everyone your folks live in a big rambling castle and that your aunt left you millions of euro in inheritance money.'

'Oh dear.' Bunny looks worried. 'I wish she hadn't. No wonder everybody is being so nice to me. I couldn't understand it. Now it's all beginning to make sense.'

'A-J thought it would be fun to make you into a star. I guess she thought she was doing you a huge favour.'

'But it's not right to tell people lies, is it? I mean people should just like you for who you are.'

'They should,' I agree. 'But they don't. That's just the way the world is. People are always trying to place people. That's why they want to know all about you. And of course now they'll want to know all about you and your new man.'

'He's not exactly mine yet though. And the answer to your question is that there were no press at the function last night. It was Johnnie's father's retirement party. He works for an insurance company. He's just an ordinary man. And Johnnie's just a regular guy.'

'Janey, he must be smitten if he's already introduced you to his parents. Wow! Are you meeting him again tonight?'

'Oh no,' Bunny says resolutely. 'A girl's gotta play hard to get, you know. His last girlfriend ran after him and he broke it off 'cos she was smothering him.'

'How do you know all this?'

'Oh, I made some discreet enquiries last night,' she says tapping the side of her nose with a smile.

And once again, I'm reminded about A-J's words of wisdom when she told me never to underestimate Bunny!

'**H**ello everybody,' I call breezily to all the bent heads in the office. Very few of them even bother to look up. I, myself, am on time but it seems everybody else has arrived even earlier – what's that all about? I mean it's not like they get paid a cent more for their diligence and devotion to the job. Anyway, I'm well aware that everyone will be watching me carefully this week, waiting for me to slip up, no doubt. I just hope to God that doesn't happen.

I'm wearing a power suit, which cost me the price of a decent second-hand car. I had to put it on a new credit card of course. It's so much easier to hand over a piece of plastic, isn't it? It's like free money. I don't pay for anything in cash anyway 'cos I never have it. As soon as I sit down Cecille is at my desk, asking me if I have any ideas for this week.

'But I haven't gone out yet,' I answer. How can I have any ideas when I've just sat down? It's Monday morning and I haven't even had a chance to turn on my computer yet!

'You need to figure out what stories you want to work on. Obviously we need lots of glamour and fun, but you also need to have something different, something nobody else has. People don't buy *Irish Femme* just to read old news copied from the papers.'

'Right. A-J left me a lot of contact numbers from PR people, will I ring them?'

'Only as a last resort. PR people have a habit of simply praising their clients and trying to get you to give them free publicity. They don't give you anything too juicy though. If they've any big stories they want to relate, they'll just go straight to the Sunday papers. If you want juice, you've gotta squeeze it yourself, honey. Anyway I'll leave it to you . . . oh just one thing.'

'Yeah?'

From the way she's speaking to me now, I wouldn't be surprised if she told me that cleaning the office toilets with my toothbrush was also part of my job!

'I need you to interview this guy who has been given his own show. According to his publicist he's a fine thing, but sure aren't they all?' She throws her eyes to heaven. 'Anyway, I'll get you his contact details and you can interview him. The sooner the better really.'

'Great, thanks.'

When I first got this gig I presumed that I'd be constantly on the phone to all these major international celebrities, chatting about love, life, and stuff. But then I found out that that's Sharon's job. She gets to interview any international celebrities while I get to interview the Irish talent, which is basically a few boy bands (too young and effeminate for me), Irish models (who never quite cut it outside Ireland), and TV presenters who do exactly what I do. They interview people too but because they do it on TV, that makes them sort of celebrities too. Get it?

Anyway, I wonder who this one is. If he's new I've probably never heard of him. I hope he's not some arrogant tosspot who's going to sit there telling me the meaning of life.

Cecille's back at my desk with a press release and photos.

'He's looking fairly hot I can tell you. I wouldn't kick him out of bed for a pack of peanuts.' She pauses to take another long look at the photo. 'So, anyway there's the details of his PR woman,' she adds. 'You can do the interview tomorrow afternoon.'

I try to answer but I can't. I open my mouth all right but no words come out. I'm totally speechless. And the reason I can't speak is because my world is rocking beneath my feet. I take the press release and photo from Cecille's hands and hope she doesn't notice that my own hands are shaking. She doesn't seem to though.

'He's hot, isn't he?'

I take another look at Connor's photo.

And couldn't agree more.

'Are you nervous?' Cecille wants to know.

'Nervous? Ah no.' I give the usual fake smile I've become so accustomed to using since joining *Irish Femme*.

No I'm not nervous, I'm bloody petrified. I cannot believe I have to interview Connor of all people. Since when did he want to become a TV presenter? Ellie had mentioned that he worked in TV but I'd just presumed it was behind the scenes. Now I've really landed myself in it. Cecille was very clear about how she thought the interview should be.

'He'll probably just try and talk all about his work and the show and stuff. They all do that,' she warned. 'But you just make sure you ask him about his love life and what his likes and dislikes are, and what female celebrity he'd like to interview, you know all that rubbish. It's what the readers of *Irish Femme* want to read about, believe me.'

I think I'm going to be physically ill. Am I

supposed to ask him about Ellie and the baby? Jesus, he'll think I'm some kind of sicko. How am I even going to go through with this? Can I get out of it though? I mean, what excuse can I come up with? I can hardly tell Cecille I can't interview Connor because his wife-to-be thinks I slept with him now, can I? I barely got a wink last night thinking about the whole thing. Why me? I kept asking myself as I tossed and turned throughout the night. I tried ear plugs, eye masks, lavender oil, reading a boring book, counting sheep, even herbal tea and still couldn't nod off. God, life can be pretty unfair can't it? I mean why couldn't A-J have interviewed him last week and it could be over and done with? I sneak off to the Ladies and thankfully nobody is there so I can check myself critically in the mirror. Although I'm tired I must admit I look fairly okay. Eating healthily and walking a good bit has started to pay off.

I got my hair highlighted yesterday evening, which was a pretty stressful experience. Arriving about five minutes late the receptionist looked at her watch and tut tutted, before leaving me to wait for twenty minutes. Then this one highlighted my hair and kept yapping on about people like Jordan and Jodie Marsh before handing me over to this skinny guy, who looked like a girl, to wash my hair but didn't rinse it properly so I left the salon with a head full of greasy product. As soon as I got home I ended up having to rinse all the conditioner out myself. But anyway, at least the strip of dark brown has disappeared from my hair line, and although I'm not terribly sure, I think I might have lost some weight as my trousers are hanging off me now instead of cutting into my spare tyre like they did, when I first bought them.

Right. Here I am sitting in the bar of The Four Seasons Hotel, trying to relax and not sit rigidly with my briefcase on my lap. I keep telling myself that I am a professional woman doing a professional job and that is that. I'm not doing a brilliant job of convincing myself though and the palms of my hands are hot and sweaty. I hope Connor won't expect a handshake.

He walks through the doors and I look up in admiration. He looks like a vision. He's wearing a dark navy T-shirt, a navy coloured jacket and light coloured jeans and there's a warmth about his smile that's irresistible. My fixed smile, on the other hand, is forced. I keep telling myself that this is a professional interview, not a date. But there's nothing professional about the way Connor grips me in a bear hug and plants a big smacker on my cheek.

'How the hell are you?' he asks me like I'm a long-lost friend. 'What are you doing here?'

'I'm waiting for you,' I reply, somewhat coolly. What a *weird* thing to say. Is he making fun of me or what?

'Good answer, you charmer. Seriously though, can I join you for a quick drink? Do you have time?'

I have to laugh. Connor is acting very strangely indeed.

'I'm a bit nervous actually,' he says suddenly, taking a quick look around the bar. 'You see, I'm doing this interview for a woman's magazine, but I've never done anything like this before. I hope they don't ask me about my skin-care regime or how many times I like to have sex in the evenings.'

And then it all makes sense. Connor doesn't realise that I'm the one doing the interview! He thinks meeting me is just a coincidence, doesn't he? But of *course*, how on earth would Connor know about my new job?

'Sit down.' I pat the seat next to me. 'You should have that drink. I believe these women magazine writers can be very cruel.'

'Yeah?' He looks genuinely worried.

'I'm only messing.' I give him a friendly punch. 'I'm doing the interview, mister. Did they not give you my name?'

'No! Actually, yeah, they said Fiona but it didn't click. Jesus, this is a coincidence isn't it?'

'Absolutely. I can't believe you were nervous though.'

'I was,' he grins, revealing a perfect line of white teeth. 'But I'm not any more.'

'I was nervous too,' I admit.

'Really?'

'Yeah, you're my first interviewee for *Irish Femme*.'

'But you know me, so it's cool isn't it?'

I don't know what to say. I certainly wouldn't have described this little get together as 'cool' though. We sit looking at each other awkwardly for a moment.

'So what kind of stuff are you going to ask me? You're not to be too mean, okay?'

'I won't be mean I promise. I already have a press release and stuff but my editor said she wants to get some interesting gossip, so if you don't mind I'm going to ask you a bit about your career and hobbies and then a bit about Ellie and the baby.'

Connor stares at me in shock. As if I've just said I was going to ask him his views on pornography or gay sex.

'Did you say you were going to ask me about Ellie and the baby?' he asks incredulously. I can feel my cheeks beginning to burn. Oh my God, I have offended him, haven't I? He's going to walk out on me now and I won't get my interview and Cecille will fire me. I want the ground to open. I've put my foot so deeply in it that I'll never get it out.

'Listen, I am so sorry. I can't believe I was going to ask you any of that,' I say quickly my words tripping over themselves. 'Please don't be offended. I'm not very good at this sort of . . . I mean, I'm only just new, and . . .'

'Is Ellie pregnant?'

Now it's my turn to be truly stunned. What on earth is going on? What kind of game is this? Well I'm not enjoying it, I can tell you. My head is reeling and I want to run away. The bartender arrives with our order – a glass of white wine for me and a Miller for Connor. I take a gulp from my glass, tempted to knock the entire contents back.

'You know she is,' I say in a quiet, steely kind of voice.

But Connor looks genuinely baffled. If he were an actor, I'd give him an Oscar for his facial expressions alone. He takes a deep breath and then gives a long whistle.

'Well *that* was fast,' he says. 'But you know, I'm happy for her. I think that's what she wants. One of the reasons we split up was because Ellie wanted to move things along too quickly. But she's only with this new guy a while I believe.

'What new guy?' Jesus, this is all a bit too bizarre for my liking. This was just supposed to be a quick professional interview but now I am sitting in The Four Seasons Hotel with my friend's ex-boyfriend who is pregnant by . . . who the hell is the father then?

'Stuart. That's his name. He works with Ellie on the travel magazine. I think they've liked each other for ages. Even when I was with her she was always talking about him.'

'But how do you know he's the father of her child?'

'Hey, I didn't even know she was pregnant! But I *did* know she was with Stuart. Sure I bump into Ellie quite a lot these days. She's involved in the new TV show. We get on fine now.'

'Is she talking about pregnancy on the new show?'

'Nah, she's going to come on once a fortnight to talk about travel.'

'My God. Let me take all this in. You and Ellie are not together. You are not the father of Ellie's baby. You are hosting a chat show but Ellie will be a guest speaker once a fortnight. Ellie is my ex-flatmate and is now going out with Stuart who recently commissioned me to do a travel piece. I met a girl called A-J on that press junket who got me a job in a magazine and my first assignment is to interview . . .'

'Me. Small world, huh?'

'Small? It's bloody suffocating! But hang on . . . I met your friend Killian on that press junket and he also told me you and Ellie were back together.'

Connor's face clouds. 'And then I suppose he made a move on you?'

I don't know whether to laugh or cry. But fortunately we both start to laugh at the same time and the ice is broken once and for all. Connor runs a hand through his dark dishevelled hair.

'*Now* I know why Killian hasn't been in contact for a while. And I'm also beginning to work out why you wouldn't speak to me in Cocoon the other night. You thought I was a bastard out getting drunk with my pregnant girlfriend home alone, didn't you?'

'Well, er . . . yes, that's exactly what I did think.'

His gaze matches mine. He looks so gorgeous now. A piece of his wavy hair hangs over his right eye. He brushes it off and smiles. If this were a movie now, we'd be kissing as the credits roll but I'm well aware that it's the middle of the afternoon, and like it or not, I still have to get the interview done. I fish in my briefcase for my Dictaphone.

'Can we get this over and done with?' I ask, trying not to be affected too much by him. I'm fighting an attraction that I suppose has always been there since the first time we met, back at the party, standing by the fridge . . . but Ellie was in the way. Now there's nothing stopping us . . .

'Now then,' I say pressing play. 'Did you always want to be a television presenter?'

'Not really,' he answers, straightening up in his seat. 'I was always more involved in the production side of things. Somebody suggested that I try out for the camera and I suppose I just did it for a laugh really. I didn't think in a million years that I'd be called back for a second screening.'

God, his voice is so unbelievably sexy. He has a soft Belfast accent. It kind of reminds me of Liam Neeson's voice. I can't wait to go home and play this tape later. I'll never ever erase his voice. Oh dear, would you listen to me? I'm like a smitten teenager.

'So what do you think makes a good TV host?' I ask, nerves taking over again, like I'm some spotty schoolgirl looking for my first proper job.

'Um . . .' He looks like he's deep in thought. 'I'm trying to think about that. Well, I think you should try to make your guests comfortable, interact with them, not interrupt, or look at your watch or be distracted in any way when they're speaking . . . God, that sounds bollocks, doesn't it?'

I laugh.

'Jesus don't write that!'

'Ooooh, the power of the pen, eh?'

'Nasty journo,' he gives me a pinch.

'Ow, you're not allowed to attack me!' I screech, oblivious to everyone else in the room. 'Come on now, let's get this finished.'

'Just say I'm a good-looking charming bastard and that I'm dating Angelina Jolie. Then I can ring up all the newspapers to deny the story and get the show blanket coverage.'

'Yeah, and I'll end up getting my ass sued. No thank you.'

'So listen, are you out schmoozing with Dublin's champagne set?'

'Yeah, well I get to go to lots of things. Some nights are good, others aren't. It really depends on the crowd.'

'So are you meeting lots of hunks at these things?'

'Are you joking! These things are full of women and gay men. Most straight men are in the pub or playing football or whatever. They certainly aren't eating sushi and sipping cocktails at the openings of hair salons.'

Connor laughs. 'God, you've some tongue on you. Anyway keep firing the questions. I'm beginning to enjoy this.'

Oh believe me, so am I, I think to myself. I have never been attracted to anybody this much. I suppose I've always kind of denied my attraction towards Connor because of all the baggage I thought he was carrying. And also, I didn't want to hurt Ellie any more than I had already.

'So are you looking for love?'

I look him straight in the eye. Thanks to that glass of white wine I'm feeling quite bold.

'Are *you*?'

'Hey, I'm not the one being interviewed!'

'Next question please?' he says teasingly.

'What kind of women are you attracted to?'

'Loud ones with hairy armpits and bad breath.'

'Oh please,' I groan. 'Come on, you've got to give me something I can actually write.'

'Well then, you must ask questions I can actually *answer*.'

'What is the meaning of life?'

'Haha, very funny.'

With that my mobile begins to ring. I see Cecille's number flashing. Christ! She's probably wondering why I'm taking so long.

'It's my boss!'

'Tell her I've been delayed and you're still waiting.'

'Okay.' I answer the phone. 'Hi Cecille, how are you? I'm still waiting for him. I think he's been doing interviews all day so, yeah . . . I know what you mean, I'll try to get something exclusive from him, something he hasn't told anybody else. Right on, Cecille. Listen, at this stage I very much doubt I'll make it back to the office with the evening traffic and all. I'd rather take my time here and get a really good interview, you know? Right, thanks very much. See you tomorrow.'

'So you want an exclusive?' Connor raises an eyebrow. 'Right then. I'm really a woman.'

'Get lost.'

'Mmm. How about this? I have met the woman of my dreams but won't ask her out for fear of getting rejected.'

He picks up his bottle of beer, swallows some and then puts it back down again. We sit side by side, an air of awkwardness hanging in the air between us. Then Connor breaks the silence. 'I think I'll have a second one of those. You ready for another vino?'

'Yeah okay,' I smile back. And then I decide I don't really want to be anywhere but here. We talk for hours about everything, off the record of course. My Dictaphone is well and truly switched off now as Connor tells me about his childhood, his travels, his dreams and ambitions. I tell him about my job in *Irish Femme* and don't glamorise my life at all like I usually do when I'm desperately trying to impress people. With Connor I don't feel I have to bend the truth. He just seems to like me for some reason. We go back to his place later (a flat in Rathgar). Connor lights a fire and we lie in front of it sipping Coke and eating a Chinese meal. I know that might sound kind of boring but honestly I'd rather be alone with Connor than in some fancy restaurant where I wouldn't be able to touch him. Connor is the type of guy that you just want to reach out and touch all the time. He's so irresistibly handsome but he's also kind and he loves cats, which is a bonus. I can't love anybody who doesn't love Timmy!

After the meal we lie side by side on the rug looking into each other's eyes, flushed with the heat from the flames. I keep waiting for him to kiss me but he doesn't so finally when I can bear it no longer, I grab him and kiss him passionately. He's an amazing kisser. And I have fallen big time. I'm just worried about how Ellie is going to take it. Connor agreed that it was a good idea to call her and gave me her new number. But what woman is ever truly delighted when their ex-boyfriend hooks up with an ex-friend?

28

I ring Ellie first thing in the morning. The call goes straight to her message minder and I congratulate her on her pregnancy. I ask her to call me back so I can take her out for lunch to celebrate. Then, feeling a lot more relieved and happier, I switch on my computer to type up the interview with my beloved Connor. Even typing in his name makes me as excited as a teenager who scribbles the target of her affections all over her copy books. I know, I know, I'm a bit sad. Then again you just can't help yourself when you fall in love. Suddenly life seems a lot more tolerable and little things that would normally bother you, don't. Anyway I'd better stop daydreaming and get cracking on this piece. But how the hell I'm going to write it without being completely biased, I don't know.

Cecille has already enquired whether my interview went well and I said that it had actually gone better than expected. Then I blushed like a ninny while she looked at me rather oddly. I just hope my roaring red cheeks didn't give the game away *too* much.

Anyway how could she possibly suspect anything? I'm just being paranoid.

I get back to work. It's hard to call it work though really – I mean I could happily write about Connor for free. But Connor is not the only thing I must write about today. I also have to go to the launch of a new eye cream at 12.00. I hope it's not too boring. I mean, a skin care product is a skin care product right? And too much alcohol can't be good for your skin, can it? So why oh why do all skin care product launches ply you with free booze, eh? Do they really think journalists wouldn't turn up if it wasn't on offer? Well, maybe they'd have a point! Basically I think most journos would turn up to the opening of a dustbin if it meant getting sloshed for free. I used to think A-J was exaggerating when she first pointed this out. Now I've no reason not to believe her.

My sister thinks my new job is the business by the way. She can't believe it's part of my job to go out to things where you get free drink all night. After all, most doctors only get drunk after they pass their exams, which is pretty regularly actually when you think about it. They're always bloody studying! God, who'd be a doctor these days? My sister says it's nothing like *ER* and none of the doctors look remotely like George Clooney.

I start to write but am interrupted by my phone ringing. Would I like to come to the launch of a new range of fine wines? Yes. The launch of a new mobile phone? No. The launch of a computer magazine? No. The launch of the latest Audi? Mmm . . . yes.

Gosh, I am in such a good mood today. I'm really beginning to love this job but most of all I am looking forward to seeing my darling Connor again. I wish I had a picture of him on my screen saver so I could drool a bit. I go into 'Google' and search his name to see if I can get up a picture. As soon as I type in his name though, the phone rings again. Drat. If it's another launch I'm not going. Seriously, I'm all launched out for the moment.

'Hello, Fiona Lemon speaking?' I say breezily.

I say this so many times a day that I've actually started answering my mobile phone like this.

'Fiona? Hi, it's Ellie.'

'Ellie!' Oh my God, it's so long since we've spoken I can actually feel my stomach twist in an imaginary knot. 'What's the story?'

'I'm not sure,' she says in a sort of distant tone of voice. 'But I was sort of hoping that *you* could tell me.'

Ellie is coming over. Yes. I know. So here I am sitting in the living room fidgeting anxiously. What can she want? What does she want to say to me that she couldn't say over the phone? Has she heard about me and Connor? Is she furious? Will she threaten me to back off? Will I agree or will I just tell her that Connor is mine now and I can't help the way we feel for each other? Will she get all aggressive or will she shed tears and beg me to stay away from Connor? I feel like a stranger is coming to see me. Not Ellie. Not my ex-flatmate whom I used to adore. This just feels so weird.

I can kind of understand Ellie's point of view. I mean we rarely wish our exes undying happiness but, at the same time, Ellie is expecting a baby with Stuart now. So she can hardly *still* want Connor now, can she?

I look at my watch. It's almost 8.00. She said she'd be here at a quarter to. Suddenly the door-bell rings and I get to my feet. It's strange answering the door to Ellie. It wasn't so long ago that she lived here herself.

Ellie smiles a terse sort of nervous smile as I open the door to let her in. She's wearing a big woolly coat so you can't see any bump. I wonder how long she's gone. As she walks into the apartment her eyes nearly pop out as she takes in all Bunny's gadgets.

I'd love to tell her Bunny has won the Lotto but I can't.

'Your friend Bunny is a big spender, huh?'

'Yeah, she loves to shop.' I smile. 'You met her didn't you?'

'I did indeed.' Ellie sits down on the sofa. 'Strange girl. She seemed to think I wanted to move back in and so she was a bit wary of me.'

'Didn't you want to move back in?'

Ellie shakes her head vigorously. 'No, I didn't. I moved back with my folks for a couple of weeks. But I *did* want to come over and apologise in person for storming out after the party. I completely over-reacted. In fact I was already pregnant at the time but I didn't know it. Stu and I had had a big fight and I thought Connor would be the perfect person to date on the rebound. I wanted to make Stu jealous. Then I saw you two together and everything just came to a head. I was upset anyway about having left my friend in the hospital and Stu had gone off on a last-minute press junket without telling me. I thought he must have got back with his ex-wife. She'd been calling him a bit too much for my liking.'

'Stu used to be married?'

'He's legally separated. So that's why I didn't tell you or anyone else about us. It was all a bit complicated. After all he was my boss too! His divorce was just about to come through, but his wife, who had initiated the whole thing, looked like she was having a change of heart. So anyway after a few days I came back here to say how sorry I was. I had lost my mobile so I gave Bunny my new number to give to you.'

'You did?'

'Ellie looks confused. 'Didn't Bunny give it to you?'

'No, she *definitely* didn't. I even asked her had you left a number.'

'I think she was threatened by me, you know. She kept saying it was her room now. I left a box of doughnuts for you and said I'd call in again soon but between one thing and another I never got around to it.'

'Hey, take off your coat and I'll stick on the kettle. I'm so glad you called over, you know.'

'Thanks. God, it's funny to be sitting here, just like old times, isn't it?' She pauses with a smile. 'Anyway, Stu told me you'd been in contact with him about a press trip so I was delighted for you. I mean, there's a limit to how much travelling I can do now,' she says patting her tummy.

'Yes! I'm so delighted for you, Ellie. In fact I thought the baby was Connor's . . .'

'Yeah well so did . . . so *does* everyone else, that's the problem. Some newspaper hack rang me wanting an interview about being the future mother of Connor Kinnerty's first child. And about an hour later a wedding magazine wanted to know if we could send them pictures of our big day! I nearly fell over in shock. I was wondering if the rumour had anything to do with you?'

'God no!'

'Well then, I reckon it was just a Chinese whisper that got out of hand.'

'A-J in *Irish Femme* told me your news. She said you'd applied for a job there but Cecille was worried that a pregnant woman wouldn't be able to go out four or five nights a week chasing showbiz stories. Then somebody else told her you were getting married.'

Ellie nearly drops her mug of coffee in shock. 'God, none of it is true. Especially the part of wanting to be a gossip columnist. You of all people should know, Fiona. I wouldn't do that job in a million years!'

'Well, I'm the new gossip columnist for *Irish Femme*,' I say in a dead-pan voice. 'At least I'm filling in for Angela-Jean Murray while she's out searching for herself in New Zealand.'

'Oh God, I'm sorry. When I said I wouldn't want to be a gossip columnist I didn't mean to insult you. I meant that I wouldn't be able to go out drinking and schmoozing at night. Not in my condition anyway. My morning sickness happens at night for some reason and I've spent more than a few nights with my head stuck down a toilet bowl. I'm afraid that wouldn't go down well at product launches, would it? Imagine if I kept asking for the sick bucket!'

I laugh at the thought of it. It's nice to see Ellie hasn't changed that much and is still her old depreciating self.

'I do wonder though, how in the name of God A-J got the complete wrong end of the stick?'

'I *think* I might know,' says Ellie with a half smile. 'I met Cecille at a lunch party in the French embassy. We had met on a travel trip before and she was asking me if I had any more exotic holidays planned for the year. I said I was pregnant so that it was hardly likely.'

'And I bet she suggested you should write a pregnancy column or something,' I laugh.

'That's *exactly* what she did. But she must have said something to Angela-Jean who was only half listening – hence the cock-up.'

'Oh well, at least we've got *that* sorted out now. Talk about a rumour getting out of control!'

'Yeah, it happens a lot in this town! Anyway, have you heard from Connor yourself recently?'

'Well . . . um, I'm meeting him tonight,' I say, and to my surprise I start blushing furiously. God, how mortifying!

'I *knew* it. I always had a feeling the two of you would end up together.'

'Well, I don't know. "*Ending up together*" is a bit too strong for my liking. We're going on a date tonight and we'll see how it goes from there.'

'But you *do* like him, don't you?'

'Yeah,' I admit. 'I like him a lot. But I wasn't with him the night of the party. I swear to God. I was just really drunk and was changing out of my wet clothes.

You walked in at a completely inappropriate moment. I know it looked bad but . . .'

'Hey, all is forgiven and forgotten. Honestly. I believe you anyway. So what time is he calling around at?'

'In about an hour.'

'God, you'd better get ready so.'

'Yeah.'

Ellie stands up and gives me a hug. I can't tell you how happy I am that the air has been cleared. I feel a ten-ton weight has been lifted from my shoulders!

Shortly after Ellie leaves Bunny arrives home. She's been out in town styling for *Irish Femme*. Her brief today was 'Make me look like a star!' She was trying to get the kind of clothes J-Lo, Kylie and Kate Moss would wear – but at a fraction of the price. Her eyes are shining and her cheeks are glowing. It's obvious that she's really happy with her new position as 'stylist'. Who would have thought it? Bunny from the sticks! A couple of weeks ago she had to hire A-J as her personal style adviser. Now she herself is advising the women of Ireland what to wear – it'd make you laugh, wouldn't it?

I have to admit though, Bunny must be the prettiest stylist in Dublin. They say money can't buy you everything but it has certainly bought her a certain *je ne sais quoi* and Ireland's hottest hunk is hanging out with her.

'Are you going out with Johnnie tonight?' I ask as Bunny dumps all the shopping bags in the middle of the floor and flops onto the sofa.

'Yes.' She looks at her watch. 'So that means I've got about forty-five minutes to get the glad rags on and make myself look normal.'

'Normal? That's a bit of an understatement. You always look fantastic.'

'My bruises are nearly all gone,' she says, pulling up her sleeves.

'That's good.'

'But unfortunately the emotional bruises are still there. You just can't see them.'

'You've got to move on though,' I say gently, aware that I must start getting ready too as myself and Connor are meeting up later.

'I'm moving on slowly but surely. It's not that easy. I'm still worried Shaney is going to come back and ruin this amazing fairy-tale that I happen to be living at the moment.'

'Forget about him. He's history. You've got a great future in front of you now with your styling and whatever. Sure it was just the other day you were wondering if you should send your CV around the shops. Now you're a style icon.'

'Well, now you're exaggerating. But yeah, I know where you're coming from. I've just got to believe in myself.'

'Exactly. Hey,' I look at my watch. 'You'd better start getting ready. What time is Johnnie calling at?'

'Nine. What time is your fella calling at?'

'Same time. Better get my face on too.'

'What's his name by the way?'

'Connor.'

'I haven't met him have I?'

'Well . . .'

'Hang on, he's not the Connor we saw in Cocoon?'

'Em . . . actually . . .'

'You mean the dad?' Bunny shrieks, her hand flying to her mouth. 'Oh my God!'

'He's *not* a dad. That was just a rumour.'

'But he's mine,' Bunny gives a funny wail. 'I saw him first!'

'Hey, you can't have *every* man in Dublin, you know. Anyway I saw him long before you. It's . . . well actually it's a long story. I'll tell you all about it tomorrow.'

'Is it a romantic story?'

Is it? Well, I suppose it is kind of romantic. But it'll all depend on the ending, won't it?

Johnnie Waldren looks a lot better in the flesh than he does on the rugby pitch. Not that I've ever seen him on a rugby pitch of course. But I've seen him on TV in his green rugby shirt, white shorts and muddy boots. He looks better now in his navy blazer, crisp white shirt and loose fitted jeans. I can hardly take my eyes off him. He's about six foot four and makes me feel like a dwarf. He's about twice the size of Bunny but I have to admit they look so cute together. He sits in our flat having a beer as Bunny is still getting ready. We exchange small talk and I ask him about his training, which thankfully he doesn't elaborate on 'cos I know nothing about rugby – I'm just being polite. And then he asks me about my column, and is polite enough to look interested as I tell him about all the launches I have to attend.

When Bunny finally emerges from her room looking like Kate Moss's twin, Johnnie looks suitably impressed. And when he looks like he is actually interested in the contents of all her shopping bags, then *I'm* impressed. The word 'metrosexual' could have been invented for this guy! I'm sure Connor would like him too. In fact I'm sorry Connor hasn't arrived in time. We could all have had a beer together and exchanged rugby 'n' shopping tips. What a combination, huh?

Unfortunately, by 9.30 Connor still hasn't shown his face though, and Bunny and Johnnie head off into the night like young love's dream. While I'm waiting I think I may as well have another beer. I wonder what's keeping him? Then again, he must be really busy, never mind pretty nervous about his new show. It's a big undertaking doing a live chat show, isn't it? After all, the critics will be waiting to pounce, won't they? They're so quick to tear apart new faces on the box. No wonder young people find it impossible to break through. I have been invited to a couple of things tonight, but to be honest I'm so tired that I can't bear the thought of going out schmoozing with a bunch of people I don't know. And besides I'm quite sure Connor wouldn't appreciate being dragged along to any of those silly events either.

I sip my beer as time slips on by, and I'm getting a bit anxious now. I mean, if he *has* been held up, why doesn't he just text me to let me know? Oh God, do you think he might have changed his mind about 'us'? Maybe he only kissed me last night 'cos he felt sorry for me. Ah no, wait a minute, I'm being a bit ridiculous here, aren't I? Men don't just snog women 'cos they feel sorry for them. In fact, as far as I can remember, men only seem to do what pleases them so I've nothing to worry about, right? Right?

It's now 9.45 p.m. Still no sign of him. This is ridiculous. He has either (a) forgotten all about our little *rendez-vous* or (b) I have been stood up. I begin to feel a bit nauseous. We *did* say 9.00 this evening, didn't we? And we *did* say we were going to meet at my flat, didn't we? I'm beginning to doubt myself now. Could he have got lost? No, of course not. Sure wasn't he here before? At our party? Should I text him? Perhaps he was involved in an accident and is lying injured somewhere at the side of the road? Ah cop on Fiona, would ya? Face up to the facts. Connor has obviously changed his mind. He doesn't like you because you're too eager. He's going to be a big star on TV and you're just a nothing who is filling in for A-J while she's on holidays. When she comes back, you'll still be a nothing going nowhere. Even Bunny has got her act together. She's out enjoying herself tonight with a rugby hunk who wouldn't have dared stand her up. But Connor didn't bother calling around. And didn't even think you were worth texting to let you know. You're not even worth a text, you big lump you. Road accident indeed!

And with that I burst into tears.

About twenty minutes later I stop crying. Only

because I hear a key in the door. It's Bunny. Oh great. Herself and Johnnie will be wanting the sofa to make out on, I suppose. And I will be expected to give a big exaggerated yawn, pretend I'm tired and retire to my room to twiddle my thumbs for the rest of the night. She's alone so I presume Johnnie must be off parking the car.

'Are you still here?' She looks at me in amazement and I hope to God my red eyes don't give me away. I don't want to have to explain to Bunny and Johnnie that I've been stood up. It's bad enough knowing I'm a loser without letting the rest of the world in on my secret.

'Yeah, I changed my mind about going out. Have you seen the weather? It's mad! I took one look outside but when I saw the rain lashing down I thought I'd better stay in and watch a DVD or something.' Bunny and I then look over at the blank TV, which has *so* obviously not been turned on this evening. I begin to feel like a fraud.

'You mean to say you stood Connor up because of a bit of rain?' she asks incredulously. 'That's the rudest thing I've ever heard! Was he not furious?'

'I just texted him but he hasn't texted me back yet.'

'I'll *bet* he hasn't. He's probably in shock. You can't go around doing that to people, Fiona. I'd be really hurt if somebody did that to me. Ring him now and tell him you've changed your mind.'

'No, I can't do that. And anyway it's not just the weather. I'm not feeling great anyway. I think I'm a bit run down at the moment. Where's Johnnie?'

'Still in the pub,' Bunny says. 'I didn't want to stay out 'cos I've to be up early to bring those clothes to the studio tomorrow to dress the models.'

'Was Johnnie not pissed off that you wouldn't stay?'

'Well, he wasn't delighted or anything. But I'd already told him I could only stay for one and I meant it. I'm not just a loser Lotto winner any more, I'm a woman with a job.'

'God, *you've* certainly changed! Fair play to you! I don't know if I'd have had the willpower to leave Johnnie Waldren in a pub by himself. Do you not think he'll have women drooling over him?'

'Of course he will. "Absence makes the heart grow fonder", so *I'm* the one he'll be thinking of. It's best to treat them a little bit mean, you know? But then again I wouldn't go as far as to stand somebody up. God, I don't think I'd ever forgive anybody for doing that to me.'

She's right, I think mournfully. And that's why *I* will never ever forgive Connor Kinnerty.

As the days drift by, and we head into the festive or rather the 'commercial' Christmas season, I realise that Angela-Jean was right about one thing. The whole social scene in Dublin is a bit of a joke. It is the exact same people on the circuit. Night after night. Launch after launch. The same old heads turn up on a regular basis. I wonder why. Don't they actually have homes to go to? Sometimes I think it's just such an empty life going to all these events. Free cheap champagne isn't such a treat when you're sipping it among a bunch of strangers.

I'm sure you're wondering if I've heard from Connor again. Well, I haven't. Not a peep even. I'm still kind of devastated and more than a little confused about it and to be perfectly honest, I found it pretty hard to finish writing my glowing article about him, which incidentally is going to print tomorrow at long last. You won't believe this, but Cecille was so pleased with the interview that she wanted to wait so she could run it as a cover story! Anyway, Connor's show is going so well that he's become sort of an overnight heart-throb. I haven't seen it yet of course because I'm in the office every day but Bunny (who only does her styling job once a week!) watches it every day and updates me in the evenings. I am still truly baffled as to why he never made contact. Eventually I told Bunny about him standing me up, but despite her insistence that I should ring him to demand what the hell was going on, I declined. I still have my pride, sort of.

I am really tired now. And I can fully understand why Angela-Jean nearly had a nervous breakdown while writing the social column and trying to juggle everything else in between. It sounds fun being out and about five nights a week but it's a full-time job: getting glammed up every day, heading into town rain, hail or snow, and *still* trying to look interested as some minor actor chews your ear about the terrible price of fame in the corner of a night-club!

The funny thing is though, that everybody sees my photo regularly now in *Irish Femme* and thinks I'm having a ball, when all I want to do is to head off to Connemara or somewhere for a week, to mingle with a few sheep who couldn't give a damn about who's in or who's out or whether Bono is going to show up.

Bunny and Dervala are still friends by the way. And I eventually made peace with Dervala too. To be honest I think she's a bit mortified about the whole incident with the Peter Andre look-alike. Anyway, neither of us has brought it up again. It's probably for the best.

Bunny ends up going to a lot of fashion shows these days thanks to her new job as 'stylist'. She never seems to tire of the lifestyle but that's because she has nothing to do all day. In fact she seems to have more PR people ringing her now than I have. And Cecille just loves her. She thinks the sun shines out of her arse if I'm to be crude about it.

A-J will be home in just over a fortnight. I'd love to know how she is getting on over there. I wonder whether she has found herself yet. And if so, has she liked what she found? I haven't phoned her. Well, that's a lie actually. I *have* in fact phoned a couple of times. Only by mistake though. You see, because A-J is the first name keyed into my mobile phone address book, every time I'm drunk I dial her number by mistake. She's used to it though. She once told me that people are always calling her at four and five in the morning, and is therefore considering shortening her name to Jean, simply so she can get a good night's sleep. Why doesn't she just switch off her phone before going to bed?

It's Thursday night. And I've just come back from the launch of a new Christmas shop in the city centre. It was good fun and there was a jolly band playing Christmas carols, even though it's only November, which is a bit ridiculous really. Still, it was highly entertaining. I ate moist Christmas cake and rich mince pies, as well as drinking more than a few glasses of mulled wine. I mingled and mixed, met lots of familiar faces (including Amy Whittle, A-J's arch-enemy who incidentally quizzed me up and down about Bunny's relationship with Johnnie), and even got a few quotes off a well-known singer for my column. In my goody bag I got three really nice expensive-looking red and gold Christmas decorations and a silver letter opener, which I was delighted with. But the thing is, I now feel kind of empty because the flat is so quiet. Bunny and Dervala came with me to the party (and I *warned* Bunny not to talk to either Amy or Faith, who was also sniffing around) but then I had to come home because *Irish Femme* goes to print tomorrow. The two girls saw me to a taxi rank and then decided to go on the batter yet again without me.

My eyes are almost closing now but I don't honestly know how I'm even going to manage to undress. I know I was tired anyway but the mulled wine has knocked me for six. Eventually I manage to haul my poor body off the sofa. I nearly trip over Bunny's treadmill which despite all our good intentions hasn't been used once since its day of purchase. Then I see the phone flashing. For a split second I wonder if Connor has left a message. I know it's been over a fortnight, but still . . . he might have been busy . . . or playing hard to get or . . .

It's a woman's voice. Drat. My heart sinks again like it always does when I realise that Connor hasn't called and at this stage, probably never will. It's a voice I don't recognise. Probably some boutique owner looking for Bunny – she seems on first names with them all these days! The voice then tells me she's phoning from RTÉ about a new mid-afternoon show and was wondering if I could phone straight back. I feel the hair rise on the back of my neck. Oh my God. RTÉ television. And they want ME to go on their show. Jeepers, this is the most exciting thing that's ever happened to me in my life! I wonder what they want me to do. Maybe they're looking for a showbiz correspondent. Yes, that *must* be it! Imagine, they probably want me to come in and talk about the stars. Wow! Isn't that just the coolest thing ever! I've *always* wanted to be on the telly. I'm so excited I can hardly breathe. The woman on the phone said to ring straight back but that was hours ago. After all it's almost midnight now. A bit late to phone back now. I'll have to wait until tomorrow morning. Oh, how am I possibly going to sleep tonight?

'And now we'd like to welcome showbiz columnist extraordinaire Fiona Lemon to the show.' Thunderous applause! I wait for the clapping to calm down before I smile directly into the camera. *'Thank you, thank you.'* I take a demure little bow. The cameras zoom in on my perfectly made-up face. Well, I *have* spent about two hours in hair and make-up being groomed to look like Cameron Diaz! All I need is Justin Timberlake at my side. *'Can we just say, Fiona, how honoured we are to have you . . .'*

Jesus! The sound of my alarm clock blasts me into the world of the living. Don't tell me it's time to get up already! Shoot! I was just beginning to enjoy my little dream. Right, Lemonhead, up you get. Today is the beginning of the rest of your fabulous new life!

It's Friday morning and the magazine is going to print. So that's probably why Cecille is ignoring me. I won't read into it too much, I think. No. I'm determined not to act in any way paranoid. It's just Friday, that's all. Cecille is never *not* under pressure on a Friday.

God, I'm fairly shattered though. I almost need two matchsticks in my eyes to keep them focused on the screen ahead. I'm dying to ring your woman in RTÉ but I'm just waiting for the right opportunity. I don't want everyone in my office knowing my business. I mean they might be a bit envious if I get my own slot on daytime television. And I wouldn't blame them. This, after all, is the stuff dreams are made of, isn't it?

I wonder how I will actually cope with being on TV all the time though. I mean I wonder will I get pestered in the street and all that. Will I be expected to hang around with other celebs and stuff? How will I handle being in the spot light? Will the show be live or will I have time to prepare? I was never confident as a child or teenager. And I wasn't ever cast as the lead in the annual school play. Far from it actually. In fact as far as I can remember I was cast as the mast in *Huckleberry Finn*. Yes, that's right. I was the mast and my best friend was the raft. She had to lie on the ground and I had to stand on top of her as Huckleberry himself pretended to sail us down the river. How embarrassing was that? I was too mortified to tell my parents about my role because my sister Gemma had been King Lear in her school play the year before and they'd been so proud. Instead I gave them the wrong date of the school play and although they were furious for having missed a big night out, at least I didn't have to witness their disappointment as I pretended to stand on Kathryn Delaney's back for ten minutes looking like a complete eejit!

My parents will be proud though when they see me on TV. Mum will be able to tell the other women in the bridge club although . . . God, I've just had an awful thought . . . maybe she'll start saying really mortifying things like 'You can't give me a ticket, young man. Don't you know who I am? I'm Mrs Lemon, Fiona Lemon's mother.' Oh no, that's exactly the kind of thing she'll start saying to people in uniforms.

Oh God. It's nearly lunchtime and the magazine *still* hasn't gone to print. I can't wait any longer. Cecille is screaming at everybody in the office, except me. She's just ignoring me. I don't know if that's worse. At 12.45, I can't bear it any longer. I rush into the Ladies and dial RTÉ on my mobile phone. When the researcher answers I try to remain composed yet my words come tumbling out nervously.

'Hi, this is Fiona Lemon. You were looking for me?'

'Who?'

'Fiona Lemon?' I repeat hopefully.

'Sorry,' she sounds confused. 'What's it in connection with?'

'Um, I'm not sure,' I answer my voice kind of shaking now. Sugar, this isn't the kind of response I was expecting. Surely she can't have forgotten me already!

'You rang yesterday. I was in work at *Irish Femme* and I'm only getting the chance to phone back now. I'm so sorry. We go to print today. It's always manic at the end of the week.' I give a strangled sounding laugh.

'Did you say *Irish Femme?*'

'Yes,' I sigh, somewhat relieved. Phew! For a moment there I thought I might have been set up or something. By one of those spoof radio shows. Jesus, I can feel myself breaking into a mild sweat. This can't be good for my heart.

'Is that where Bunny Maguire works?' the voice at the other end enquires as my heart plummets. Oh, oh . . . *I* get it. They weren't looking for me at all, were they? No, of course they weren't. I am such a stupid moron! God, I am so pathetic. How on earth could I have possibly thought . . .

'Are you still there?'

'Oh yes,' I say miserably. 'Sorry yes I am. You were looking for Bunny were you? Well, she'll probably be at home now if you want to try her. She only comes into the office here about once a week.'

'Oh that's good. So she'll probably be available to be our resident stylist on our new show?'

'I can't see why not,' I answer. 'Well, good-bye.'

I switch off the phone.

God, I think I'm going to be sick.

31

From: <u>AJ44@hotmail.com</u>

To: <u>Flemon@irishfemme.ie</u>

Subject: Promotion

Hi Fiona,
How are things? Sorry I haven't been in touch so far.
New Zealand is wonderful. Honestly it must be the
most beautiful place on earth – absolute paradise.
And the people are so lovely as well. How is dreary
Dublin? Are you sick of flat champagne and mini
quiches yet? Unfortunately I'll be back in a fortnight.
But the good news is that Cecille has been in contact
and offered me a promotion in *Irish Femme*. She
didn't say exactly what it was but I reckon it must be
the position of deputy editor. Wow – can you believe
it? Anyway this means that the permanent position of
social editor is up for grabs. Has Cecille spoken to you

about it yet? Maybe I'm not supposed to say anything to anyone yet, but I just had to warn you not to be too amazed when you're offered the job. Anyway I'm in an Internet café right now. If you reply I might not get your email for a few days, but write back anyway. Miss you loads. How's Bunny by the way? Has she been fired as stylist yet? Is she still going out with that hunk? Let me know all the news,

luv A-J

XXX

From: Flemon@irishfemme.ie

To: AJ44@hotmail.com

Subject: RE: Promotion

Hi A-J,

God I'm so jealous. It's hard to believe you're the other side of the world. Everything's fine here, except that it's been raining solidly for the last ten days. I just interviewed one of the Westlife guys this morning but he wouldn't give me much scandal. They've a new album out this week and he was just basically saying how excited everyone was about it. This morning was manic. Cecille was in foul humour as usual. She hasn't mentioned anything to me yet about the social column so I don't want to get my hopes up too much. Bunny is loving her styling job. And yes, she is still very much with Johnnie. They were out at a function last night and there's a big picture of them in today's

Irish Mirror. She's become quite the little star – just as you predicted. Everyone seems to want a piece of her. Cecille wants to put her on the cover of *Irish Femme* with Johnnie. She asked her if she wouldn't mind. Bunny discussed it with Johnnie and they've agreed to do it. He said that it'd be good for her profile. In the mean time I'm exhausted. Everyone thinks being a social editor is fantastic fun but it leaves me drained in the evenings. All I want to do tonight is go home, put my feet up and have a glass of wine . . . or two. I have far too much news to put in an email. You'll have to wait until you get home to hear it all. Remember that guy Connor? Well he's not with Ellie now and she is pregnant by Stuart in her office. Connor's on the cover of next week's *Irish Femme*. I had to interview him and all. It's a long story though. Anyway better go. Any men in New Zealand by the way?

Love Fiona.

When I get home, I sink into the sofa. Bunny is going out again. Where does she get the energy? She emerges from her bedroom looking radiant. The first thing she does is sit down beside me to give me a huge hug. 'Thank you, thank you, thank you.'

I disentangle myself from her awkwardly. 'For what?'

'For everything. I mean, where do I start? For the TV show. My God, it still hasn't sunk in yet!' she says, her eyes shining. 'For my job in *Irish Femme*. For

introducing me to a life I could never have dreamed
of. It it wasn't for you, I'd never have met Johnnie
either. He's the best thing that's ever happened me.
Do you know we're going to be on the cover of *Irish
Femme*?'

'Yes, I'm so delighted for you.'

'Well, Cecille says sooner or later somebody is
going to want to interview us. And rather than deny-
ing our relationship, we thought we might as well go
public about it. Just to stop us getting hassled.'

'Yeah . . . er, why not?'

I'm trying to muster up some enthusiasm for all
Bunny's good news, but I'm finding it hard. All
Bunny's sudden success has made something die
within me. I can't explain it. What is wrong with me?
Why can't I even pretend to be happy for her? Am I
really that bitter?

'But I really want you to know how grateful I am
for everything you've done for me. I'm thrilled about
everything, especially the new position as social
editor. I don't know how I'm going to pull that off! I
really hope you don't mind showing me the ropes.'

Hang on a minute. What is Bunny talking about? I
straighten stiffly.

'Social editor?' I feel my throat constricting.
'Social editor? Social editor for who?'

Bunny looks at me blankly. Then confusion masks
her face. She frowns. Then she opens her mouth and
speaks very slowly.

'Oh my God, you don't know, do you?'

'Know about what?'

'Oh Jesus,' she covers her mouth with the palm of her hand. 'What have I done?'

And suddenly it hits me like a slap in the face. It all makes sense, doesn't it? *That's* why Cecille was ignoring me all day today. I'm about to be let go. Oh my God, that's it. I'm going to be fired. And my replacement is none other than Bunny!

The door bell rings.

'Oh fuck, there's Johnnie,' says Bunny. 'I'll tell him I'm not ready yet, will I?'

'Don't be daft.' I give a forced smile. 'I'm fine. My job was never going to be permanent anyway so . . . I'm pleased you got it. You're doing very well, Bunny,' I say fighting to keep the deep disappointment from clouding my voice. 'I'll get something else. When one door shuts another one opens. Isn't that what they say? Go on, I'll be fine. Have a great night. And don't celebrate too much.'

Bunny stands up hesitantly. 'God, this is really terrible. I feel awful for leaving you here.'

'Don't. Honestly. I'm looking forward to a night in.'
Another one.

'Anyway I need to get my head together. Sort out my life, you know.'

The door bell rings again.

'Well, if you're sure . . .' Bunny trails off.

'Go on, before I push you out the door.'

And then suddenly she's gone.

Timmy and I exchange glances. He looks at me darkly. He looks as depressed as I feel. Although, that's probably just 'cos I haven't fed him yet.

'So Timmy, let's pop open the champagne, eh?'

He looks at me in disgust as I feel an intense pain in the middle of my forehead.

'Don't look at me like that, Timmy. This is serious stuff. How the hell am I going to keep paying for your Whiskas? There'll be no cat stocking for you this Christmas. I'll just have to stick your smelly old mouse in the washing machine, dry it and wrap it up again this Christmas. You won't know the difference, will you?'

Timmy just shifts his position so that he ends up facing away from me. God, I hope I haven't insulted him. Timmy is all I've got left now and even *he* thinks I'm crap. I'd love a beer now but I refrain. What'll I have instead? Oh, I don't know what I want. Water? Coke? A life maybe? A job even. That would be nice. Yes. And it would be even nicer if Bubbly Bunny moved out. I can't bear to have her around me any more. Princess Bunny. Bunny who always looks on the bright side of life. It's all A-J's fault, of course. Bunny had no confidence when she first came to Dublin. She was so bloody grateful for everything. Now everybody wants her. And that's a fact. And they don't want me. Another fact. Fiona Lemon is all right to be a temporary stand-in but not good enough for anything else. Oh God, I'm so depressed I think I want to die.

I think I'll go to bed now. Yes. I'll consider my options about things again in the morning. Everything always seems that much better in the morning, doesn't it? At night everything is dark. And bleak. And things always seem a little more hopeless.

As I crawl into bed the front door bell rings loudly.

Who the hell is that, I wonder?

Did Bunny forget her keys?

Do you think the Peter Andre look-alike or his brother would have the chutzpah to come back here again for another night of 'fun'?

Or could it be my mother with food for Timmy? Too late. I've just fed him.

I look out the window but can't see anybody.

No sign of my mother's car.

Nor my father's.

And I don't know anybody else who'd be driving around aimlessly on a Friday night.

'Hello?' I call out. 'Who is it?'

A shadow steps into the street light. A man is standing outside. He looks up. Immediately I recognise his menacing face. Shaney.

'What do you want?'

'I'm looking for Bunny,' he snarls.

'She's not here,' I say coldly.

'That's fine. I'll wait.'

'You bloody won't,' I say. 'If you're not gone in five minutes I'm phoning the police.'

'You do that,' he says. 'I'd like to speak to them. About my money.'

'What money?'

'The Lotto money – half of it is mine.'

I slam the window shut. My heart is racing. Oh my God. He *knows*. He knows about the money. He could take Bunny to court. This is bad. Very bad. She'd find it pretty hard to prove that he didn't give her the money for the ticket. Shit, what'll I do? Shall

I phone Bunny? Then again I don't want to upset her. She always said he'd be back.

The door bell rings again. Jesus, he must be nuts. He's obviously seen Bunny in the papers with Johnnie and completely flipped. Christ, if he takes Bunny to court it'll be all over the news! Then all might be revealed about Bunny's brother being in prison and everything. If that happens she wouldn't be flavour of the month with Dublin's jet set anymore. I know what they're like. Any whiff of scandal and they run a mile.

And Johnnie might not want to get involved in a public fight about lottery money. Newspapers love those 'Lotto gone wrong' stories. They always make great copy. What would happen then? Would RTÉ decide not to have Bunny on their show? Would people think Bunny was a thief? Might they believe she actually *stole* the lottery ticket – Jesus! Her fifteen minutes would be well and truly up then. Hell, what'll I do?

I open the window again.

'Are you still there?'

'I told you, I'm going nowhere. I can't be got rid of easily. You should ask Bunny all about that. She'll tell you.'

His voice sounds so horrible and threatening. I think of Bunny and how delicate she is. And how all her dreams are about to come true, even if some of them *are* at my expense.

Never underestimate Bunny. That's what A-J said. She'd always maintained that Bunny was well able to look after herself. And in a way it was true. Within a couple of months, Bunny had become toast of the town. Maybe she wasn't so innocent after all. She had fairly pushed her way into this flat and made it very clear to Ellie that she couldn't have her room back. She had also quickly adopted Dervala as her new friend so that she'd always have somebody to go out and get drunk with. And to top it all, she had effortlessly snapped up Johnnie Waldren, a guy that most women would give their right arm to date. And now, not only does she have her own TV slot, but she has my job too. *My* job. For such an innocent girl, she really knew how to find her way around town without a map. Her brother was in prison and she rarely mentioned her family background, preferring to gloss over it at every opportunity. So maybe . . . maybe Bunny *did* steal that lottery ticket. Maybe half the money did belong to Shaney.

'Where is the bitch anyway? Out partying is she? Sheems to forget where she came from. I'll shoon remind her.'

He's slurring his words now and I can see he's got some kind of bottle in his hand. He takes a swig out of it and then the bottle smashes. Pieces fly everywhere but Shaney doesn't even seem to notice.

'I will call the police, you know.' I'm shivering in my nightie now. It's bloody freezing out there. Why won't he go away? He's out to destroy Bunny, that's obvious. He's incensed that Bunny has moved on. She has everything now. There's only one person who can take it all away.

And he is standing outside.

'I'll teach her what's what when I get my hands on her.'

'I think you've put your hands on her once too often,' I say, my voice like steel.

'What ya talking about?'

'You know exactly what I'm talking about.'

'I sh'poshe she was telling ya I beat her up.'

'She didn't have to. I saw the bruises.'

There's silence for a moment. It's so quiet out there. I can almost hear my heart pounding. Where has he gone?

Then his voice resounds through the chilly air. 'You can't prove anything.'

'We can. We have photos.'

'She plans to shet me up, doeshn't she?'

'She doesn't need to. We have evidence. It's all there on polaroid. We also have medical witnesses from the hospital. Bunny had to be admitted and the nurse took a statement while she was there. She wanted Bunny to press charges at the time, but luckily for you she didn't. We also have a beauty therapist who was shocked by Bunny's bruises. She doesn't mind giving evidence either.'

There's no reply. Shaney is just standing there staring.

'So,' I call out for the last time. 'Do you still want me to call the police?'

32

'Oh my God. I don't know how to thank you,' Bunny sits on the sofa, shaking her head in disbelief.

'Well, relax now. I'm sure we've seen the last of the bastard,' I say switching on the kettle.

'Hopefully. Anyway how dare he come around stalking me like that! He knows damn well he didn't give me the money for that lottery ticket.'

'Are you sure you're telling the truth?'

'I swear on my parents' grave.' Bunny looks at me steadily. 'And I don't do that lightly, believe me.'

'Good riddance to him then.' I stand up and pour the coffee into two mugs. I need a strong dose of caffeine and by the looks of it so does Bunny. I wonder why she is up and dressed so early. It's not like Bunny to join me for breakfast!

'How can I ever thank you?' she asks as she accepts the mug and then bites into a large croissant.

'Don't worry.' I give her a smile. 'I just did what anybody normal would have done. I was lucky that I just happened to think on my feet.'

'And to think I didn't even want you to take those photos!'

'Yeah, well it was a good move. It was A-J's idea so you have her to thank for it!'

'A-J has been very good to me. So have you,' Bunny says with a frown.

'Why the long face?' I ask jokingly. She looks like she's carrying the world and his mother-in-law on her shoulders.

'It's just that . . . well, I feel so guilty about taking over your job and everything.'

'Don't worry about it. Whenever a door shuts another one opens. That's what I believe.'

Well, maybe I don't believe it at all. But I'm forcing myself to. I have to. Otherwise I would simply lose my reason.

'Can I have a word with you, Fiona?'

Cecille is looming over my desk.

Okay. Big dramatic sigh. This is it obviously. The dreaded 'talk'. I am *so* not looking forward to getting fired for a second time in a matter of months. Well, I'm not *exactly* getting the chop, but A-J is coming back next week and Bunny will be taking over the social column. It still hasn't hit me yet. Everybody knows the news. It's the talk of the office apparently. So I reckon this is good-bye. I wonder will I get a 'going away' party too – with pepperoni pizza and warm wine. Or will I be given the much more unappealing 'clear your desk' option?

Do you know what? I think, as I follow Cecille into her office. I really don't particularly care any more. If Cecille shows me the door, it doesn't matter. It's not life or death. I'm going to make a success of my life anyway. With or without *Irish Femme*. I've done bloody well during my stint here and I'm going to have a long career in journalism no matter what anybody says. I'm going to *be* somebody some day. Hang on, let me rephrase that. I *am* somebody. I'm somebody now.

'Take a seat,' Cecille motions to the chair opposite her.

I do as I'm told.

'I'm very pleased with this week's cover story, Fiona. Connor Kinnerty looks great. And the interview you did was most impressive.'

'Thank you,' I say. This is all a bit confusing. It's not fair to praise somebody you're about to fire, is it? I wish she wouldn't bother. I just want this over and done with.

'As you know, Angela-Jean will be back next week.'

'I know,' I say, determined to retain my dignity.

'And as you may or may not be aware, I've asked Bunny to be our new social editor.'

'I'm aware,' I say stiffly and refuse to let my real emotions show. She's not going to break me. Not now. Not ever.

'Well the thing is,' Cecille takes a deep breath. I look at her steadily. 'The thing is . . .'

She's struggling. Why? I thought Cecille would have no problems showing me the way out. Maybe she *does* have some feelings after all. Well, there's the surprise of the century!

'It's okay,' I say. 'I know A-J has been promoted and I'm delighted for her. I also think Bunny will do a fantastic job as social editor. She really has come in to her own recently.'

'That's very diplomatic of you, Fiona. Anyway I'm hoping you'll be able to make the good-bye party this evening.'

Good-bye? I *knew* it! I knew she was going to let me go. But I didn't think I'd have to go until next week. This is a real slap in the face. Oh God, I hope my expression doesn't give my feelings away. I had psyched myself up for the disappointment but this I guess . . . well this makes it all fairly final, doesn't it?

I stand up awkwardly. Oh God, I need some fresh air. I'm not looking forward to going out to face the pitying glances of the rest of the *Irish Femme* staff. Mind you, they've seen so many people come and go through these doors, they're probably used to it.

'Hang on, where are you going?' Cecille asks sharply. 'I haven't finished with you yet, Madam.'

Too surprised to answer back, I resume my position on the chair with a thud.

'I will be making an announcement later on,' Cecille continues. Oh God, does she have to? I mean it's embarrassing enough being fired without having to let everybody know so publicly. 'But until then,' she leans forward mysteriously. 'Until then, what I'm about to tell you must remain completely confidential.'

'Uh okay.'

Janey! What's the big surprise? I must say I'm intrigued!

'I have bought *Irish Femme*. I am the new owner of the magazine.'

'You have? You are?' She has? Well, what can I say? Does she want me to congratulate her? I'm not being smart here but I genuinely don't know what I'm supposed to say, so I just nod contemplatively.

'Therefore I can't be both editor and publisher.'

'I see,' I say frowning, pretending to be interested. What the hell is she on about? Can't she just let me escape?

'So Angela-Jean will be the new editor of *Irish Femme.*'

'Really?' I perk up. Now *that* really is a bit of news. Oh gosh that's great. If A-J is the new editor then maybe she could commission me to write a few features or do the odd styling job. That would certainly keep the wolf from the door while I looked around for something else.

'Well I'm delighted. So er . . . will that be all?'

'You seem in a terrible hurry to get going. Is there something urgent you have to do?'

'Well you know, I'd need to clear my desk and get everything sorted for . . .'

I trail off as I spot a look of panic on Cecille's face. Oh God, surely she's not going to stand over me while I do that? Come off it, I'm not going to *steal* anything!

'Clear your desk?' she echoes dully.

'Isn't that what you want me to do?'

'Darling, if I could get a word in edgeways, I was just getting to my next point.'

Which is . . .?

'I'd like to offer you the position of deputy editor.'

'Me?' She's pulling my leg, right? 'But what about Sharon?'

'Sharon is also going to New Zealand to find herself, just like A-J, only she intends looking a bit longer. She'll be there for a year.'

'Really? Why didn't she tell anyone?'

'Sharon has been telling everybody all morning. The only person who didn't seem to be listening was you. Hey, are you okay, Fiona?'

'Um, yeah, yeah I'm fine.'

'So the restaurant is booked for six o'clock.'

'What restaurant?'

'I've booked a lovely little restaurant for Sharon's "going away" do.'

'No pepperoni pizza?'

'Not this time.' Cecille laughs. 'Sharon has been with us for over seven years. She deserves a proper send-off.'

'A-J will miss it.'

'Oh well, she'll be back for the Christmas party. So we'll see you at six o'clock?'

'Sure.'

'You can bring someone along if you like.'

'Like a date?'

'Yes. That's if you want to of course.'

'Oh, thanks, Cecille, but there's nobody special in my life right now. But thank you, Cecille. For this opportunity. And er . . . for everything.'

Cecille's face softens so that she looks almost human. 'Listen, I don't do people favours. I'm running a business here now. You earned this promotion, don't you forget it.'

'Thank you.'

'And stop thanking me. Okay?

Last night was good fun. Bunny couldn't make it as herself and Johnnie had plans but I enjoyed the meal and relaxed for the first time in weeks. Everyone got on great – I didn't even find Cecille as painful as usual. She got pretty drunk and at one stage started shouting about how she was thinking of becoming a lesbian. She had her hand dangerously on my thigh as she said this, so I told her Connor Kinnerty was still single. Just to give her hope.

'Well thash good,' she said animatedly and then proceeded to sit on Old Mike's knee and tickle his beard.

However, today it was business as usual and Cecille was back at her desk, with her glasses on her nose, and no sign of a hangover. Just a bottle of unopened Lucozade beside her phone. How do herself and A-J do it? If I get that drunk I usually spend the next day wrapped around a toilet bowl!

Anyway, my liver is delighted that I'm no longer the social editor of *Irish Femme*.

I'll be paying my own way from now on. No more disgusting free cherry vodka drinks, no more ghastly openings of shoe shops, trendy bars, night-clubs, book launches, album launches ... no more PR people ringing me with 'Hi, how are *you*?' like they're my best friend or something. No more red wine-spattered press releases lying around my bedroom floor for weeks simply because I don't have the energy to pick them up. No more scanning rooms full of wannabes in the vague hope of spotting the big celebrity who is always *rumoured* to show up, but never does. No. I'm all done with that. This weekend I can just go to the local pub and buy my own drink. And sit up at the bar without anybody wondering who I am or why I'm there. I'll chat to everyone and anyone without desperately hoping they have a 'story' for me. And back in the office I'll quite happily sit at my desk from 9.00 a.m. to 5.00 p.m., Monday to Friday, writing light-hearted features.

Yes. From now on I'll be living like a nice *normal* person again. And do you know something? I can't bloody wait!

Back in the flat, Bunny is doodling over the *Woman's Way* crossword. Cecille has told her she must read all the rival magazines now so that she'll be aware of outside competition. Somehow I don't think she meant Bunny to do all the crosswords!

'Hi Fiona, The Great What? starring Steve McQueen. Six letters.'

'Escape. Ah c'mon, Bunny. You should've got that.'

'I'm a bit hung over today. I was in Renards till all hours. That's why I'm being a bit slow.' She puts down the magazine. 'Listen Fiona, I've been doing a bit of thinking. I've decided to turn down the position of social editor in *Irish Femme*. I don't think I've enough experience. And I honestly don't think I'd be any good at it.'

I look at her in surprise. 'Nonsense. Don't be talking like that. You'll be well able for it.'

'I don't want it,' Bunny insists, pulling nervously at her fingers.

I know she's not telling me the truth. I know the only reason she's saying this is to make me feel better.

'Listen Bunny, don't worry about me. I've just been promoted to deputy editor.' I give her a reassuring wink, and tell her about my earlier chat with Cecille.

'Oh my God, that's great news. So, we'll be like happy families in *Irish Femme!*' Bunny exclaims brightly.

'Yeah, apart from Cecille being the owner. She'll still be watching over us like a wicked stepmother.'

'We'll have to figure out some way to butter her up,' Bunny suggests. 'Let's send her on a spa treatment holiday – for a month!'

'Ah, if only . . .'

The door bell interrupts us.

'Oh Jesus! Do you think that's Shaney back again!' Bunny nearly falls over in fright.

'No way, it can't be,' I try to assure her rushing to the window.

'Oh my good God!' I scream.

'What! Is it him?'

'No, it's . . . it's Connor Kinnerty. What does *he* want? What is he doing here? I can't answer the door. I haven't any make-up on.'

'Here, run into your room and put on some slap,' Bunny offers. 'I'll stall him. I'll tell him you're still in bed or something.'

My heart is racing. 'Oh Jesus, I dunno. Are you sure? What can he want?'

'I don't know, do I?' Bunny says excitedly. 'We won't know until we let him in. Go on, run.'

I rush into my room and look in the mirror. A crazed-looking version of myself stares back. Oh no, I have *seriously* dark circles under my eyes. And as for my hair? I could fry chips with the grease! Would a hat be too obvious? I *can't* let him see me like this. I fish out my Flawless Finish foundation and smear it all over my face. Then I apply some deep red lipstick and several coats of mascara. My mind is racing. What does he want? Hang on a second though. What am I fretting about? *He* stood me up, didn't he? Why am I even humouring him? I should tell him to piss off really. Curiosity has got the better of me however. I'm just bursting to know why he's here.

Now. Calm down, missus. You'll soon know what this surprise visit is all about. Go on, you look fine. You might not give Cameron Diaz anything to worry about but you'll definitely pass. Anyway he is *only* a human being, *and* he owes you an apology.

'Hello,' I say shyly, convinced that my face is

redder than Ronald McDonald's hair. I am mortified.
And okay I take it all back. He is *not* just a human
being. He is a god. He's so amazing looking and has
the sexiest way of looking at you. I can't take my eyes
off him as he sits back against the sofa, a mug of coffee
(with my name on it!) balancing on his lap. 'Um . . .
how are you?'

'Fine, great thanks. Bunny has made me feel very
at home.'

Bunny laughs. 'Anyway I'd better go and get
ready.'

'Where are you going?'

'To the gym, to work off all the calories I consumed
last night!'

Gym? Huh! I thought Bunny hated gyms. I
thought that was the whole *point* of getting our own
treadmill. But as Bunny gives me a 'you're on your
own from now, buddy' look, I suddenly get it.

'Would you like something to eat?' I sit down
beside Connor as Bunny disappears. He's wearing
aftershave. I can't place it but it's nice. God, this is so
embarrassing. Connor is sitting beside me in my own
home. Last time he was here I was in bed. *We* were
in my room. And he was drying my hair. Oh the
shame!

'I'm fine with just the coffee thanks.' His leg
lightly touches mine and I feel a wave of electricity
soar through my thigh.

'I've got a bit of a hangover from last night,' he
says.

'Just like Bunny, haha. Where did you go?'

'We started off in the Ice Bar in The Four Seasons and ended up in Renards. I think we were probably the last to leave.'

'Oh, Bunny was in Renards too.'

'I know. I saw her there briefly,' he says and then suddenly his face turns scarlet. 'I don't think she saw me though.'

And then the penny drops. Of *course*. It's so obvious why Connor is here. Yep, it's as clear as crystal. He's here 'cos he fancies Bunny. Well, what do you know! I might just throw myself out of the window. And then you know, Bunny can live here by herself. And adopt Timmy – he won't care as long as he's fed. And then if she ever breaks up with Johnnie or whatever . . . she won't have to sob too much. No. Because dear old Connor will be standing in the wings only *dying* to take Johnnie's place.

'Right then.' I stand up. 'I'd better not keep you. My mother said she'd be calling over this evening.'

'Oh, oh. Listen, does Bunny have a boyfriend?'

Oh my God. Talk about being *obvious*! He doesn't give a damn about my feelings, does he?

'Sorry, I have to go out to the shops. We're out of milk,' I say dully, refusing to look Connor in the eye. 'And my mother won't drink tea without milk. Anyway, it was very nice of you to call around. Bunny should be ready in a minute. Then you can ask her yourself if she has a boyfriend. Bye.'

I grab my coat, run out of the flat and down the stairs. And tear off down the road as fast as my poor legs can carry me. I run and run and run. I know I might have acted a bit crazy in there but I no longer care what Connor thinks. How dare he treat me like that! Does everybody think I have absolutely no feelings? I'm only human, you know. I can't help it. I keep running with the wind in my face, ignoring my rage.

I hear somebody calling out my name but I don't turn around. Instead I run even faster. I don't give a shit. I don't want sympathy. I am all out of pride at this stage.

As soon as I reach the shop I dart inside, and go straight down the back. Only then do I stop, pretending to examine the range of gaudy Christmas cards on display. I try to get my breath back while secretly cursing A-J and her silly little experiment. *She* was the one who thought she'd make something of Bunny, simply to amuse herself. And now she's not even around to make things right again. I jump as a hand touches my shoulder.

'Fiona.'

'Leave me alone.'

'Fiona, I need to talk to you.'

'Well I don't want to talk to *you*!'

I turn to face Connor. I see the sympathy in his eyes and I can't bear it. I am sick of everybody feeling sorry for Fiona Lemon. They can all fuck off.

'I've hurt you, haven't I?'

'Don't flatter yourself, Connor,' I sniff.

Connor offers me a tissue, which I refuse. I want nothing from him. Except of course to never see him again.

'Bunny said . . .'

'. . . that she's taken. Oh what a shame! I could have told you that though.'

'Hang on a minute, do you think I called over 'cos I fancy Bunny?' Connor looks completely stunned.

Now it's my turn to be shocked. Could somebody please tell me what the hell is going on?

'Hey.' Connor grabs my arm and forces me to look at him. 'I came over this evening for *you*, Fiona. Not Bunny. I have no interest in Bunny whatsoever.'

'Then why did you ask me if she had a boyfriend?'

'Here, come outside. People are looking at us.'

'Don't care.'

'Come outside, Fiona,' he says firmly. 'And stop being so ridiculous.'

I follow him out of the shop like a bold sulky child. My arms are folded. I'm not prepared to give an inch.

We sit on the wall.

'Hear me out,' says Connor. 'The reason I called over this morning was because I saw Bunny out last night with Johnnie.'

I look at him blankly. I'm lost. What is he talking about?

'I thought he was *your* boyfriend.'

'You did?' I ask, my head spinning.

'When I called around that night to take you out, I was about to get out of the car when I saw Johnnie Waldren pull up in his BMW. Then he got out with a massive bunch of flowers and walked towards your front door.'

'They were for Bunny.'

'I know that *now*. But how the hell was I supposed to know at the time? I didn't have so much as a miserable plant with me. There was no way I was going to call to your door and stand empty handed beside the biggest, most fancied bloke in Ireland.'

I sit there in silence waiting for all this to sink in. Then I can't help smiling. 'You thought Johnnie was my boyfriend?'

'I just jumped to the worst possible conclusion. I'm an idiot, right?'

We stare at each other and then I look away. I can't get my head around this at all.

'But you never even contacted me,' I then accuse.

'I didn't want to make a fool of myself. The next day I asked somebody if they knew if Johnnie Waldren had a girlfriend.'

'And?'

'And they said he was going out with some wealthy society bird from *Irish Femme*.'

Neither of us knows what to say. This is just so weird.

'Well, it's obviously not me. I'm neither wealthy nor a society darling. Another case of Chinese whispers?'

'I guess.'

'But why didn't you phone?'

Connor stares at the ground. 'I didn't want to worry you. I wasn't thinking straight. My mother was ill. We didn't think she was going to pull through.'

'God, I'm sorry, Connor. I'd no idea.'

'She's fine now though. She's going to make it.'

'Thank God.'

'Come on, let's get out of here.' Connor takes my hand and squeezes it. 'I can think of spending our evening somewhere more romantic than on a wall.'

'So where are we going?' I ask getting to my feet.

'Out. Let's be sociable.'

'Out where?'

'Wherever you want.'

'Well, I don't care where I go. As long as I don't have to go to a launch, and drink anything with a sheep's eye floating at the bottom of the glass or an orange and pink umbrella sticking out of it.'

'Fine. Let's just go somewhere quiet for supper and a dirty big pint. Somewhere with sawdust on the floor and toilets with no doors,' Connor says with a cheeky grin. Then he stuffs his hands in my coat pockets and kisses the tip of my nose. 'Listen, I don't care where I go. As long you're with me.'

'Aw, you're too smooth, Connor Kinnerty,' I smile and kiss him back. 'But keep talking. I'm beginning to enjoy this . . .'

34

I've just got a phone call from A-J. She's home, having flown in yesterday as a surprise. I'm so thrilled she's back. She's not as thrilled as I am though. No. In fact she says her stint on the other side of the world has only made her realise how much she needs to change her career direction.

'But it'll all be different in *Irish Femme* now that you're editor,' I say encouragingly.

'Hmm. I'm not sure about that,' A-J mutters. 'I mean I'll still be answering to that silly old cow. She'll probably be even worse now that she's the owner. Anyway, I'm not sure I want to continue working in women's magazines. It's a bit like being back at school, with the bullying headmistress and all.'

'But what else would you do?'

'Well, I wouldn't mind getting back into newspapers. I kind of miss the thrust and grind of working for a tabloid.'

'Really?'

I'd almost forgotten that A-J had cut her teeth in journalism working for one of the biggest selling red tops, door-stepping innocent, grieving people and asking them how they felt about their relatives being brutally murdered. She once told me she'd nearly had a breakdown with the stress of it all, being on call for almost twenty-four hours a day, getting zero thanks for it, and phoning people who gave her dog's abuse when they found out she was a reporter. Why on earth would she consider going back to that?

'The pay is better,' she states matter-of-factly. 'And you're out and about, not chained to your desk like a bloody prisoner.'

A-J's negativity is kind of getting me down. I'd had such high hopes for all us working on the magazine together like one happy family. I hope to God that she's not going to backtrack now.

'I have so much news for you,' I say, suddenly anxious to get off the subject of work.

'Do you?'

'Yeah, Bunny's ex called over the other night threatening to expose her. But I told him that we've photos proving that he abused her and I basically told him where to go.'

'And he went off just like that?' A-J sounds surprised.

'Well I threatened to call the police. I'm sure he wouldn't have liked that. By the way, A-J, you *did* get those photos developed, didn't you?'

'No, actually I must do that soon. It's something I keep meaning to do. So any other news? Is Bunny still Ireland's favourite IT girl?'

'Oh yeah, the press love her, believe it or not. It's mad the way it's all taken off. God knows where it will all end though.'

'Well, she needs to keep her wits about her,' A-J says sagely. 'The press are great at building you up. But they love to tear you back down to earth again.'

'Oh, I'm sure she'll be okay. Everything's gone surprisingly well so far. She's quite a star now, thanks to you. You know she's even been offered her own TV show?'

'So I've heard,' A-J says without emotion. It's hard to tell if she's pleased for Bunny or not. 'Anyway I'd better let you go. I need to start on sending out my CV.'

'So you're serious about leaving *Irish Femme*?' I ask, my heart sinking.

''Fraid so. Once a grubby hack, always a grubby hack,' A-J laughs. 'I don't want to go to any more fashion shows serving cheap champagne, or listen to any more PR women bleat on about anti-acne cream over the phone ever again. I'm sick to the teeth with all that kind of stuff. From now on I want to write serious news. Leave the fluff to the fluffy people, that's what I say. Listen, let's meet up soon and you can fill me in on all the goss. Okay?'

'Sure. And A-J, you won't forget to get those photos developed, will you?'

'Trust me, I won't.'

Bunny is delighted when I tell her that A-J is back in town. Immediately she wants to throw a little party in A-J's honour but I tell her she's probably exhausted, having flown across the world.

I also tell her that A-J won't be coming back to *Irish Femme*. Bunny's face falls. She genuinely looks as devastated as I feel. 'So who will be the new editor then?' she asks, voicing my exact thoughts.

'God only knows,' I say yawning. It's late. I'm too tired to even think about whom A-J's replacement could be. I look at my watch. Jesus, no wonder I'm exhausted! It's almost midnight.

35

I can't sleep. No matter how hard I try. I toss and turn and then I toss again. My mind is racing and a million thoughts are taking up my brain space. One minute I keep thinking about Connor and how lucky I am to have found him, but the next minute I'm wondering whether I can trust him. Would Connor leave me if a more attractive offer presented itself? I also wonder if men are capable of being faithful to the one woman for the rest of their lives or whether they're just opportunists who pounce on any female with a pulse.

At 4.30 a.m. I am still awake. I have no idea why. There is an exceptionally annoying magpie perched on a branch outside my bedroom window. He is squawking continuously and I swear if I could get my hands around his little neck . . . I don't know why I'm so restless. I feel exhausted but I can't explain why sleep is eluding me. However, the more I fret about not getting to sleep, the more awake I seem to become. I close my eyes and start to count sheep going through a hedge. But I'm still going strong at number 350 and the sheep are now talking to each other and dancing with each other and some of them are actually sitting on top of the hedge, while others are sitting beside it wearing little red caps. I decide to think of blank paper instead. Sheets and sheets of it. Before long I begin to drift off, peacefully. I'm dreaming that I'm on a rowing boat drifting in the middle of a turquoise sea. The hot sun is blazing down. I'm all alone on the boat and I'm not sure where I've come from or where I'm going, but it's very peaceful. And the water is smooth and tranquil. Suddenly the sky begins to cloud over and darkness falls like a curtain. The temperature changes and it begins to rain. Heavy, menacing drops. The boat is shaking now and the waves are rocking the boat. The mood has changed and out of nowhere a flash of lightning strikes. A crash of thunder follows as the clouds above hurl themselves against each other. The noise is deafening. There's another smash. And another one. And then I wake up.

Somebody is in the sitting room.

I sit upright, frozen in the darkness. My heart is beating so fast I think it's going to burst. I listen hard hoping I might be wrong about the noise. But then I hear another crash. Followed by a piercing scream. Bunny. Oh Jesus! Oh good Jesus, no.

My entire body has broken into a cold sweat. I'm completely paralysed by fear. It must be him. Shaney must be in the flat. She must have let him in.

Oh God, how could she have done that?

For a few seconds there's no noise. I slowly ease myself off the bed, terrified of making a sound. I know my mobile phone is somewhere in my bag but I don't know where my bag is. I have a feeling that I've left it on the sofa out in the sitting room. Fuck. Then the shouting begins.

'You're a whore! A fucking little whore. Fucking your way around Dublin like a piece of unwanted meat.'

'Shaney, listen we should sit down and talk about this. Fighting isn't going to get us anywhere.'

I stand at the door trembling. I don't think I've ever been so petrified in my entire life. This is like a horror film without the music. And without the prospect of a happy ending. I feel like I'm going to vomit. But there's no time for that. I have to think quickly. There's a window in my room. I could jump out, but suppose he heard me? Suppose I broke my ankle? Then I wouldn't be able to run anywhere to raise the alarm.

'You've made a fool out of me. Everyone at home is laughing at me while you're up here shagging rugby players and thinking you're somebody for taking off your knickers.'

'It's not like that, Shaney,' Bunny says, her voice full of terror. 'You've got it all wrong. Don't you know that papers just make things up? I'm just friends with that rugby player. There's nothing going on.'

'Jesus, stop lying to me, you little bitch!'

Another crash. Another blood-curling scream. I

can't bear it any longer. I open the door. Bunny is cowering in the corner shielding her head with her hands. Shaney has a massive steel saucepan in his hand. The surrounding floor is covered in broken glass.

'Leave her alone,' I command in a trembling voice.

He turns around and stares.

'Who the fuck are you?'

There is a crazed look in Shaney's eyes. It's completely terrifying. This is the face of a man so consumed with hatred that he will quite obviously stop at nothing to wreak revenge.

'I'm Bunny's flatmate,' I say, anxiously scouring the room for my bag. I see it half opened on the kitchen table. But how the hell I'm going to reach it, I have no idea. I start praying frantically. It's all I can do now.

'Oh yeah,' he turns his attentions to me, his eyes narrowing. 'I know who you are all right. You're the slut who tried to get rid of me the other night, aren't you?'

'You'd had a little too much to drink,' I say with a calmness I definitely don't feel. 'You weren't making any sense then.'

'Well, I'm making sense now.'

I look at him blankly.

'Aren't I?' he repeats menacingly.

Shaney's eyes bore through me. He takes a step forward, his arm raised. I recoil in horror. He's not going to hit me, is he?

'Leave her alone!' Bunny screeches, managing to distract him. 'She's done nothing to you.'

He turns back to her, lifts up the saucepan and with full force slams it into her face.

Now it's my turn to scream. Good God, can nobody hear us? Bunny stumbles back, her mouth pumping blood. On falling, she wallops the back of her head against the wall and slowly slumps to the ground.

I make a dive for the mobile while Shaney still has his back to me. He is now kicking Bunny's head repeatedly, shouting like a maniac. I rush to my room and with trembling fingers somehow manage to dial 999.

Please answer, I silently beg as the phone rings. I'm paralysed with fear. Please, please answer.

The voice on the other end asks what emergency service is required.

'Six A Rosebush Terrace. I think my friend might be dead.'

I keep one petrified eye on the door. Bunny is no longer screaming. Everything is deadly silent and my voice sounds like a loudspeaker.

'Six A Rosebush Terrace,' I repeat, my voice crumbling.

'Terrace?'

'Six A Rosebush *Terrace*. He's still here. Oh God, I'm afraid he's going to kill me . . .' I trail off, seeing a shadow in the doorway.

Christ.

'Are you now?' Shaney is speaking in a dull

monotone voice. He looks as though he's hiding something behind his back. Probably the saucepan. 'So you're afraid I'm going to kill you? What kind of monster do you think I am? What kind of lies has that little trollop been feeding you?'

'Shaney, listen I know you're upset . . .'

'Yes, indeed I am, especially now that you've gone and called the police,' he says with a menacing smile. 'Yourself and Bunny are well matched.'

I take a step back. He takes one forward.

'Bunny!' I screech.

'Oh, she can't help you now,' he says calmly.

'The police are on their way,' I warn in a frantic last-minute ditch to scare him off.

'That's okay,' he smiles again. 'I might as well be hung for a sheep,' he says after a while, unbuckling his belt. His other hand is still behind his back. 'Why don't you and I have some fun while we're waiting?'

Terror numbs me as I watch him slide off his belt. It falls to the floor with a thud.

I grab the nearest object – a wooden lampshade. With both hands I swing for his head. He catches it with one hand and throws it at the window. The window smashes. I don't turn around to see the damage. I keep eyeballing Shaney. And now I see what he has been hiding behind his back. A knife.

We both stand looking at each other for what seems like an age. Then Shaney takes another step forward. 'You don't want that pretty little throat of yours slashed now, do you?' he whispers.

He pushes me on to the bed. I'm hysterical now.

There doesn't seem to be a way out.

'Put the knife down, Shaney,' I plead with him, the tears streaming down my cheeks. 'Please.'

He's on top of me now, the sharp tip of the knife scraping my neck. I close my eyes, terrorised. 'I don't trust you,' he says and I feel his breath on my face.

I struggle with all my might, and when the front door bell finally rings, every inch of my body feels the relief. The bell rings again and I try to open my mouth to scream but Shaney covers it with his hands.

'Shut the fuck up, bitch.'

Suddenly I'm filled with uncontrollable rage. I'm not going to let him harm me any more than he already has. He can burn in fucking hell first. I lift my forehead off the pillow and with full force, I whack it against his.

He is momentarily stunned. I push him off with all my strength and wriggle from underneath the weight of his body. Grabbing the side of the bed, I try to find my balance before making a dash for the door. Blood is pumping from my right hand but I don't care. Then without warning, Shaney hurls himself towards me. Panicking, I try scrambling out the door. But he grabs my ankle and I whack my head against the doorknob. I try pulling my leg away. If I could just get out of the bedroom . . . I hear the front door crashing down. The police are in the flat. I'm safe, I think just before I feel a searing pain through my right shoulder blade. I fall forward, the knife deeply imbedded in my flesh.

'Hi.'

It's my sister Gemma. She's standing over me. So are my mum and dad. What are they all doing here standing by my bed? This is so weird. And then I feel the pain. It's excruciating. Like I have been hacked to pieces and sewn back together again. Gemma tells me I've had twenty-one stitches.

I remember now.

The police want a few words in private. They're very kind. I ask them if they've spoken to Bunny yet. They haven't. Bunny hasn't regained consciousness. I start to cry. So do Mum and Gemma. Even Dad looks like he might start.

Mum tells me A-J is outside. Apparently she's not allowed into the ward because of my condition. My hand is broken and in a cast. I feel desolate.

Gemma says she'll go out and tell A-J to come back later. I nod gratefully. I can't talk to anybody right now. I'm in so much pain. I want to close my eyes and sleep forever.

Gemma leaves the ward and to my surprise, comes back two minutes later with A-J. Even though her familiar face is somewhat comforting I can barely manage a smile.

'I'm so sorry,' she says, kneeling down by my bed. 'I called over to you this morning and the neighbours told me what happened. I got here as soon as I could. I hope you don't mind.'

I shake my head weakly. The walls are closing on me. I can barely stay awake.

'She's on strong medication,' Gemma tells her. 'Why don't you come back later?'

A-J remains on her knees. 'Fiona, what happened?'

'Shaney . . .' I'm struggling. 'Shaney broke into the flat.'

'And he stabbed you? Is that what happened? Did he stab Bunny too? Is Bunny okay?'

'He kicked her. He hit her in the face. He hit me and he . . . had a knife. He must have . . .'

'Honestly, Angela-Jean,' I hear Gemma's voice. It sounds a million miles away. 'It's time for you to leave now.'

The whole day is a blurred mess. Every time I wake somebody is asking me something. Bunny is still on a life support machine. She has suffered two broken ribs as well as head injuries. I am inconsolable. Only the other day, I had been so happy.

So how did everything go so wrong so quickly?

Mum and Dad are being brilliant, as is my sister Gemma. She has sort of taken control of the situation. It's at times like this that you realise how much you need your family. I haven't told anybody else I'm here. Not Cecille and not even Connor. I don't want him to see me like this.

It's not until 11.00 p.m. that word reaches us that Bunny is going to pull through. Gemma wheels me into her room. The sight of her horrifies me. I barely recognise her. Her eyes are like two black and purple holes in her face. Her lips are cut and swollen and her nose has been broken as well. Nevertheless she still manages a half smile when she sees me.

'Look at the state of us,' she says through tears. 'I'd give you a hug but I'm afraid I can't move.'

'We'll just pretend we've given each other hugs,' I smile.

'I heard you had to have stitches,' she says in a tiny voice.

'I'm going to be okay.'

'You saved my life, Fiona. You do know that, don't you?'

'Well, Shaney will go to jail over this, and that's the main thing,' I say grimly. 'He'll get what he deserves.'

'I still owe you my life.'

Gemma wheels me out again. She asks me whether I had any idea about Bunny's situation.

'Well, I knew he was violent but I didn't think he was capable of this,' I say.

Gemma shakes her head. 'Women never think that. But I saw this kind of thing a lot when I worked in A&E. Violent men just don't go away. They get worse.'

'Well we won't be seeing him again of course . . . until we get to court. I hope he gets put away for life.'

'Hmmm. He might not get life.'

'Won't he? But he *must* be put away for a very long time. He assaulted and hospitalised both of us, not to mention . . . not to mention . . . Jesus. Gemma, for a moment I thought he was going to try and rape me.'

Gemma's hand flies to her mouth in horror. 'Oh God, did you tell that to the police?'

The shocked look on her face frightens me. The

enormity of the situation has just hit me like a slap in the face. It's been a delayed reaction.

'No, Gemma,' I say as the tears start to flow uncontrollably down my cheeks. 'I just blocked it out of my head.'

She takes my shaking hand in hers and just holds it.

'Everything will be better in the morning,' she promises gently.

38

But everything gets a lot worse. I wake the next morning, along with the rest of Ireland, to the national news of our joint brutal assault.

Every paper in the country has run the story. And Bunny's photos are splashed across the pages. The ones with Bunny covered in bruises. The photos I took with the disposable camera. The sight of them, laid out for the whole world to see, make me feel sick to my stomach.

Yesterday I thought things couldn't possibly get any worse. But they have. Today my darkest hour has arrived. I feel completely helpless.

A-J has sold out on us. Yes. She has betrayed us, her own friends – for a story. Or ten different versions of it. I have lost faith in humankind. I feel so empty. I'm quoted in all the stories. There are no quotes from Bunny.

There are photos of myself, A-J and Bunny at a society function. *The girls in happier times*, the captions read. There's a photo of Shaney, looking like a thug. There's a photo of Bunny's brother and a story running about his dodgy past and run-ins with the law, as well as Bunny's lottery win.

The closet of Ireland's latest IT girl has well and truly been laid bare.

It looks like A-J has gone all out to get herself the scoop of the year while her two friends battle for recovery in hospital. I never thought she'd do this to us. I never thought a story was worth more than a friendship. I was wrong. There's a photo of Connor in the papers too. I'm sure he won't be pleased about that.

My phone rings. God, maybe it's Connor! I haven't had the chance to phone him yet. I wonder has he read the papers yet? Does he hate me for dragging him into this mess?

It's a reporter. Would I have a minute? Well, I'm stuck in bed, aren't I? Of course I have a minute. I have the whole bloody day! I tell her that I'm recovering well. She asks me not to talk to any other newspapers as she wants an exclusive. I feel like telling her where to go, but I don't. Instead I explain that I'm not doing any 'exclusives'. But I know she'll slap the word 'exclusive' on top of the piece anyway. They always do that.

The phone rings again. It's another reporter. How is Johnnie Waldren coping? I raise my eyebrows in disbelief. How is Johnnie coping? For fuck's sake! Was he stabbed too?

'I'd better go and see Bunny,' I say to Gemma. 'If

I'm getting all this hassle from reporters, her phone must be hopping too. Can you wheel me in?'

'A couple more days? Ah, Johnnie, I have to see her to find out how she's coping. She won't mind. Come on, let me in.'

But Johnnie doesn't budge. His huge frame blocks the doorway. 'I'm sorry, Fiona, I really am. But she told me not to let you in.'

'Why not?'

'Because of the photos. She says you took them. She says it was a set-up. She also says you gave interviews to the press yesterday without telling her.'

I feel nauseous at the injustice of it all. 'But I *didn't* talk to the press yesterday,' I exclaim. 'I only spoke to A-J.'

Gemma wheels me back to the ward. I feel deflated as I crawl back into bed. I close my eyes just wishing I could disappear. When I open them again, Gemma has disappeared and Connor is sitting by the bed instead. I don't think I have ever been so pleased to see someone in life. His eyes, full of concern, search mine.

'Sorry, Connor. I should have told you sooner.'

'I know,' he says softly.

'I just didn't have the energy to phone anyone.'

Connor strokes the top of my head gently. 'I came into work this morning to find you plastered all over the papers. Can you imagine the shock? Seeing your girlfriend like that?'

'I'm sorry,' I repeat, secretly delighted that he has

referred to me as his girlfriend.

'I drove straight to the hospital. I must have broken every set of traffic lights. Jesus, Fiona, you gave us all some fright.'

'I gave *you* a fright?' I give him a smile. 'Well as you can imagine I fairly terrified myself as well. God, all I ever wanted was a quiet life. There's so much to tell . . . I don't even know where to begin . . .'

'Hey,' Connor says quietly. 'You relax now, do you hear? You can tell me again. There'll be plenty of time later for the post mortem. Go back to sleep now if you can. You've had a real shock and . . . I'm not going anywhere for a while.'

So I obey, closing my eyes again, trying not to look pleased. His *girlfriend*? Did you hear that?

It's day three now. The doctors are telling me I can go home tomorrow, but obviously I'll have to take it easy over the next few weeks. Bunny will be kept in a while longer for observation.

I don't particularly fancy the thought of going back to the flat and staying there alone. I'm not sure what I'm frightened of. All I know is that I'm scared about what happened to me. About being so close to death. If things had gone wrong that knife could have sliced my neck as well as my hand. Or I could have been raped. My life would have changed forever.

Gemma can't stay because she has to go back to Cardiff to work. Dervala says she'll stay. In fact she's more than happy to. Dervala, by the way, has been in her element since the whole story broke. Yesterday she was in all the papers as the 'concerned friend'. Funny how Bunny hasn't frozen *her* out of it though? In fact Dervala was in Bunny's room earlier on today helping herself to chocolates sent in by Bunny's adoring 'fans'. Not a peep has been heard from A-J however. Word has it that she got so much money for our story that she had the money to go straight back to New Zealand.

'That one was only ever out for herself,' Dervala says as she sits on the hospital bed skimming through the papers and admiring her own photo. I'm tempted to say something about the pot calling the kettle names, but refrain of course.

'My hair looks very bright in those photos,' she says frowning. 'I must get a few lowlights in the next time I'm in the hairdressers. So,' she says brightly, looking from Gemma to me. 'Any good-looking doctors in this place?'

Gemma opens her mouth as if to say something smart, but as she does so, somebody appears in the doorway of the ward. It's a clearly pregnant Ellie carrying the most beautiful bouquet of richly coloured flowers that I've ever seen. I am so thrilled to see her.

She sits on the side of the bed and patiently listens to my story. She asks if Connor has been into visit. Feeling myself flush slightly, I tell her that he has. 'Connor had to dodge past the paparazzi waiting at the door of the hospital, but he came to see me as soon as he heard,' I explain, propping myself up so I can smell the heavy fragrance of the flowers. She just nods her head silently listening. For a moment it's like old times when we used to live together in the flat. Me, sitting in bed like a complete mess, spilling out all my problems while Ellie sits at the end of my bed calmly offering all the solutions.

Then I tell her that Bunny isn't talking to me.

'Well, I hope she's talking to *me*. I have a little present for Bunny in my bag,' she says brightly. 'I thought I couldn't visit one of you without the other.'

'Hmm. I doubt she'll see you.'

'Well it's worth a try.' Gemma stands up.

Fifteen minutes later she's back. And she's smiling.

'Let's get you into the wheelchair,' she winks. 'Bunny is asking for you. I think she misses you already.'

40

If I met A-J on the street I would still say 'hello'. Yes, I definitely would. Of course I wouldn't stop for very long but I wouldn't snub her either. I just kind of feel sorry for her now. She'll die never knowing the real meaning of loyalty and true friendship.

A story runs for just one day, at the very most two. But if you sell a trusted friend down the river for it, you can never win that trust back. No newspaper will ever offer you the same loyalty as a friend. You're only as good as your last story anyway. As a journalist you're oh-so replaceable, and anyone who thinks otherwise should put their foot in the ocean and see how quickly the hole refills once they take their foot out. A-J will burn out. Most do in the end.

I'm willing to forgive, although Bunny doesn't quite share my views. She says if she ever sees A-J again she will cross the road to avoid her. I can't blame her. After all, it wasn't my family history that got splashed all over the papers for everybody to read about. But as I said, I'm not one to hold grudges.

Shaney's court case is looming and obviously I'm not looking forward to it. But it could be worse. Bunny could be dead. And so could I.

Bunny and I are closer now than ever before. Of course she realises that I had nothing to do with the photos being splashed all over the papers. But at the time, she says she was too distraught even to think about it. Bunny resumed her television slot last week, and her fan base is rapidly growing. Despite her initial concerns, all the publicity that followed the attack served only to boost her profile even further. The power of the media, huh?

My life is back on track. The wound on my shoulder is healing nicely. My emotional scars are worse than my real ones. But they should all heal in time. Connor has been an absolute rock in recent weeks. I've had nightmares, sometimes waking up at 3.00 or 4.00 a.m., drenched in sweat. I've rung him in a panic and he has softly talked me back to sleep again. His younger sister, a mobile hairdresser in Dublin, comes to my house every second day to wash my hair as I still find it difficult to do simple things since my hand was broken. She tells me that he's mad about me, but says I'm not to let on. She needn't worry. I'm not *that* silly.

At the moment I'm sitting in Cecille's office. It's the last Friday before Christmas, and the magazine, with all its New Year diet tips, has well and truly gone to print. The night of festive fun stretches ahead and is full of promise. It's time to put my feet up. Cecille has produced two Waterford Crystal flutes and a bottle of bubbly. The rest of the staff have gone home.

'I thought if we were going to do this, we might as well do it in style,' she smiles, sitting across from me. 'So how do you feel about becoming editor?'

'Oh I think I can cope,' I grin as she pours the champagne and it spills over onto her desk, soaking a tray of mince pies. 'After all, since A-J left us high and dry I've been doing most of the editorial work anyway.'

'Indeed you have,' she says. 'And you've done a damn good job of it I can tell you. Now,' she says raising her glass with gusto. 'What will we drink to?'

'How about the future of *Irish Femme*?' I suggest unsurely, thinking that might be the right thing to say.

But Cecille just laughs at my eagerness. 'Listen, it's Christmas, love. Forget office politics until the New Year. I'm human too. Just don't tell anyone, okay?' she says with a wink. 'So how about making a toast to, say, life?'

Life? Well, why not indeed? That's definitely worth toasting.

'Cheers!' I clink my glass with hers and sip slowly, letting the bubbles carry me off to another world. Mmm, this is good. In fact life is good. And it's about to get better. I've had my darkest hour. And it was blacker than I ever imagined. You know that of course, because you were there. But ahead lies the dawn. It looks promising. And I'm going to rise with it. Yes, life is worth toasting right now . . . I'll certainly drink to that.

You can buy any of these other
Little Black Dress titles from your
bookshop or *direct from the publisher*.

FREE P&P AND UK DELIVERY
(Overseas and Ireland £3.50 per book)

The Men's Guide to the Women's Bathroom	Jo Barrett	£4.99
I Take This Man	Valerie Frankel	£4.99
How to Sleep with a Movie Star	Kristin Harmel	£4.99
Pick Me Up	Zoë Rice	£4.99
The Balance Thing	Margaret Dumas	£4.99
The Kept Woman	Susan Donovan	£4.99
Simply Irresistible	Rachel Gibson	£4.99
I'm in No Mood for Love	Rachel Gibson	£4.99
Sex, Lies and Online Dating	Rachel Gibson	£4.99
Daisy's Back in Town	Rachel Gibson	£4.99
Spirit Willing, Flesh Weak	Julie Cohen	£4.99
Blue Christmas	Mary-Kay Andrews	£4.99
The Bachelorette Party	Karen McCullah Lutz	£4.99
My Three Husbands	Swan Adamson	£4.99
He Loves Lucy	Susan Donovan	£4.99
Mounting Desire	Nina Killham	£4.99
Accidentally Engaged	Mary Carter	£4.99
She'll Take It	Mary Carter	£4.99
Step on it, Cupid	Lorelei Mathias	£4.99

TO ORDER SIMPLY CALL THIS NUMBER

01235 400 414

or visit our website: www.headline.co.uk

Prices and availability subject to change without notice.